She Starlight

She Starlight

Gordon Hall

First Printing, May 2025

ISBN 978-1-0686941-5-8

www.lakefell.com

This book has had a long gestation
which has meant that my friends and family
have had to put up with my creative idiosyncrasies
and weird mutterings for several years!

To them I offer my apologies, and my thanks.
In particular I would like to thank Margaret
for creating 'to order' her wonderful book cover.

Prologue

"It's nothing but a bloody shambles. A complete farce, you should never have let it get this far."

Michael Pederson, mediocre politician and now Parliamentary Under Secretary of State at the Home Office, was clearly taking considerable pleasure in berating his Permanent Under Secretary responsible for domestic security.

"If we had been involved earlier it wouldn't have come to this. Now you tell me that we need to take 'Positive Action'. Well I don't like your sort of positive action, and I certainly don't need to know anything about it."

Hugh Strickland, was only partly listening to the tirade from his political master. His thoughts were more tuned to mapping the intricate path that would allow him to exonerate himself from any blame for the whole regrettable business.

"We are taking all the necessary steps," said Strickland,

"I really don't want that sort of information. Not in detail. If we can't gain control ourselves then we must at least make quite certain that no one else does, and for goodness sake make sure that we keep our noses clean."

"Indeed. We will of course be tying up any of the loose ends."

"Such action is entirely operational," said Pederson, "and thus falls within your remit, not mine."

"We are gaining a better understanding of the scope of the situation. It is just a little unfortunate that as yet we do not have access to the data."

"Unfortunate! Unfortunate! I'll give you 'Unfortunate'. If you had intervened sooner we would not be in the position we find ourselves in now. It's not just 'unfortunate'; it is turning into a bloody cock-up, and possibly worse. Under no circumstances do I want this to be an embarrassment to me, and I should make it clear that if things don't go smoothly it is likely to be a good deal more than an embarrassment to you."

Hugh would have to be careful not to allow this rotund and rather florid little man from some northern constituency to get out of hand. "I am not saying that you are wrong, Michael, but there are some positive aspects to this whole affair that I think we can build upon."

Pederson mopped his rapidly balding head with a large spotted handkerchief. Such mopping was not strictly necessary, but was a clear warning sign to those that knew him well that he was on the point of violent explosion. Instead of the expected eruption however his manner became calmer and his voice dropped an octave. He turned away from the high, bullet-proof window that gave out onto the Thames and turned to face his thinner, fitter and slightly older Permanent Under Secretary.

"What we are dealing with here is very sensitive indeed. If word was to get out then the consequences are unthinkable. It goes way beyond HMG, indeed way beyond this country. It is of vital importance that we stop these freelancers and either terminate the whole thing, or perhaps better, bring it in hand."

"You can rely upon the Service to sort things out Minister."

Hugh felt comfortable in this rather forbidding room even if he was far from comfortable about the grilling he was getting from this bumptious politician. The walls were oak-panelled and hung with oil paintings depicting conflicts past. How much simpler life was then, you gave the nod to a rich young aristocrat and within a month he had a regiment fully clothed and horsed at his own expense, ready to do or die in the cause of King and Country.

Michael was plodding on. "Right. So, we have sufficient resources on the ground?"

"Indeed, a very good man, seconded from our Friends Over the Water. They say that he is totally reliable and, thank goodness, with some considerable expertise in the field. There is no doubt that in co-operation with the Friends we are well placed to ensure things go smoothly," said Strickland with quiet satisfaction. He had said enough to ensure that if things went badly he could start to shift the blame in the direction of the Secret Intelligence Service, commonly known as MI6.

"Never mind that. What are our chances of taking on The Project ourselves?"

"The assessment to date is that conditions are not ideal for our participation in the near future without the close cooperation of the current Principals."

"Come on, man, speak English." Michael reached once more for his handkerchief, thought better of it and returned it to his pocket. Where did these mandarins learn to speak such gobbledygook? Back up north a horticultural articulating implement was called a spade.

Strickland spoke slowly, annunciating his words clearly. "We are not capable of running it without the expertise of at least some of the people who are currently involved."

"Well see to it then. It would be preferable for U.K. Inc. if the work could continue, but better to lose it entirely than have it fall into the wrong hands."

Sir Hugh nodded his agreement. "If Fielding continues to be involved with The Project then we need to find out what makes this chap tick."

"You tell me he is a professor at Lancaster, so presumably he is bright enough, but is he a bleeding heart or made of sterner stuff?"

"Enquiries so far suggest that he is reliable." Hugh liked that term. It meant a great deal to those in the Service, but he feared that its full meaning might be lost on this self-important politician.

"Hmmm. But does that mean he will play our game?" said Michael.

High took a deep breath. He would have to spell it out rather more clearly. "It would appear that he is, potentially, 'one of us'. I have had a brief word. By all accounts he is a thoroughly good chap. He was at a half-decent school, went up to Cambridge where he carried a sound bat and read philosophy. He then followed an academic career path."

"Right, so he might be persuaded?"

"It would appear to be a possibility."

"Well that is something of a relief. Now you said that there was a positive spin that we could put on all this?"

"Yes," said Hugh, realizing that this man was more politically astute than he had given him credit for. "We cannot set up our own laboratory in total secrecy, particularly if Fielding joins us. I would therefor advise that it would be appropriate to do so openly, promoting our involvement, and thereby showing that HMG is increasing funding for academic research."

"Obviously without revealing the nature of that research." said Michael.

Hugh would work on this. But in the meantime there was a lot to do. He liked having long-term objectives. Furthermore, and of greater importance, he could at last see how he might extricate himself, his career, and his KCMG from this nasty little affair. A few words with his oppo responsible for Higher Education and the judicious leaking of this 'new Government Initiative' would soon create media interest in the 'initiative', providing the positive result that Michael wanted.

"Very well. I think we can leave it there. The details of this are, as I have made quite clear, operational decisions that I must leave entirely to you. Just give me a few hours warning before going public with the investment in education story. Oh, and arrange a briefing note so that I can make a short statement to the House."

One

It is time to make contact with a world where systems and timing and regulations are the rule. Where the tick of time sweeps us along remorselessly in the only direction that humankind knows, thus maintaining that thin line between order and chaos. Now, the need to re-establish such order is paramount and necessitates a rare intervention.

The pilot knows the rules by which she must now abide. They are not her usual parameters. She has a natural distaste for conformity and a reluctance to enter a situation where at least a degree of conventionality will be required. But there is no moment of hesitation as she reaches across the control panel and switches the aircraft radio to One One Nine Decimal Nine Five.

"Blackpool Approach this is Beechcraft Golf Echo Tango Mike Echo, in-bound from Cyprus, currently twelve miles south of Blackpool, requesting joining instructions."

"Golf Mike Echo, Approach, descend flight level thirty to intercept localiser. QNH is One Zero Two Five. Call at POL."

"Golf Mike Echo, descend three zero. Call at POL."

It has been a long and tiresome flight hardly helped by the constant whine of the small jet's propulsion. If she were a demonstrative individual, she would be feeling relief that she had negotiated her way thus far. She has made too many landings, organized too many refuelling rigs, suffered the groping of too many sweaty and lusting hands since that dusty-red take off from the improvised airstrip in the Outback. She savours the memory of that parched ancient landscape, so different from the chequerboard lushness of this, her destination. Perhaps she should have travelled in a less physically demanding manner, but it is better to ease herself into this assignment and to have accomplished this journey by conventional means.

Dressed in grey flying overalls that make not the slightest attempt to flatter, she rubs her hands over her spiky hair trying for the umpteenth time to reposition the headphones that are crushing her ears in their clamshell grip. She thinks of the shower that she will enjoy as soon as she can find a bit of personal time. Of sluicing the cleansing water down over her head, her shoulders, her whole body. She will rinse the dust from her hair and scrub the grime from her pores.

Bliss!

But before that she will be caught up in the maelstrom of bureaucracy occasioned by an incoming international flight. She is alone, but nevertheless there will be a mound of paperwork that must be completed signed for and docketed.

She is not worried about leaving Egon and the others; this is not the first time she has done so and they will be ready for whatever she needs, or whatever she sends them. She must do what she must. She is a little apprehensive about what lies ahead. She does not wish to cause unhappiness. That said she is confident in her ability to handle tricky situations, and is resolute in her purpose.

She is well travelled but it has been a long time since she has seen the north of England. She remembers it well enough, nevertheless it will take her a while to find her bearings. Places will be different and there will be a number of changes since she was last here. There will be new people whom she must contact, befriend and re-assure. Only then can she start to weave and spin her way into the nub of that which she must accomplish. She has a mission to complete and although her youthful looks belie it, she has more than sufficient ability to perform the task. It will only take a few days, certainly less than a week, and then she will be on her way back to the Others. She is concerned that because of her actions they too may have to fight their own corner, in a different place and different time, in that red desert dust.

"Blackpool Approach, this Mike Echo, at POL."

"Mike Echo, call Tower on One One Eight decimal Four Zero. Good-day"

"Good day." She fiddles again with the radio, changing the frequency.

"Blackpool Tower, Mike Echo, Good morning."

"Mike Echo, runway Two Eight, you are number one, cleared to land. QNH One Zero Two Eight ."

"Mike Echo, cleared to land."

Moments later the private jet taxies noisily across the bitumen to the light aircraft parking area. There is little activity; it is a small airport. There are no other private planes parked here today, Blackpool is hardly a popular destination in late November. The pilot signs off with the Tower, concludes the shutdown checks and jumps down from her aircraft. She finds the refuelling rig and directs it towards her aeroplane.

She is aware that to the rig operator she will appear to be in her early twenties, but looks will deceive.

"Good flight, luv?"

She looks at him. He will see her as quite petite, with striking deep blue eyes and a wide mouth, wearing no discernible make-up. She does not appear as conventionally beautiful but exhibits an inner strength and vitality.

"Not bad. I need to sign off, and then grab a shower."

She is aware that she is making a lasting impression on this man, as she does with most of those with whom she comes into contact.

"Admin block, over there. You can sort out the paperwork with Mike. Just ask him about the shower and he will get you sorted." He points to a single storey building over to her left.

She waits until the refuelling is complete and signs off on the tally sheet.

"Thanks."

She heads for the concrete-rendered functional building. She will need to travel on for less than an hour. There are a few basic preparations that she must see to before she can start her work.

Two

The dawn was making a reluctant effort to put in an appearance, it being a lazy time of year for the sun; one of those late November mornings when it seemed disinclined to part company with the horizon and thereby fulfil its allotted purpose.

"Seeing your lover again this evening, Miranda?" I asked, glancing at my wife across the breakfast table. I had to admit, if only to myself, that she was a good-looking woman with her auburn hair cascading down around her shoulders and her intense blue eyes smiling at me.

"I'll be in the lab until late."

"Another all-nighter?"

"I've got so much to do, and only that bloody little Simon to help me."

"I thought Simon was your bosom buddy?"

Some time ago I had indeed suspected this to be the sordid truth, however of late I had come to realise that I might well be pissing up the wrong lamppost.

"I can't imagine why I saddled myself with such a very passé Doctor of Mathematics, when I could be enjoying the enthusiastic commitment of an energetic young physics post-grad."

I knew that this wife of mine was referring to the scientific ability of a suitable postgraduate rather than any of the physical attributes that such a youth might exhibit. On the cerebral-carnal scale Miranda was unflinchingly allied to the beauty of the thought process rather than gratification of the flesh. Thus she and my occasional drinking companion, Simon Pennick, were to be cooped up together for yet another evening without even a frisson of attraction to relieve the mighty experimental steps that they would be taking into the unknown.

"What about your evening; perhaps you could amuse yourself by chasing some floozie?"

"What an anachronism. Anyway I haven't done anything like 'chase a floozie' for aeons . . . . well at least a couple of months."

"That's just as well. I am always worried that you will catch something unmentionable from these one-night stands of yours. You must look after yourself."

"It's OK, Randy, I'm careful."

Despite our problems we look after each other.

Perhaps because of my own occasional dalliances it was a surprise for me to learn that it was Miranda who had gone the whole hog and immersed herself in a serious liaison. She was entirely honest about having an affair but she never let on to me who her lover was, and I did not consider it appropriate to ask.

Thinking back a couple of years it now seems ridiculous that the two of us made the mistake of getting married. We were barely passed the Signing in the Registry stage before we both admitted that it was a singularly foolish thing to have done. Entirely our own fault, we should have foreseen the problems, but did not, and the deed had been duly enacted.

Miranda had said to me that it wasn't that we were not fond of each other and, savouring the double negative I had admitted that we had stumbled into the arrangement without thinking it through. As it was living together was convenient and comfortable and our situation did not warrant anything as drastic as divorce.

After a few attempts to indulge in sexual intimacy we had admitted that we were incompatible. In order to avoid anything too Ruskin-esque we had, in the first week of marriage, achieved a physically painful, emotionally wretched, but nevertheless legally binding, form of consummation, following which we each retreated, both spatially and metaphorically, to our own comfort zones, and stayed there.

"It was daft of us to marry," Miranda had said, "It was only because of my parents, poor things, they just couldn't wait to get me properly coupled off, and you really were the candidate of least harm."

It was a great sadness to us both that Miranda's parents only just had time to see their eldest daughter bolted firmly into wedlock before they perished in that awful ferry tragedy in India. It was such bloody bad luck, stupid too, that boat was way over-crowded, they just copped the disaster that was inevitable.

Breakfast over I set out from home at the same time as my wife, the pair of us enjoying the extravagance of separate cars, she bound for her laboratory and I to my tutorial; convenience getting the better of eco-conscience.

"Stephen, I know you have prepared some work, perhaps you would care to give us the benefit of your thoughts on the subject?"

The student in question was not really called Stephen but boasted a Chinese name foreign to the Western tongue.

I turned to the sanitised view offered to me through the plate glass of the window. Only three months ago that ragged looking fuchsia was in full bloom providing nectar for its adoring collection of bumblebees as they paid homage to its sugary flowers. Now this charming but isolated plant will have to fend for itself as the winter closes in upon it. Beyond, there is a dearth of aesthetic delight in the ocean of rye grass mono-culture that stretched to the boundary of the campus. Close to me, at the very margins of this cropped green desert, those executioners of horticulture, the university's gang-mower brigade, were unable to reach any beautiful alien intruders to cut and tear them to shreds. Only here, I mused, along this meagre unkempt strand, can the fuchsia, and a thin smattering of fellow pioneers of summertime individuality, inch themselves cautiously up the 1960's grey walls of these, the cell blocks of academe.

I turned back from the window to scan the dozen expectant faces. I spoke quietly and without undue frustration. "We have done Death; that was last week; now we are concentrating on the consequences of dying. "

I started to build a philosophical analogy of the horticultural escapees. They existed as great minds, freed from the order imposed upon them by the World State. Swarming around each would buzz their acolytes, a dozen bees, each eager to taste the exquisite fruits of original thought; thence to fly homeward bearing with them sweet droplets of metaphysical truth.

I focused my attention upon the serious but lacklustre presentation from a Chinese called Stephen.

"Excellent work, Stephen," I said as the diatribe swooped, slowed and, toppled with the finality of a landing glider, coming to a faltering halt. I had failed to listen to more than a few words of this inelegant chinoiserie but that hardly seems to matter. Such millstones as these were my bread and butter, and essential to help fund The Project that Miranda and I had been working on this past three years.

By early evening, after a day on campus, I was just comparing the relative merits of a cold empty home with the more compelling cosy companionship of the saloon bar of the Kings Head when my mobile burst into a wayward love song, thus interrupting my imminent departure for the pub.

"Bugger off," I said to it.

It did no such thing.

I reached for the offending device and hit 'receive' only to find that it was babbling Simonese. "Duncan," it said with just a trace more West Country lilt than is normally present in Dr Pennick's delivery. "It's Miranda, she's badly hurt. Get down here to the Lab pronto. I'm pouring water over her."

Bits of this message make sense, but why the hell is Simon dousing Miranda in the wet stuff?

I made it to the lab in great time but in greater perplexity. Miranda was usually so very careful about practical experimentation; however, I was not sure that Simon was as cautious. I also know she was working with some decidedly noxious substances, including radioactive isotopes.

Miranda was lying in a crumpled heap over on the far side of the room. I lowered my frame floor-wards to better catch the few words that she was attempting to mumble. The linoleum was wet, my knees were wet, my wife was exceptionally wet.

"I found her like this" said Simon. "I've secured the Lab and phoned for an ambulance."

"What the hell happened?"

"I don't know. I went into the cuddy to make us both a mug of tea, I heard an almighty crash and Miranda was lying sprawled out on the floor. There was a smell of burnt hair and her face was very hot; all I could think to do was to pour lots of water over her."

By this stage Miranda was attempting to stagger to her feet, but without demonstrable success. I lent a hand and with some help from Simon deposit her upon a swivel chair. The chair rotated a full turn and the bloody thing came to the end of its thread and deposited itself, its passenger, Simon and myself under a solid workbench..

We decided by mutual consent, to conduct further communication whilst sitting on the floor under the bench. It was not exactly cosy, but it was convenient enough.

"I'm clearly going to die," said Miranda.

"What the hell happened?" I said.

"It was the brain-scan laser. I must have overclocked it. But you know what, the experiment damn nearly worked. I reckon I just about captured the evidence. It's what we have wanted all this time."

Simon was sitting with his mouth open but keeping very quiet.

Miranda continued, "Dunc, we need to face the inevitable."

Much as I would have liked to hug the bearer of such burdensome news my ability to do so was more than a little constrained by my sitting squashed underneath the bench. All I could do was to provide a sympathetic nod of the head.

Miranda went on, "If the authorities find out about this accident then The Project is doomed. You two must fix it with the University and the Hospital to make it seem that I'm in the terminal stages of cancer caused by a malignant brain stem tumour. This will explain my post-accident symptoms. Do you think you can do that?"

I knew my wife, her strong will, and her clarity of thought. Nevertheless, it was a long speech from someone facing their imminent demise, considering that only a rotating chair ago she was unable to utter anything remotely intelligible. Miranda had however cracked the problem of how The Project might be saved. With Simon's help I now had to set about achieving a massive cover-up of the accident.

Our unhappy little under-the-bench party was rudely torn asunder by an inrush of figures clad in yellow and green, their radios bleeping and sundry equipment trailing. Simon, ever the practical one, curtailed their attempts to extract me from beneath the bench and to load me onto a gurney. He pointed an accusatorial finger at the female member of our small group. "She is sick," he intones, "she is in the terminal stages of cancer caused by a malignant brain stem tumour." Simon made up for that which he lacks in intelligence by possessing an an excellent memory

With consummate ease the dying Miranda was rolled onto a stretcher, dumped across the gurney and rushed from the scene.

I decided that the time had come for Simon and I to resume vertical status.

I said, "Hospital Chairman."

Simon said, "Pro Vice Chancellor."

We went our separate ways to heap deception upon harsh reality.

It took Miranda nearly a month to die.

Three

Food!" I say, better to ensure that I understand myself. "Better do something about it."

My search for digestive inspiration meets but scant success. Home with Miranda was hardly heaven upon earth, but without Miranda it is almost entirely unwelcoming. Talking to myself is hardly a substitute for her, but perhaps it relieves the emptiness.

As ever the choice, due to my culinary incompetence, is a limited one: demolish a can of baked beans or order a pizza. The latter is easier, but entails the inevitable wait for delivery. It is a tedious conundrum that I face on an almost daily basis.

"Time against work; a moral dilemma. Hell, Duncan, you are slithering headlong into your own philosopher-speak."

Like Balaam's Ass I stand unable to choose between these alternatives, prepared indeed to starve upon the horns of my indecision. But a butterfly flaps its wings in the Caribbean, unnumbered forces, great and small, act upon the planet, the pendulum swings, and decisions are made.

"Tonight, the beans have it!"

I extract a recalcitrant can from the upper cupboard and wrench at the ring pull.

"Bugger!" I say to a weary and unheeding world "Can't get the bloody thing undone."

A small circlet of metal now adorns my index finger whilst the can remain otherwise untouched and untroubled by events.

"Duncan," I say to myself, "you're falling apart."

"Nonsense," a more practical part of me replies, "It is just that it was one hell of a sight easier when they expected folk to use a tin opener. Now it's is all 'Pull the Ring', and if it comes off in your hand what are you supposed to do?"

I mutter Dark Things to relieve stress. I cast around in a rather futile way, rummaging in several drawers before discovering an old-type opener cowering behind a disused egg timer fearful that it is destined for the Tip. I hold the tin securely on the worktop and stab at it hard with the pointed bit of the device. The resulting gash is too near the centre of the tin.

"Bugger!" I say again, to a world that has no intention of replying, and would undoubtedly have terrified me if it had. I stab once more, this time with rather greater accuracy.

The tin's defences are now breached at a more appropriate point. I insert the opener and work it around the can until it makes the full circle. Still using the tool, I try to lever up the jagged edges. The opener slips.

Blood flows.

"Bugger!" I say for the third time, sucking my finger. The world remains unimpressed and unmoved by my plight.

"Come on Miranda," I say, uncertain as to whether I should be looking towards the stars or the fiery depths as I address my late wife, "stop rolling around with laughter at my incompetence. I know that neither of us were particularly expert on the domestic front, but you could have at least given me a celestial hint or two about how to deal with this blasted can."

Mournfully I inspect the gloopy morass within the tin, think better of indulging in such a blood-bespattered meal and drop the offending proto-meal into an already overfull bin.

"OK, Beans one, Duncan nil!" I admit to a totally unresponsive rack of kitchen knives that is hanging forlorn and unused on the wall to the right of the sink. "Tonight, is not the previously billed Night of the Bean. Tonight, we have a change of schedule. Tonight is – boom – boom – boom - Pizza Night!"

I wander into the downstairs bathroom, sucking my finger, in search of solace and sticking plaster. I glance into the basin mirror. Staring back at me is the adequately handsome face of a man who, as the forces of middle age wash over him, is happy to bend to their onslaught rather than take up arms against this particular sea of troubles. He wears his hair just a shade longer than is acceptable, even for someone in his profession.

I can hear Miranda's voice chiding me. "You poor old sod, you're turning grey."

Close inspection reveals just one or two light strands are beginning to pepper the dark brown masses.

"Not so," I respond, "such picturesque adornments merely add to my air of academic distinction, they are hardly harbingers of an onrush of senility."

Finger duly plastered I make my way to the sitting room. I pick up the phone from the small inlaid table beside the window. I prod at a couple of buttons on the handset.

"Hi, is that the Pizza Palace? This is Duncan from 27 Druridge Street".

The voice at the other end is female, remote and entirely disinterested in all things Duncan.

"Hi, Donna, how are you doing?"

The reply is as intelligible as a call centre from Pluto: distant, noncommittal and meaningless.

I continue unfazed by this unusual coolness, "Well tonight I reckon I'll treat myself and go for your regular Hawaiian with, err, Nachos."

The order having been successfully accomplished I replace the phone and flop my long bony frame into the larger and rather more comfortable of the two easy chairs. My meal should be delivered in about thirty minutes. I pick up the remote and flick on the T.V.

Disconcertingly I find myself suspended in a helicopter staring down vertiginously from above a sea-wracked cliff hounded by a Hitchcock-esque flock of wheeling, crying seabirds. The cliffs look terrifying; the sea gnaws cruelly at their base. The birds ebb and flow above the sheer walls. My mind spins in anguish at the precariousness of it all. A well-modulated voice oozes from its perch in the helicopter describing the tousled scene with untoward sanguinity.

The theme jingle for the ten o'clock news starts me from my doze. Reality barges in and ensures that my attention is refocused towards another bank crisis, a kidnapping, hurricane damage in the Caribbean - the news is either awful, or predictable, or both.

The front doorbell rings. My stomach gives a Pavlovian lurch. The pizza has arrived. I stumble through to the hall switching lights as I go.

Fumbling, I unhook the security chain and release the lock.

"Pizza for Professor Fielding!" sings out a clear voice from under the hood of a grey anorak.

The pizza is thrust forcefully towards my midriff. As I make to receive the box I find to my alarm that it is not being relinquished, indeed, propelled by it, I am being hustled backwards through the hallway. I make pitiful efforts to stem the advance of pizza and its deliverer, but fail.

"Who the hell are you. What sort of shit is this?"

The perpetrator, this head-down Hoodie, slams the door behind us with its foot.

The suddenness of such unprovoked invasion neutralises any possibility of resistance.

Fear overwhelms me.

No chance for a pause. Instead I am swept up in the moment, unresisting, uncomprehending, a passive victim of uncalled for circumstance.

I want to shout, to scream, to defecate. Instead I find myself continuing to be forced backwards through the hall and into the kitchen.

"Help!" I shout to a deaf world, "Help, I'm being mugged!"

I am being pushed hard up against the right-hand wall near the sink, and still this Hoodie is not letting go of the pizza box.

Is this a mugging? At what stage does a firm push become a physical assault – and then a mugging?

Where are this person's accomplices?

Are there any accomplices?

Words are not being spoken.

My assailant does not seem to be bearing a weapon any more threatening than the pizza box. My apprehension level that has been so cruelly elevated now retreats a notch to just below 'high'.

I remain slammed up against the wall. This is not a position that I feel comfortable in.

My assailant backs off a bit, still holding the pizza box. I am less immediately threatened, but most uncomfortable. There is a definite impression of a sharp ridge just below my shoulder blades. Of course, it is the knife rack. I always knew that I had put it in a stupid place, a fact that Miranda had reminded me of on innumerable occasions.

"Stop!" I say, finding a voice of indignation, "what the hell do you think that you're up to?"

"This is your pizza delivery, sir."

"No it isn't, this isn't the way that pizzas get delivered." I know I am correct about this. Over the past month I have, perforce, honed up my personal experience in the pizza deliveree department.

"This is a special delivery, a very special delivery, a very special delivery just for you."

It takes a while for the idea to dawn upon me. Very cautiously I feel behind my back with my left hand until I locate the rack. This is tricky, there are at least half a dozen knives dangling precariously from their magnetic catches. I have an aversion to sharp knife-like things falling off racks under the influence of gravity thus effectively transmuting my back into an involuntary pincushion. My hand moves cautiously upwards and detects a large blade. That will do. One gentle tug and I have it in my palm. At least I now have a weapon.

"I didn't order, nor do I want, any sort of Special Pizza Delivery."

"That's a shame, after all the trouble that I've gone to in providing you with such a personal service."

"Well just leave the box here and get out."

"I think it would be a whole heap more friendly if we were to share it, sir," comes the response.

"The Hell we will" I say, clutching grimly to the knife but, emulating Mac upon his Sidewalk, manage to keep it out of sight.

This is far from good. I have not yet been assaulted, but it can only be a matter of time. Young people that burst into middle class homes late in the evening are, in my vast experience, motivated by bad deeds rather than good intentions. Probably supporting a drug habit. It would be best not to escalate the situation; I am in enough danger as it is.

"What can I give you? How much money do you want?"

"Hey, relax, it's OK," says the interloper, "Please don't be frightened, I mean you no harm and certainly didn't mean to scare you."

I am a rabbit petrified in car headlights. Of course I am scared. Bloody scared.

The Hoodie removes her jacket revealing a head of spiky close-cropped yellow hair and an altogether pleasing young lady, perhaps in her mid twenties. "Hi," she says.

"Who the hell are you?"

"You can call me Starlight".

"That's a very strange name."

"You'll find it less strange than my real one," says the female who calls herself Starlight. "Come on. Don't worry. Nothing's going to hurt you. Let's sit down".

Why should I do what she is telling me? I am in danger and it would be considerably more effective to be standing when it comes to defending myself. My instant judgement however is that this Starlight person is not one to be trifled with. Perhaps it's best to take the line of least resistance – for now.

I sit.

I really do not understand what's going on. Why is she picking on me? What is the point of this Starlight girl barging in on my evening? The situation is decidedly discomforting. I suppose that she might have come from the Pizza Palace, but I have never seen her before. She has an air about her more akin to a film star or royalty than a pizza delivery person. This could hardly be some sort of food promotion; after all I am being invited to share my food with her, food that I have paid for with my own money. This is no free hand-out that I am being coaxed into buying.

"This isn't a food promotion is it?" I ask, knowing full well that it is not.

"Not very likely," comes the reply.

I am almost sure that this girl does not mean me any immediate harm. That is not to say that I am out of danger, just that the risk of incipient injury has receded. As a gesture of conciliation, and to steady my nerves, I bring my hand round from behind my back and carefully place the knife down on the table in front of me, being sure to position it within within easy reach.

"OK" I say, trying to defuse the situation. "Here's the deal. You and your friends stop threatening me and I'll leave this weaponry, this knife, where it is."

The girl looks at the knife lying on the table and then stares me straight in the face. A smile plays around her mouth and her blue eyes twinkle with merriment.

"Threaten?" she says.

"Yes, "

"Weaponry?"

"Yes."

"But that's a bread knife."

I look down, and sure enough the weapon of choice for the defence of my mortal body is but the saw-toothed, blunt-ended slicer of my morning toast-fest. I feel foolish.

The girl smiles the most gorgeous smile I have ever seen. "Serious weaponry I see!"

I look at her, look at the bread knife, and capitulate. "I don't suppose it's that much of a threat." I too am grinning now.

"Come on let's eat." says Starlight, "I'm starving!"

Whilst she tucks in to the pizza with considerable gusto I find that one slice is sufficient for me. I really ought to be handling the situation differently, but what on earth should I do? This is a gross intrusion upon my property, my privacy, and my life. I was taken unawares or this would never have occurred. I have yet to discover why

I should be entertaining, at my own expense, an uninvited guest at ten fifteen on a cold Monday evening.

"Look," I say, "that's my pizza you are eating."

"I thought we were sharing it."

I try hard to remember if I have seen the girl before. It flashes across my mind that she might have attended one of my seminars over the past couple of years, but I cannot place her. I am almost certain that she is not one of the regular delivery people from the Pizza Palace.

"Who are you? Have I met you before?"

"Conceivably!" says the girl who calls herself Starlight.

"What do you mean 'conceivably'? Have you come from the Pizza Palace?"

"Almost certainly."

She is really quite attractive. She has draped her jacket over the back of one of the kitchen chairs revealing a well filled white T-shirt. She is a good deal shorter than I am, not thin, but well proportioned. Her spiky blonde hair is just a shade lighter than her eyebrows. Her eyes are of the most intense dark blue and her demeanour is friendly and relaxed.

She calls herself Starlight, but has said that this is not her real name. I wonder what that is. Even if she has come from the Pizza Palace that would hardly explain her actions. Perhaps she has bribed one of the regular delivery staff so that she can bring my pizza to me; but why me? If she intends me no harm, and I am by no means convinced of that, then what is the point of a young lady of undoubted attractiveness breaking into the home of a crotchety old widower at this time of night?

I just might rephrase that 'crotchety old widower' bit. It hardly does me justice. How about 'eligible philosopher exuding maturity and wit'? God, that is worse! It sounds like an advert for speed dating at Saga. I toy with this analogy for a full minute with just a trace of a smile forming around the corners of my mouth. In doing so I abandon the attempt to couch myself in more flattering terms.

"Have you come here alone," I say, trying to make it sound casual.

"Probably." says Starlight.

"Look here, it's about time that you gave me a straight answer!"

"Hey, don't get cross. Chill, just go with the flow," says my potential assailant.

I definitely fancy this girl. I wonder what my bodily systems are making of having to switch from 'full fight' mode to 'incipient desire' mode in such a short space of time. My whole endocrine system must be approaching overload. I resolve that whatever the state of the various hormones doing battle within this temple of humanity known as me, I must remain very cautious of this young lady. The sexual stirrings she is arousing in me are all very well, but my situation remains perilous. If I weaken to my baser nature I will be laying myself open to all sorts of future accusations. The situation is too fraught to take any chances, especially those that might be considered as compromising. Perhaps I should phone the Pizza Palace to see if she is indeed one of their delivery girls. On the other hand how about giving a spot of direct action a try?

"I'm going to chuck you out." I say. "You can't just wander in on me like this, violate my house, eat my food, and speak in monosyllables."

"The words 'conceivably', 'probably' and 'certainly' have three or four syllables each."

"God-damn it. Get Out!"

Starlight does not seem in the least dismayed. She looks at me with, to my concern, a slightly pitying expression. She makes as if to say something but apparently changes her mind. She pushes her chair backwards across the floor with sudden resolve. She rises to her feet. She smiles slightly at me. She crosses to the kitchen sink. "I need some water."

I soak up her youthful figure appraisingly. What am I supposed to do now? I can hardly manhandle her out the door and throw her bodily into the street. Perhaps I should call the police, but that might land me in fairly hot water, depending upon what she says to them. It would be fairly easy for her to maintain that she was innocently delivering a pizza and that I hauled her into the house against her will and thereupon set about ravishing her.

I play that bit back again so that I can maintain the scene a little longer I really rather like the verb 'to ravish'. I try to remember whether I have ever ravished anything or anyone in my whole life, but nothing comes to mind. Pity really, it is a waste of a really good word if it is not put to sound practical use.

The girl calling herself Starlight bends over the sink. Her upper body curls around as she opens her mouth beneath the cold tap and drinks water directly from it. Her left foot lifts from the floor as her torso bends and her leg extends. Wow, I really fancy this girl.

She turns and sees on my face what can only be an expression of drooling lust, with just a morsel of Ravish still remaining. "Do you want to fuck me now?" she says.

Four

London was having one of its bad days as its arteries teetered towards a collapse into chaos. The drizzle of the wintry morning had persisted late into the afternoon bringing shame upon the weather forecasters and misery to all. Christmas shoppers were colliding with things animate and inanimate throughout every cranny of the capital. The gutters of the side streets, swollen by the remorseless rain, bore a slush of discarded rubbish pulped by crushing wheels into a festering morass. Buses bulged with bodies crammed beyond the limits of personal space; squashed, soggy, irritable refugees from that even harsher world of the streets. Dry, fortunate, and grateful, the smug few had commandeered the remaining black cabs thus achieving the ultimate goal of the day in distancing themselves from the reality of the seething, dripping masses.

Helen Marston buttoned her chic coat against the elements, snapped her umbrella open and stepped into Devonshire Street. She bothered to make two futile attempts to hail a taxi before accepting the inevitable with a slight sigh of resignation. She had little option but to turn her back to the wind and rain and hurry off in the direction of Great Portland Street underground station.

Battling to keep her brolly as a protective shield behind her Helen smiled wryly as she recalled her last clients of the day. She knew them as a small but ambitious firm of builders based in Enfield. Goodness knows what sort of scam they were pulling in hiring her company's suite of meeting rooms at such vast expense, but she had set the whole thing up for them beautifully. Their 'punters' would have had no idea that the chameleon-like offices of 'Room for Business Ltd' were not the London headquarters of a major civil engineering firm.

Helen was good at her job and enjoyed the games that she was able to help her clients play in renting out her buildings for their possibly slightly nefarious purposes. She could create all that was required: offices, boardrooms and company headquarters as well as provide 'virtual office' facilities such as phone lines and e-mail addresses. 'Corporate Prostitution' she had called it, creating a semblance of reality, a vision created of smoke and mirrors that could be made to disappear with one stroke of her magic wand. She was not sure that her staff would appreciate their hard work being so described.

She had remembered this time to get her building supervisor to replace the temporary nameplate at the entrance door with the real one. Details mattered in her business and it had been embarrassing a month or two back when the team had overlooked a simple nameplate change. Now she had made sure that the building was set up for the small informal meeting that one of her regular clients had scheduled for tomorrow morning. No deception involved with this one, but again it had to be right.

Helen had been devastated by the death some three weeks ago of her older sister. Miranda had been just two years her senior and throughout their lives had been very much the leader. Miranda had been the clever one, with her University Fellowship and her long list of published works and then her position leading a cutting-edge research team. Helen's own achievements seemed to her to be rather feeble by comparison. "Mind you," she thought, "I'll be earning a damn sight more money than Miranda ever did."

The funeral at what had been their parents' home village of Cartmel, and then the memorial service a couple of days later in Lancaster had been satisfactory. Duncan had dealt with the whole rigmarole of coroners and undertakers before she had arrived up north and she was sure that she had been wise, and indeed quite happy, to go along with Duncan's suggestion that she should not view her dead sister's body. "Best to remember her as you knew her in life," he had said. It was one of death's many clichés, but she knew Duncan was right.

The wake had been a little harder to cope with. She had not known many of Miranda's friends and such conversations as she had joined in with had been tediously academic, but Duncan had kept an eye on her and had come swooping over to the rescue as and when help was needed. She had spent the minimum time up north before returning to the boutique home in Islington that she had, until very recently, shared with George.

Helen dipped into the station, flashed her plastic at the card reader, and was fighting her way through the crowds on the eastbound platform just as a tube clattered to a halt. No chance of the sanctuary of a seat during the evening rush hour, but she only had to endure for a couple of stops. She suffered the squeeze down the carriage and hung on with grim determination to an overhead strap. She would have to change at Kings Cross. There was a momentary wait at Euston Square, then the train lurched viciously into action again playing its usual sport of skittles with its passengers, who cannoned each other towards the end doors of the carriage. They were plunged into the dry darkness before hurtling into Kings Cross and St Pancras. The doors opened and Helen allowed herself to be ejected from the tube along with the outgoing crush of passengers and baggage.

There was the usual mêlée; people turning, twisting, crushing, changing direction. She made for the Victoria line. Arriving on the platform she pushed her way forcibly towards the far end in search of a little more space. There was a collective intake of breath from the crowd behind her; she looked round. Someone screamed. There was a shout of "No" as the executioner howled out of its tunnel, brakes locked, iron wheels scrabbling ineffectually against the remorseless destiny of the rails.

"Oh Bugger," said a respectable looking man to no one in particular. "Another bloody jumper, that's all we need."

Helen, to her shame, felt much the same. "Incredible how inconsiderate people are to do this sort of thing at Rush Hour," she thought, and then "Oh, my God. Look at what living in London has done to me!"

The Unfeeling Monster of the Underground, made her way to the Northern Line platform, suffered an even more intimate transportation experience, alighted at the Angel and walked homewards along Liverpool Road. It continued to rain.

Helen had been fortunate to buy the house in Bewdley Street about three years ago. It was a fashionable enough address and she had very much set her heart on it. The price had been high and repayments of the resulting mortgage were towards the upper limit even of her income, so that generous contributions from the recently removed George had been particularly welcome. Now that he had left (and "bloody good riddance to the wanker" she thought) she would have to plan her retail therapy with a little more care. She needed to be sure that she could continue to cover the repayments.

She unlocked the oiled oak door, deposited her wet, and ridiculously expensive, coat in the hall, picked up the post, and kicked off her shoes. She glanced into the mirror and gave her medium length exquisitely styled dark brown hair a quick primp. She wandered into the dining area to pour herself a drink. The two gold bracelets on her left wrist clinked together as she waved the gin bottle generously at an eager cut glass tumbler.

The house boasted a Spartan rather than a luxurious style of furnishing. Those pieces it did contain were expensive and interesting rather than comfortable. There were three exquisitely chosen paintings that reflected both her excellent taste and George's ample wallet. She sank, ever so slightly, into the plush cushions of a green chaise that was one of but a few outstanding pieces.

Half a glass of G&T, a gas bill, a credit card statement and an appeal from Oxfam received appropriate treatment. Helen picked up a small white envelope with her name and address typed on it. It did not look like a bill and bore none of the hallmarks that denote a charitable appeal. With slightly quickened interest she slit it open. Inside was a single piece of white paper, folded in half. It read:

'FROM WHAT DID MIRANDA DIE'

That was all; displayed in bold capital type. Nothing more. No address. No signature. Not even an interrogation mark. Helen looked at the postmark. The letter bore a legend denoting that it had been posted yesterday in Preston.

She sat looking at the message trying to divine further meaning from its simple text. Her first thought was that it must be a hoax, although in the very worst of taste. Someone wanted to upset her by casting totally unjustified suspicion on the sufferings of her poor sister. She wondered about George but, pig as he was, he would not do such a thing to her. His metier was a needle-sharp caustic wit, not the abusive pen. She was surprised to discover herself suddenly missing the undoubted benefit of George, or to be more precise the benefit of George's logical brain. It would have been good to talk this through with him. He could be relied upon to smother any desperate crisis with the dreariness of a finely tuned legal mind.

She had indeed wondered about the progression of Miranda's startlingly rapid death. She knew that cancer could strike quickly and conclusively, but Miranda's behaviour was hardly consistent with the sister that she knew. Miranda had not confided in her about her illness, and that was highly unusual. Helen readily admitted that she had not known anyone who had died from an inoperable brain tumour, so she accepted that for all she knew the speed and unexpectedness of the diagnosis, and the rapid progression of the disease, were entirely normal. But it had seemed wrong that Miranda had not spoken of it to her.

Duncan had seemed quite satisfied with the care that Miranda received. He, after all, had a lot more to do with the hospital authorities than she. Now she felt guilty that she had only managed a one-day visit to Lancaster. Perhaps she should have stayed up there during Miranda's short illness, but what use could she have been? Whilst she loved her sister dearly, they had never been 'touchy feely' types and the thought of holding Miranda's hand and watching her die filled Helen with the deepest dread.

Helen's phone rang.

It was George.

"I thought I might discover you sola domi," he said. "Following our recent minor contretemps and your rash ejection of me and mine from chez nous I distinctly remember your catchy phrases that, roughly translated, suggested that you were not at all enamoured of the idea of setting eyes upon me again. Well, in these changing times water has flowed, so to speak, and I have tidings that I need to impart to you over foul food and fine wine."

Five minutes earlier Helen would have screamed a string of obscenities at this master of the flowery phrase and flung the receiver down. Even now this would have given her a great deal of satisfaction. She was sorely tempted. However, the needs of the moment prevailed and instead she said, in an almost conciliatory voice tinged with only a small element of canine command, "Come here now, George. I need to talk to you too!"

Five

Come on", says the girl who calls herself Starlight. She moves away from the sink, "You've been lusting after me for the last five minutes. If you want me for Christ sake let's get on with it!"

I consider her proposition. Perhaps I am in the grip of some sort of male fantasy thing. I am well aware that the lust for non-consequential sex is an almost inseparable part of the universal male condition. The Man-thing is to fantasise about sex being offered free of commitment and without emotional attachment. And now here it is; that offer of a golden opportunity. This is my chance to indulge myself with no long-term commitment and without guilt. That said I am still very doubtful about the motives of this girl. Sex is all very well but I can think of no reasonable cause for her to be offering herself to me on a serving dish.

"Look, I don't know what is going on," I say, "but you can hardly consider me much of a 'catch' so there must be some motive for your being here other than providing me with the opportunity of a quick shag. Could you please tell me just what the hell you are playing at?"

It seems to me that I am being set up for a criminal act or, at best, some frightful scam. It will be best to refrain from doing anything that could be considered compromising. The situation that I am in is fraught with all sorts of hazard and despite enticing sexual favours being on offer I must make sure that I minimize those dangers.

Perhaps it is some form of morality test and by declining her very attractive offer I will have shown myself to be less animalistic than the average male. Furthermore, it might help me gain a better understanding of what is going on if I could discover more about Starlight; where she comes from, and why she has barged into my house in such extraordinary circumstances.

It is just a possibility that this girl, who calls herself Starlight, is not real. Indeed, the pizza might not be real either and it is conceivable that I could still be dozing my way through the television news. I am not sure whether the question of reality is of great consequence.

"You know, "she says, "there is only the flimsiest of boundaries between the dreaming and waking states, between reality and illusion."

It is as if she knows what I am thinking. I ponder over which of those states I am in, awake or dreaming, sensing reality or creating illusion. Perhaps I am lucid dreaming? If I play along with the situation will I discover the answer? Of course, there may not be an answer. I opt for enlightenment against gratification.

"No, not just yet," I say in answer to Starlight's original question "although I could always change my mind."

She gives me a fleeting smile. "I'll take my clothes off anyway", she says, unzipping and stepping out of her jeans, "I'd like to be ready, just in case you do."

Blast! I've got to stop this. It is leading me into very dangerous territory. "No", I say, "No, don't do that. I don't know why I mentioned changing my mind, I really have no intention of doing so"

"Why not, are you scared of me?"

"No. Well yes a bit, but it's not that."

"Well what is it then?"

"You would not be here in my kitchen if all you were looking for was a bit of sex. You may have come with criminal intent, but I'm beginning to doubt that, so what is the reason? Is this some kind of test?"

"Possibly," she says.

It is hard to read these enigmatic replies, but I get the impression that I could take that as a 'yes'. If so then I have indeed passed this test, although it is ludicrous position to be in. As if in confirmation of my reasoning Starlight bends down and, with only the slightest show of reluctance, pulls up her jeans. She zips them up and sits down.

There is a long silence.

"Could get a bit Pinteresque, this", she says.

I nod my head.

"I suppose in a way we are all actors," I say, verbalising my train of thought.

"In what way?"

"On occasion we exist, that is both our bodies and our lives, in a moral vacuum that allows others to pull the strings for us."

"You feel that you are playing a part in a life written for you by someone else? That's perilously close to suggesting that all our actions are predetermined."

"Not that. I believe strongly in free will," I say, "No, it's just that sometimes we feel or behave as if we are characters, manipulated very lightly by some external force. This still allows us to expand on that template using our own free will. We, as these characters, are playing out our lives as if on a scroll that is continuously unravelling. It results in us having to accept at least the road towards our individual destiny whilst contriving as best we can to modify it by means of our personal input."

I am concerned that I have not put that very well.

"Perhaps there is also a detachment from reality. The sort of feeling that's experienced when waking after an anaesthetic, where dream and reality exist side by side and it's possible to flip from one to the other without awareness of which state you're in."

The girl who calls herself Starlight is looking at me critically. I am sure that she understands me perfectly.

"Do you think there is more than one way of expressing reality?" I ask.

She is letting me do the talking, letting me explore the notion of consciousness. Why should she want me to do that? There is a strange quality to this girl that makes me wonder if she is playing even more of a role than I have just considered; a role that goes beyond mere illusion into a different sort of reality. Now this is getting interesting, this is my field of work, the possibility of human thoughts being capable of accessing more than one state of existence.

"Where are you from?" I ask, with perhaps a little too much interest in my voice.

"That does not matter."

"Of course it matters. What are you here to do?"

"I'm here to talk to you."

Perhaps another person or organisation has assigned her to this role. Is it possible that she, or they, are after information from me about the research project that Miranda and I have spent so much time and effort working on? If that is the case what could they possibly want from it? I need more information about her.

"Who the hell are you?" I ask.

"Your delivery girl," she responds.

"Pizzas do not come with their own free gamines; at least not ones that join me at my kitchen table."

"I was called for," she says.

"Not by me."

"Oh yes, it was all in your phone call".

"Nonsense, I quite clearly only ordered a large Hawaiian with Nachos. I emphatically did not order you, or anything like you."

Starlight looks mildly affronted "With some orders," she says "you can get more than you bargain for."

Too right, I think. But say aloud, "So did you come from the Pizza Palace?" I am damned if I am going to let this drop in a hurry.

"Possibly not," says Starlight, "but tell me why it matters."

I am a little stumped by this. I speak as the words come into my head. "Things need some sort of logic to them. You are here now and you were not here before, so you must have come from somewhere else. You came bearing Pizza, so it seems logical that you came from the Pizza Palace."

"Possibly!"

"No, not 'possibly', but 'definitely'."

"There are things that you're not letting yourself understand," she says.

"There are things that I can't understand; like you!"

"If you think too hard you won't gain understanding. When you cannot remember a name it does not help to keep trying to recall it, you just relax, do something else, and in a minute or an hour or a day it 'll just pop into your head."

"That's my subconscious at work."

"Probably, but it's not the process that matters, it is the analogy."

"I think you are just trying to stop me from questioning the Who and the What and the Why about you."

"I know it's not easy, but you must let go a bit, allow yourself to feel things, not just think them."

"So perhaps I should have screwed you?"

"No," she says. "No, because whilst your body was sending signals to your mind saying 'fuck her', your mind was not relaxing at all. Its powers of concentration would be devoted to the shagging experience, more particularly because you are a male of the species, not that I'm totally excluding women either. If you want to come to a better understanding of what is going on your mind must be relaxed and receptive."

I reel somewhat under this. Who am I talking to, this pleasant young person who, despite some slightly questionable morals, or possibly because of them, seems to be as normal as any such that I have encountered of late. She has an uncanny ability to understand my feelings and also has a firm grasp of my thought processes, yet I am failing to get to grips with who she is. Her way of behaving, of interacting, is leading us in directions that are unfamiliar to me.

I wonder if I am in danger of focusing on the wrong part of this experience. I still need a whole heap of answers. It is time for me to return to the attack.

"Perhaps you would like to tell me why you came," I say.

Starlight looks at me. "You know why I came."

"My dear young lady . . . " Damn, that sounds just terrible, I am being hopelessly patronising, "err, sorry for that. What I mean is . . . Look here, Starlight, we need to get some things straight. I 've no idea who you are, I've no idea where you've come from, and in particular I've no idea as to why you're here".

"I know," says the girl.

"That's not good enough, you have got to tell me something about yourself."

"I wonder if it might help if you think of me as a sort of angel."

"I really don't think so." I say, "partly because I don't believe in the Christian concept of angels but also because if I did it is quite clear to me that you're much too contentious to be an angel, and finally your morals would never pass the angel-test." I rather like the notion of an 'angel-test', perhaps it should be widely adopted.

"That's a bit unfair, "says Starlight. "I'm not for one moment saying that I'm an angel. I just suggested that you might find it easier for you to think of me as one. Anyway if I was a real angel I don't see how I could have behaved much better. I've fed, you, offered you decent sex on the kitchen floor, and entertained you with my sparkling wit. Hell, I'm even clearing up your house."

Saying which she scoops up the remains of the pizza box and shoves it into the protesting and over-full rubbish bin with such force that the recently rejected can of beans squirts part of its contents over her T-shirt.

"Bugger!" says Starlight.

This is my very own favourite kitchen-word and she has appropriated it for her personal use. I am not sure that I can complain to her about it though as she is, at this very moment whipping off the T-shirt and running some warm water over it in the sink. I find myself staring lustfully at her naked breasts.

"Look", says Starlight, "let's get this sex thing sorted once and for all or it's going to be a real distraction. If you find a mixture of sodden T-shirt and cold beans so stimulating why don't we just set to on the kitchen table?"

"It not the T-shirt or beans!" I say, 'It's your tits."

"That's just it," says Starlight, "here I am trying to have a conversation with you about angels and all you can offer by way of a response is get too randy about my boobs."

"Just a few moments ago I was wondering if you were real or not."

"It is entirely reasonable for you to question my reality, after all you're a philosopher. However you need to be careful in that the logical progression from that line of thinking is that you will find yourself having a virtual shag because you fancy my virtual wobblies. Well, real or imagined, it just will not do."

So saying she wriggles back into the now rather wet T-shirt.

"Tell me what you do at the University?" says Starlight.

So I am right. I suppose that she could assume I work at the Uni given that she knows that I have a professorship, but all the same it is a very leading question. She might well be after information about The Project. This calls for caution.

"Oh, I don't know, it's rather boring"

"Bollocks, you wouldn't be working there if you were bored. You're not that sort of person."

"How do you know what sort of person I am?"

"I have information about you."

"You sound like a credit agency."

"That's quite perceptive of you," she says, "you see relaxing the mind is working."

"You don't look like the sort of person a credit agency would employ."

"Looks can be deceiving."

"I'm not talking about your appearance; I mean the sort of person that I think you are."

"In the broadest sense though you are right. Credit Agencies gather financial information so that they can assess the state of your monetary worth. My sort of agency is not interested in your financial worth."

"So what are you interested in?" said Duncan.

"You."

"But why?"

"We need to get out of this place so that I can explain some things to you," she says. "We've got an awful lot to do."

I really do not like this suggestion at all. It is dark, it is cold, and by this time of the evening there is hardly anywhere that we can go.

Does she not realize that it's winter in Lancaster and options for even a pint in a pub are now non-existent?

"Why leave!" I say, "It's getting late, it's a hellish cold evening and I'm rather enjoying your company here in the warm. That's despite the extremely disturbing manner of your arrival and a certain enthusiasm on your part to keep taking your clothes off."

"We need to explore some boundaries," says Starlight, "and to do that we're going to have to make things happen. We need to go places, see things, experience things. We need to start to build up a proper picture in your mind. And we don't have that long."

What on earth can she possibly mean by this? As far as I am concerned plenty of things have happened already and I doubt if we need to go out looking for more. I am also puzzled by her saying that we do not have long. Does she mean that we do not have long together? It is all very much a mystery.

How far can I trust this girl? I certainly feel a good deal more relaxed about her, but it seems to me that she has been working on establishing just that relationship. She might have accomplices outside waiting to mug me, or do me in, and then ransack my house. Perhaps she has been sent into my house with the express purpose of getting me to leave it for a couple of hours so that the gang can clear out all the contents. I have read about this sort of thing happening in the area and it is most disturbing. I cast around for a weapon more suitable than the abandoned bread knife.

"You need to trust me," says Starlight.

"What makes you think I don't?"

"You've been wondering about it, haven't you? "

"Not at all."

"Liar!"

"Well, OK then, but you can see why I'm worried."

Starlight gets up and walks over to me. She takes my rather cold hand in her warm one and presses it gently. "Come on," she says as, despite myself, I rise to my feet, "stay with me, trust me, we've a long way to go together."

I hesitate. How can I possibly trust this young Hoodie who has shown such scant regard for convention? I have been more or less forced to communicate with her because she has invaded my home, and all things considered I reckon that I have done so in a very tolerant way. Now I am being asked to travel onwards with her to do unknown things in unspecified places.

"I can't trust you," I say.

"If you don't then you can hardly be a philosopher."

"Nonsense, philosophy has all but nothing to do with this situation."

She laughs. "Oh, what lies you do tell when it suits you."

"That's not a lie."

"Look, Mr Philosopher, at your level of expertise we are discussing abstract thought, conjecture, and Ionian Enchantment. You think the unthinkable, you guess, you hypothesise; and only then do you look for a comfort zone of reason, or faith, or science to provide credibility for your position. So, when I ask you to trust me that's exactly what you must do. Not to do so would be to close off your mind to everything that I have to offer. You can't ask me to prove that you should trust me; enlightenment just doesn't work like that. Now do you understand me? "

She's right. I know it. I nod my head in acquiescence. By doing her bidding I will be putting myself in a very vulnerable position. There might well be no going back, but not to trust, follow, or explore would be so much worse. I am after all a philosopher, a seeker after truth, and wherever that truth takes me I am compelled to follow.

"Where's the car, out here?" She moves into the utility room and puts her hand on the door to the garage.

"Look you'll perish with just that wet T shirt on", I say.

I find myself entirely happy to be led by Starlight and am rather hoping that she will not decide to put anything over the wet T shirt that is displaying the perfection of her nipples plastered to the inside of the wet fabric.

"Nonsense", says Starlight, "It's a bright summer's day out there and we're going to enjoy it. Anyway, we've got to make good use of this smart car of yours."

In an act of role-reversal she opens the driver's door so that I can get in and closes it. Once I am seated, she swings into the passenger seat beside me. She puts her hand on my arm, "go on put the hood down."

"Look, Starlight, or whatever you call yourself, it's very cold, it's very dark, we'll freeze to our deaths with the hood down."

She turns to look at me; the deep blue of her eyes is both commanding and reassuring. "Do it, Duncan. It'll be just fine, believe me."

I release the top clips of the hood catches and hold the 'down' side of the rocker button. The roof disappears behind us, carefully folding up and stowing itself into what little storage space the Alfa Spider possesses.

"Neat," she says, "Now open the garage doors."

I reach down for the key ring, press the control and the door starts to lift; as it does so sunlight and warmth flood into the garage as if a blast furnace had been opened. It is, quite naturally, a warm summer's afternoon. Birds sing, bees hum, butterflies flutter about doing whatever it is that they do on flowers. "How on earth did you do that?" I say.

"That wasn't my doing", says Starlight buckling her seat belt. "Think carefully. What did you expect?"

"Dark and cold."

"Oh no you didn't," she says. "If you had then it wouldn't have turned out to be a lovely day in summer. Right, my trusting philosopher, let's head out to Langdale."

Six

Fifteen minutes later, treading very warily, as if they were two alpha dogs sniffing bums, they were making polite noises at each other. Helen looked at him afresh. George, she considered ought to be, perhaps should be, considered as 'getting on a bit' by now. Two marriages, two divorces, three children and an ex-partner to support would drain most men of their cash and vitality, not so George. He was balding slightly but fit and lean. He wore an Armani suit. His deep tan was mainly, although not quite acquired thanks to their summer break in the Maldives. With some reluctance she admitted to herself that he had made a rather better job of tanning than she had. Achieving her lightly tanned elegance back in this country had cost her nearly as much as the holiday flight. George, in his late forties, was the best part of ten years her senior; she concluded that he was not by any means perfect, but he would do.

Had an outside observer been unaware that she and George had recently parted with a high degree of acrimony they would have considered them ideally suited.

"Why do you want to see me, George?" she said.

He explained with an air of casual indifference that the position that he had agreed to accept was now almost certainly a non-starter. There would be no move to Paris. This was because there was a bit of a rethink going on at the French end and George was well aware as to what 'rethink' meant in these perilous financial times. He had discussed the matter with his fellow senior partners in the City and there was a general acceptance that if George wished to remain in the London office then George should so remain. Indeed, he was most welcome so to do.

"Thus," he explained. "Sedit qui timuit ne non succederet. I am but putty in your hands, do what you will with me. I await your verdict, O Caesar."

"Well you showed you true colours in saying that if I didn't want to go to France with you that was my problem!" Helen was still nettled by George's casual indifference to her, her life, and her career. He had decided that he would very much like to civilize Paris and that he was determined to go gallivanting off to the capital of France with or without her. She really was not prepared to give up her business, sell the house, and dump her friends to follow this poor apology for a Pied Piper. The resulting row had been bitter, prolonged, vengeful, and the most enormous fun for both of them.

"Perhaps we both enjoyed the argument so much that we forgot why we were arguing," George had said.

The two of them glared at each other for a bit. "George," said Helen, thinking more of those generous contributions towards the mortgage rather than the man, "Does this mean that you have pretensions of moving in here once more?"

"I'm so delighted to be invited. Thank you. Would tomorrow suit your domestic arrangements."

"I didn't invite you."

"You graciously posited a return scenario which I humbly accepted."

"You've never done anything humble in your life. And I didn't say that I would allow you to return."

"Helen, my dear, I plead with you to accept these, my apologies, for any minor transgressions that I may have committed. I long to return to your welcoming bosom - that was a figure of speech you understand – and to pay homage, and half the mortgage, to you."

"There will be one condition."

"You command, I obey."

"If I allow you to return then you must, forthwith, get down on your knees. There you must grovel out a few well-chosen lines of the utmost sincerity about rings and registry offices."

"Is this a sine qua non?"

"Yes, it bloody well is. I'm not going through all this nonsense again without having a stranglehold on your bollocks."

"I have the deepest doubt as to whether it is technically feasible to strangle bollocks."

"You want me to try?"

George looked at her in a resigned and hopelessly unromantic manner.

George remained seated at the table in the dining area and addressed his finely tuned speech to a rather striking but small bronze statuette that was the sole occupant of the alcove to the right of the Victorian fireplace.

George spoke in the lifeless, abject tones of the now thrice defeated.

"Helen, will you marry me?"

"Yes," said Helen in a rather perfunctory manner and slightly to her own surprise, "but before we turn our minds to such mundane musings, I need your brains."

"First my bollocks, now my brains. Go on take of me what you will."

Helen passed him the letter.

"Mmmm, "said George, "This really is not kind. If it's a hoax, which I should say is the most likely explanation, then the perpetrator will have ensured that you, and whoever you show this to, is bound to have a few sleepless nights. On the other hand, if what it's suggesting is true then it's going to kick off the most almighty row that's bound to hurt everyone, and create all sorts of untoward scandal."

"What do you think we should do about it then?"

"What you should do," said George, "Is take it to a nice friendly policeman. The local constabulary will no doubt send it to their Lancashire people and I suppose they will investigate it with the hospital. Not that I imagine they'll spend much time on it, but in the process they may rake up all sorts of stuff that might best be left well alone."

"I think that might upset Duncan."

"Oh, I don't know, he was pretty sensible about the whole thing from what you told me."

"But it's one thing having your unfaithful wife die on you from a properly diagnosed disease. That's both decent and respectable. It's quite another having her death raked over by the county plods and no doubt blazoned across the front page of the local rag with such scandal as they can unearth. Apart from which it's unsettling for me. I really would like to be sure of what was wrong with Miranda."

"I wonder if Duncan perpetrated her demise by means of an undetectable South American poison?" said George.

"No he did not," and then realizing that George was teasing her, "Oh, wind your neck in. "

Helen didn't like the idea of taking the note to the police. She thought it might be better if, before doing that, she should go and see Duncan and talk it through with him.

"I think I'll go to Lancaster," she said. "What are you doing this next couple of days, George?"

"Apart from arranging my third and final stag night?" he replied. "No, I've got to go through a ghastly fraud thing with some frightful clients in Southampton. If you go North you're on your own, I'm unable offer you the unique pleasure of my company."

"I'll go the day after tomorrow, just as soon as I can get away. Should be back late on Friday evening."

"Shame, that means you'll be feeding yourself courtesy of Virgin Rail and I'll be denied providing you with the product of my culinary expertise, at least until a later occasion."

"George, you can't cook"

"That is an irrelevance. I provide food. Such provision is generally welcomed, even on occasion, dear lady, by you!"

"Just wait until you are married to me, you won't get off so lightly."

It never for one moment occurred to George that he would.

The question of the rest of their lives together seemed worthy of a decent restaurant. There was a pleasant little place that had recently opened in Upper Street and it was thence that Helen and George made their way. The food was good, the service appalling, the wine excellent, and the conversation lengthy. It was therefore approaching midnight before they arrived back home and headed for bed.

Helen tried Duncan's number from her bedside phone. It rang for a long time. "I suppose he must be out," she said, "Can't think what he is doing, unless, of course, he's fast asleep. You'd think that he might have a messaging service, wouldn't you?" She put the receiver down.

George was already gently snoring.

Seven

I am surprised at how very little traffic there is here on the M6. On a bright summer's day there ought to be a lot more than this. The motorway unravels ahead of us at exceptional speed promising sometimes two, mainly three, lanes of tempting tarmac for the Alfa to hoover up with relish.

Conversation normally comes easily to me but the attitude of this girl who answers my questions, or responds to my observations, with vagaries, is more than a little unnerving. Every time I try to start talking about her, or about what it is that we are going to do, she stops me short with a terse rejoinder. Conversely, she is quite at ease asking questions of me and clearly wants me to talk about myself. She also seems particularly interested in Miranda.

"Did the University employ both you and Miranda as lecturers?"

"Yes, but that was only the bread and butter of our existence, and of course for me still is. For nearly two years though the important work in Miranda's life was her involvement in what we called simply The Project."

"Presumably she employed assistants?"

"There was a succession of trainees, almost invariably postgraduates, who gave her a hand from time to time, but Miranda was the only scientist working on it full-time."

"And did you have any professional interest in her work?"

"It seems an odd combination, a philosopher and a neuroscientist, but it was a strange project. At first the work was largely conceptual and at that stage we worked together, but as The Project moved towards number crunching and experimentation, I took a back seat. Later still, with the work becoming less and less abstract, Miranda needed some practical help so she involved an acquaintance of mine, Dr. Simon Pennick."

"Who's he?"

"Simon started his career as a particle physicist, I suppose he still is, but he's also a solid mathematician who can crunch numbers as well as anyone I know. I came across him some years back when he was working on a military project, but he has been at Lancaster for a couple of years now. When Miranda needed some help it was natural to suggest him."

Now that we are away from Lancaster I am finding it easy to disregard the unsettling arrival of this girl. I am beginning to think of her as a mature postgraduate, someone with whom I can discuss my work freely and whose opinions I am likely to value. It occurs to me that she is a little over-inquisitive, but I do not feel in any way threatened by this, in fact I'm rather pleased to have someone with whom I can analyse things in a neutral and relatively disinterested way.

We turn off the motorway at Junction 36 and slow our pace once we negotiate the Plumgarths roundabout. It makes for easier conversation in the open car.

"Are you going to tell me more about this Project?" asks the girl who calls herself Starlight.

"It all came about from a conversation that Miranda and I had about four years ago. She was talking about dark matter. She said that that there needed to be a lot more dark matter in the universe than there was matter."

"But that was common knowledge amongst the scientific community wasn't it?"

"Miranda had originally graduated as a quantum physicist so she was a bit ahead of me on these things. Our conversation turned toward parallel universes. There was then, and still is, an hypothesis that these are spun off from 'our' universe every time a decision is made or an action taken."

"Meaning millions of such universes."

"She wasn't disputing that hypothesis, but couldn't see how it helped with the dark matter thing as this had to be within our own universe, not in a parallel one. Miranda postulated that there was more than sufficient dark matter within our universe to construct two worlds that were equivalent to our own."

"So not separate universes, but separate worlds?"

"It shouldn't be considered as a halfway house between the individual universe and the multi-universe model, this is a different concept from the latter."

"So how would these other two worlds work?"

"This dark matter is within our universe; we just cannot see it or make any sort of connection with it."

'But if it was possible to make some form of connection . . "

"That's what she wanted to explore. It's also where I put in my two-pennyworth. You see these two other worlds have existed for thousands of years, at least in western thinking."

"Heaven and Hell."

"Just so."

We have negotiated Windermere and are heading north towards Ambleside. The lake is close to the road on our left side and beyond it we can see the wooded slopes of the Claife shore and then the high fells in the far distance. There are no boats to disturb the ominous tranquility of the lake. And although it is difficult to be certain I gather the distinct impression that there is no reflection of the far shore in the stillness of the water. Our road is almost completely devoid of traffic and we pass through the outskirts of Ambleside without seeing a soul.

"What will happen to The Project now that Miranda is dead?"

"She was so near to a conclusion, or at least a theory of sorts. She needed to test her ideas, and that's what she was concentrating on. I really don't want to lose the work that she did and I am keen to have the joint Paper posthumously published. The trouble is that I've a limited understanding of the physics and only a vague grasp of the neuro-biology. I've set Simon on to do what he can, and with his input I think there's a sporting chance that I can tie up nearly all the loose ends. That will allow me to finalize 'Thought-Energy - a route to The Parallel Worlds of Dark Matter'. "

"And Simon, is he good to work with?"

This causes me some difficulty and I answer Starlight with a degree of circumspection: "He's good at what he does. He's sound and predictable. The real problem I have with Simon is that he's over-ambitious."

"Does that affect you?"

"He keeps pestering me to include his name as joint author of the academic Paper, and that I will not allow. It would diminish Miranda's standing in this ground-breaking work."

We lapse into a slightly uneasy silence. Somewhere near Elterwater I rather foolishly ask Starlight what she is thinking about, but her reply is abrupt to the point of rudeness. I am reluctant to ask her anything further about herself for fear of getting my head bitten off. I realise that I am not going to learn anything more about this strange young lady, at least not for the time being.

We head along the country lane that leads into Great Langdale. The High Fells are crowding in around the car as we approach the head of the valley, travelling nearly as far as the road is able to take us. I pull into the New Dungeon Ghyll car park, where, surprisingly, there are no more than half a dozen other vehicles. Normally on such an afternoon the car park would be almost full, and the place buzzing with people.

"We're here!" says Starlight, standing on the seat and leaping from the car without bothering to open the door, "That was such fun."

"I thought you were asleep half the time," I say, exiting the car in a rather more conventional manner.

"You just never can tell," she says, and starts off ahead of me on the well-worn track out of the car park.

We are in spectacular scenery. Above us are the Langdale Pikes, providing some of the best-known climbing routes in the area. The fells rise abruptly out of the flat, lush valley bottom. We appear to be back in summer and the sun is well advanced in ripening the meadowland that will shortly produce the year's only hay crop. Over the last three decades hay has largely given way to big bag silage but its function as fodder for beef cattle remains the same, and some farmers still like to produce a bit of hay if the weather is on their side.

Stone walls run up the fell-sides, I turn to Starlight, "the lower walls with gentle curves and rounded corners show Tudor enterprise in grabbing chunks of common land outside the main thirteenth century lowland wall. The higher walls, that run straight and true up the fells, are a legacy of lines pencilled upon maps during the C18th Enclosures Acts. Just below those the craggy fell tops, on the scattered scree runs, you can find remains of the stone axe heads that were traded from here as far south as northern Spain."

She looks at me as if I'm on another planet.

"Do your pupils ever think your lectures are boring?" she asks.

To start with we walk out on a well-made path across fairly level ground but the gradient soon increases. We come to a band of rock that we both easily scramble over.

"Granny-stopper", I say.

"What?"

"Granny-stopper. If you're infirm or ill equipped and you get his far you may find that you can't manage the minor scramble over the bluff. So you have to turn back; and just as well or you're highly likely to become a statistic for the Ambleside mountain rescue team".

"You mean it warns off Old Grannies!"

"Exactly."

I have made this walk up to Stickle Tarn many times before. The surface, although of stone, is not natural but one that has been reconstructed over the past forty years using the centuries old technique of pitching. The path has become a victim of the beauty of the area, unable to sustain the erosion damage caused by the thousands of feet that tramp their way up and down this route every year.

"Been here before?" I ask.

Starlight shrugs her shoulders "Possibly," she says.

Her inability to provide a direct reply to anything I say is getting beyond mere irritation.

"Look", I say, stopping and leaning my shoulder on a rock. "I'm only trying to be sociable; I didn't ask you into my life, and I certainly didn't expect to come here today. For some purpose that I simply don't understand you have inveigled me into bringing you here for a reason that totally escapes me. I love this area. I would love to share my thoughts about it with you. I would very much enjoy hearing what you have got to say about it. At the very least you could try to be civil!"

"Oh, bugger off," she says and continues to climb.

We tramp up the path together in sulky silence.

On this bright sunny day Stickle Tarn looks delightful. I prefer the winter when one can appreciate the 'bones' of the countryside, however the vast majority of visitors come to the Lake District in July and August; just when visually it is looking at its worst.

The tarn twinkles blue and silver against the dark, sheer crags of Pavey Ark, a hundred metres or more of vertical rock beloved by the climbing fraternity. There are normally several small tents near the water's edge, better for their inhabitants to enjoy the rock climbs on that dour, forbidding slab. Today there are no tents.

We skirt around to the right, circling above the tarn, and then begin to climb in earnest, knees taking the strain, as the path changes into a jumble of rocky obstacles. It is a good walk this; wilder than the path that brought us as far as the tarn. The sheep trod veers off from the rushing beck and as we climb away from the mini-waterfalls we leave its cheery sound behind us. It becomes strangely silent; there's something a little unnerving about the stillness of this scene.

There is nothing like a decent bit of physical exercise for rubbing off a grudge or two, so by the time we are well above the tarn we are exchanging the normal pleasantries of a couple of fell walkers.

"Mind the loose rock just there."

"Bit slippery by that moss."

"Ooops! Sorry about that," as a stone clatters its way down the hillside.

I am certainly not super-fit, but am quite surprised to find that we are climbing clear of the valley and I am not even a little bit out of breath. Ahead of us across the almost flat grassy landscape is the craggy summit cone of Sergeant Man. Over 2000 ft climbed from the valley floor and in just over an hour.

"Hey," says Starlight, "Well done, old timer!"

"Not so much of the 'Old Timer' please," I protest, "I can still give a stripling like you a good run for her money."

"Want an orange?" says Starlight, passing one to me without waiting for an answer.

Where did she get that? I did not see her carrying anything up the hill and a couple of oranges would most certainly have shown if they had been shoved into the pockets of her tight-fitting jeans. Anyway, an orange is just what I want so I accept it gratefully and decide against asking her anything more about it, I don't want to incur her wrath again. I lift the corner of a rock and shove the peel underneath. "Biodegradable", I say by way of an explanation.

Up to this point I have, as Starlight has suggested, very much 'gone with the flow' of this experience that I have been swept up in. I am curious about what is happening to me but, rather oddly, not unduly so. It is almost as if I am watching what I am doing from outside my own body. I am concerned that if I try to think about things in any depth then the whole dream-like sequence might just dissolve. I feel slightly disconnected from what is going on. Things are certainly odd but it feels strangely acceptable. I will just let it all happen and see where it decides to lead me.

"I know what you are thinking," says the girl calling herself Starlight.

"Yes, I think you do," It almost seems as if this oddly perceptive girl is inside my head. When we first got into the car at Lancaster she told me to drive to Great Langdale, but although I never asked her where our ultimate destination was I instinctively knew that she wanted to bring us here, to the summit of Sergeant Man.

"I'm deeply puzzled," I falter. "I really don't have a strong grip on what's happening, there's a sense of other worldliness about this whole experience, including you, and about my being in this place with you."

"That's why we're here," says the girl who calls herself Starlight. "Reality versus illusion. Let's have a go at sorting things out a bit."

"Okay," I say, "Shall we start with your name?"

Starlight shakes her head. She looks at me. She gets to her feet, still holding my gaze with hers. She stands quietly, relaxed, unmoving in front of me. "What do you see?' she says.

"I see you."

"No you don't," she says, "You see only what you think of as me."

"Well I can only see what I think you are, my eyes can't see anything else, and my brain interprets what my eyes see."

"Try looking at me without using your eyes."

"How am I supposed to do that," I protest. "If I shut my eyes then I can't see you!"

"But am I not still here if you shut your eyes?"

"Yes, that's true. But if I don't see you then I can hear you, or touch you. That way I know that you most certainly are here."

"That's not enough," says Starlight. "What happens if I take away all your senses?"

"Then there's nothing that tells me you are here. It's like that old chestnut about if a tree falls in the forest and no one hears it fall then did it really make any noise."

"Well of course it didn't," says Starlight.

"That's right. The tree falling makes no noise, it's the sound waves reverberating inside our ear and setting in train a physical process that our brain interprets as noise that is the sound of the tree falling. Without a human ear to perceive it the falling tree makes no noise."

"Exactly. But consider the converse. Use your imagination. I could in almost every sense be here if you imagined me here"

"Yes, I suppose so," I say. "Then I would see you in my mind's eye just as I imagine you."

"Right," says Starlight, "your imagination would allow you to see what you imagine to be me, so you would see me."

'Hey, but that's not quite right," I say. "If you take my senses away and get me to imagine you then that will only be my version of you. It wouldn't be the real you, the you of reality."

"What then is the difference between having senses and not having senses?"

"With senses I know that you are real, without them there is no reality, just imagination or illusion"

"But why"

"Because without senses I have to use my imagination, there's no reality.'

"No. I'm real to you because you imagine me to be real. I'm real in your imagination."

"This is going around in circles."

"OK," says the girl who calls herself Starlight "let's do this rather differently. We need to stop theorizing and deal with things on a more practical basis. I want you to imagine me, but I'm not here. Imagine me as being an impossibly large distance away. Let's say on the moon. I want you to make that image of me so real that it becomes your reality, do you understand?"

"Yes, I think so."

"Right! Stand up! I want you to shut your eyes. You can hear nothing. You can smell nothing. You can taste nothing. Nothing touches you."

I do as she says. There is no sound here at the top of Sergeant Man. I can feel no breeze on my skin. I do not smell the heather. I positively ignore any sensation of touch from the ground on my feet.

I am swaying very slightly, but my mind is quiet and still and receptive.

In the reality of my illusion Starlight is approaching me. She's standing directly in front of me and I sense that she has her eyes tight shut, swaying ever so slightly as if concentrating very hard.

I cannot take this! "I can sense your body," I exclaim.

I open my eyes, and fling out my arms meaning to crush her to me only to find she is standing some three metres away.

"No." She cries, "Fuck off. What's wrong with you? You've really cocked the whole thing up now."

"Bollocks," I say, "I could smell your skin, I could sense its warmth, I knew you were there for me. I knew that was what you wanted before I opened my eyes. OK so I was using my imagination and you were trying to prove that I could conjure you up. But I really do not give a toss about imagination or you on the Moon. You were here. Right in front of me, and you were real."

"That's just it. You imagined me to be close to you, you imagined my smell, my warmth. And then you just threw it away; and you call yourself a philosopher. You just wanted to trade in your imagination for your reality. You lusted to touch me, to feel me, to hold me as a tangible object, something you could physically drool over."

"Well that's my reality isn't it?"

"No, you fool. It's just one reality. And in that reality it seems as if your whole concept of me is something for you to rut over."

I glare angrily at the girl. Where is this leading? I am being fooled with and stripped of the dignity of my own arguments. If I can see her and hear her and smell her and touch her, even possibly taste her - although that would be a fine chance - then she is as real as I am. This imagination thing is unnecessary; nothing but an unwelcome distraction. Blast the creature, this whole thing is just a monstrous tease and she is leading me on and making an idiot of me.

"Look here, Starlight, or whatever your real name is, I've eaten pizza with you, I've driven 50 miles with you, I've climbed my way up this fell with you. All this time I've seen you and, I admit, fancied you. This isn't imagination. You are as real as I am so don't play me along with all this illusion stuff – just tell me what the hell is going on."

"You great gangley stupid heap of bones," cries Starlight. "Why the hell have I spent so much effort in trying to explain things to you? You're as thick as two short planks and . . ." at this stage it becomes apparent that because she is hopping up and down with rage her breasts are bouncing around under her T-shirt in a most provocative manner, " . . . and you, you're about as subtle at controlling your cock as a Rhesus bloody monkey."

Up to this point I have pretty well kept my cool, but this is too much. Not content with making me feel stupid she is now mocking my all too obvious sexual arousal. I start towards her, arm raised, lips pulled back. I feel rejection. I want out of here. I want her away from me, out of my life. In my anger and despair I take a wild swipe at my tormenter my open hand swinging towards her cheek.

Nothing happens.

My hand does not connect with anything.

The force of the intended blow swings me round to my left and I therefore presume that Starlight has just ducked away to my right. I turn in that direction, already deeply ashamed of my loss of temper. There is no sign of her. Here on the top of this fell there is little cover, she could not possibly be hiding anywhere. She has just gone.

No sooner is this brought home to me than I realize how dark it is getting. Not a gathering gloom as at the end of the day, but a very abrupt and frightening darkening, with the daylight turning directly into night. In the last legacy of the dying light I squint at my wristwatch. Ten minutes past two.

I have got to get the hell out of here, down off this fell. Whatever weird spirit may have possessed me has now deserted me and I am just a nearly fifty-year-old man alone, cold and pretty well lost high up in the fells, without proper clothing on a bitter winter's night.

It is cold, but at least it is dry. There is no moon, but I can make out some stars. There must be a partial cloud cover. I know that I need to head almost due south – perhaps just a little east to get down to Stickle Tarn. Once there I am fairly confident that I can make my way down to the New Dungeon Ghyll.

I look carefully at such stars as I can see. "Find the Pole Star," I say out loud. I recall that there is something about Pointers. If I can just find them then I have got a chance of identifying the Pole Star and that will give me an idea of where North is.

For a moment the clouds to the right of High Raise shred and there, surely, are two Pointers and the Pole. Yes, that must be north, so all I have to do is walk the other way.

I step out confidently. This is not going to be so bad after all. Five paces, ten, my progress is quickening.

Crunch! The tussocky sward under my right foot disappears throwing me headlong into some boggy ground. Ouch! Damage to my ankle. I should have been more careful. I scramble back to my feet again. I try my weight very gingerly on my right foot. Hellfire it's damn painful, but I will be able to walk on it.

I look back again at the sky. There are no stars to be seen behind me. The cloud has claimed them back. "Anyway," I say, "I know which way I'm going."

Almost immediately I stumble into some standing water. Both feet are wet and freezing. "Not as bad as it might be." I say to encourage myself, "at least cold water is the right thing for my ankle". I start to giggle a little hysterically, realize what I am doing and shut up.

I hobble on. Christ I am getting cold. What on earth possessed me to come up here with that girl? Was it really bright daylight?

There is a dark mass of crag ahead of me. I skirt it to the right. Good, I am getting better at this. Time to press on a bit. "Probably the biggest danger is exposure," I say out loud. I start to move at a sort of swinging trot, leading with my left leg so as to protect my right ankle as best I can.

"That's better," I say. And as I do so I step out into the void. "Shit. Pavey Ark!"

My body is falling, faster, faster, . . .

Eight

Beneath the teeming, sweaty, rain-sodden heart of the capital city there runs a spaghetti of tunnels. These conduits are built for a multitude of differing purposes, but the goal they all share is connection. They join together tube stations, they provide space for secret cable runs, the post office sends parcels through them, whilst others form the vast interconnected sewage system. Some of these subterranean routes are large and public such as the Underground, some very private such as the tunnel that runs under the Thames from the MI6 building. It was through one of these small private sub-ways that Dr. Simon Pennick was making his way. He had never been here before and did not want to be late for this meeting. The particular tunnel that he had taken was shepherding him from the car park underneath the Ministry of Justice building to an address in nearby Queen Anne's Gate.

Simon was not in prime condition and as he hurried along this admittedly rather warm rat-way he swept his forehead clear of a shock of sweaty red hair and dabbed at his face with a blue handkerchief. His outward appearance, and indeed his mannerisms, very satisfactorily concealed a darker side to his personality. He was obsessed by an ambition that had started to drive him in early childhood, had seen him through school and Cambridge, and which had become overwhelming during the succeeding years. It was a desperate need for recognition, public acclaim. It gnawed away at him tainting everything that he turned his hand to; an insatiable lust for personal success and fame. It was this defect in his character that had brought him to this place today. He was aware of the failing but such was his addiction that he could not help himself. Most attractive of all was the glittering goal of a Nobel Prize.

Simon had left Joe with the car. This bruiser of a man had already been supplied with the requisite clearance to bury the vehicle two floors beneath pavement level in the government fortification that currently doubles as the Ministry of Justice. Simon had worked with individuals like Joe before but when this square-built chunk of humanity had picked him up, as arranged, outside Green Park tube station he was pleased, given the size and bearing of the man, that he was to be a colleague, not a foe.

"Morning, Boss," Joe had said as he had pulled the large black Mercedes to a stop on the double yellows.

"Joe Hardisty?"

"Dead on. Boss."

There did not appear to be a lot more to discuss as the large man drove them skilfully along Grosvenor Place scattering the London traffic like seed corn in a strong breeze.

It was clear from his proprietorial stance once he emerged from the car that Joe would stay in charge of it until otherwise instructed. He wore a spotless, if slightly undersize, chauffeur's uniform, but he could hardly be described as a chauffeur. No, if Joe had been the proud possessor of a job description, which as a freelancer for a private security firm he certainly was not, he would have been billed as an Enforcement Officer. He would have liked that, especially the 'Officer' bit. However, the organisation that he worked for on an almost full-time basis these days was not big on job descriptions for its Joes.

The Ministry of Justice building had been constructed in the late 1970s for the Home Office. It could surely, even in the midst of the Provisional threat, have been designed to show a friendly face towards the public that it purported to serve. Instead it had all the charm of a modern-day concrete bunker, clearly conceived to keep at bay the rioting mobs that would no doubt wish to shred such incumbent Minister as might goad them into an hysterical fervour. Just around the corner however the architecture was of a different age. It belonged to an era equally used to violence but also accustomed to a now outmoded concept, that of honour. That was a time when decent men stood, when in a crisis, to face down crowds. They would take responsibility for their, or their subordinates' indiscretions and actions, and not cower behind bullet proof glass and platitudes. It was to one of the buildings of these former years that Simon was rapidly making his concealed subterranean way.

Twenty feet below street level Simon came upon the small direction pointer that he had been told to look out for. He stepped aside from the main tunnel, pleased to be escaping its dry dusty heat and faintly fetid smell, and entered a four-man lift. In the gloomy yellowish light he could make out that there were only two buttons. He pressed that which said 'Top'. The doors squeezed themselves shut and the lift gained six floors with surprising rapidity before ejecting him into the lobby of a corporate boardroom.

This particular branch of The Service that now demanded his presence was, by its own design, unknown to the general pubic. It had the very strongest aversion to publicity; indeed secrecy was essential to most of its work. To ensure anonymity it did not use any of the recognisable public buildings that were in its ownership, meetings of this nature being held in offices rented by the hour from suitable business support companies. In this way privacy was maintained and the presence of those whose faces might be recognised would not arouse too much comment. This was the first time that this Queen Anne's Gate boardroom had been used. It was ideal for purpose.

Simon was both embarrassed and disconcerted to discover that the two people whom he was scheduled to meet had arrived ahead of him. He glanced quickly at his watch to reassure himself that he was at least ten minutes ahead of the scheduled start time, not that such punctuality offered much of an excuse when he had kept these senior officials waiting.

Barry O'Connell was a tall, well-built man with a courteous turn of phrase and exquisite personal appearance. Standing next to him was the attenuated figure of Hugh Strickland, who was wearing a dark coat over a black suit.

This rented boardroom was light and airy, capable of seating at least twenty-five people around the large ovoid table covered with green baize. Further cushioned chairs were ranged along the sides of the room. The Georgian windows cast their gaze well above the traffic that surged in rolling waves along Birdcage Walk. The view out across to the green island of St James' Park was soothing, and a less obvious management tool than would have been the installation of a tank of goldfish.

The only way into the boardroom was through the lobby, the principal access to that being via double doors from the main building. These doors were now firmly closed and bolted against any unwarranted intrusion. The lift by which Simon had entered the lobby was the only other way of accessing the boardroom. It was screened from the rest of the lobby and even on close inspection might have been taken for no more than a dumb waiter.

O'Connell greeted Simon in a clear, deep voice but in a slightly distant manner. "Come in, Simon. I see that you've eventually managed to discover us. We need to be away as soon as may be, so let's get settled. I think you have met Hugh Strickland?

Simon nodded to Strickland. He was not surprised by the lack of warmth in the greeting. He did not expect these people to like him, or to be more than even fleetingly civil. That was not what he had come to expect from O'Connell and his people. He did however hold a grudging respect for Barry O'Connell who displayed a degree of forthrightness that seemed to elude Strickland, whom Simon had only met once previously. Simon understood that Barry was an MI5 'handler', but thought it would imprudent to enquire as to his precise standing.

"Simon, we're satisfied with that which you have achieved for us so far. I do hope that you have been adequately recompensed?"

"Oh yes," said Simon, "Most generously."

"I understand that the unpleasant business of removing Professor Miranda Marston was concluded in a satisfactory manner?"

"It was," said Simon thinking back with some pride at the way he had engineered Miranda's accident. "It all went according to plan, and I'm sure that no one suspected anything except, just possibly, Miranda herself. The only thing that did not go as we had intended was that she was not killed outright."

Strickland looked up sharply. He spoke with a voice that would cut glass. "But you assured us that you had planned this matter most carefully. We sanctioned it on the basis that it would proceed without any deviation."

"It must have been the radiation dose. I certainly set it for the agreed amount, but there must have been a minor miscalculation. It took Miranda the best part of a week to die in Lancaster Hospital. But there's no need to be concerned, if she ever regained consciousness she would have been totally incoherent given the dosage of drugs that she was being prescribed."

"I see," said O'Connell "but she must have known that you were the perpetrator. Are you sure that she didn't say anything about that to anyone?"

"She regained consciousness shortly after the accident when both her husband and I were with her. She never mentioned the cause of the accident, she was much more concerned with ensuring that the Project would continue."

"But why," said Strickland, with just a trace of disbelief in his tone, "why did she keep quiet?"

"Immediately after the accident, and whilst Miranda was still lucid, all three of us agreed that the thing that mattered was The Project. Obviously Duncan did not know about my role in Miranda's death, but for his wife's sake he was as keen as Miranda and I to ensure that the 'accident' was hushed up. I imagine that Miranda thought that any accusation she might make at that stage would have been a distraction that might well have derailed The Project."

"And did you square it with the Authorities?"

"Yes, with the help of the University and the Hospital that went very well. There are very few people who know it was not cancer, and only we three here today know that Miranda's death was not an accident."

"You are sure," said Strickland, "that she never spoke of your involvement once she reached the hospital?"

Simon explained that Miranda had never fully regained consciousness whilst she had remained in hospital. She had mumbled things from time to time but these were very disjointed thoughts and were limited to things that he and Duncan should do to ensure the completion of The Project.

"Good. We are done on that front then," said O'Connell. "It could have been a bit unfortunate for your well-being if this scientist had been able to implicate you."

Simon noted that O'Connell had said 'your well being'. He had little doubt about just how unfortunate it might have been for him.

O'Connell continued, "Now that we've cleared the hurdle of Professor Marston we are able to proceed with this operation. Perhaps Strickland you would care to just rehearse our overall scheme and Simon's continuing mission."

"This is strictly on a 'need to know' basis, "said Strickland. "The removal of Professor Marston was an absolute necessity; it was the only way that we could stabilise control of The Project. It was imperative that you should engineer her removal without arousing suspicion. I would like to think that there will not be a significant delay in our obtaining the sole rights to this work now that she has, as it were, departed.

"It's important that we move quickly at this stage," interjected Lord O'Connell.

"Quite. As I have indicated, we need you to step in and gain ownership before any sort of academic Paper is published. In our judgement The Project is a vitally important piece of research that might well pose a real threat to a great many people if its findings were to become public knowledge. Clearly it would be possible simply to destroy the work that has been done at Lancaster, but we consider that it is of such potential that we should assimilate it within our own ambit and continue the work that the unfortunate Miranda had made such strides with."

"You will appreciate that we are most concerned that nothing relating to The Project should be made public," said Lord O'Connell.

"Anyway, to continue, I have had an assessment carried out on the very little data that you have provided us with, and whilst we must be cautious about the potential outcome it is clearly a worthwhile to aim for just that. I am naturally just referring just to the science. Does that tally with your thinking?"

"I think that's just about spot on," said Simon. "I'm confidant that Miranda and Duncan were correct with their original thinking and that the general hypothesis is sound, although nothing has been proven yet. Before Miranda died she was beginning to take me into her confidence. Her death has thrown Duncan into some confusion, but I have, as you instructed, managed to get close to him. He is encouraging me to get more involved than ever with Miranda's side of the work. I hope to gain a comprehensive understanding of the whole Project within the next few weeks."

"And your own role," said O'Connell, "will you be able to persuade Professor Fielding that he should pass on Miranda's data to you so that it can be carried forward?"

Simon replied, "I'm fairly certain of it. He must have doubts as to whether he can conclude it on his own."

"Excellent," said Strickland.

Barry said, "We consider it important to keep Professor Fielding involved with The Project, at least whilst we evaluate his data. I realise that his input has been theoretical and he's not up to speed with the science, but he's the only person now, besides you of course Simon, who has a grasp of the objective."

"In due course we will need to encourage him to give up The Project willingly once we have his input," said Strickland, "otherwise it might prove necessary to make alternative arrangements."

Not for the first time since he had been in contact with these people did Simon get the feeling of just how ruthless they were prepared to be. Admittedly there had been the killing of Miranda, but that felt different to him, Miranda was firmly set against his further involvement in The Project and it had been quite clear that nothing was going to change her mind. Her death was a necessary casualty on his way to a Nobel Prize; collateral damage in the pursuit of his Holy Grail. As such it had hardly been a crime, more an indiscretion that should be quickly glossed over. To make 'alternative arrangements' for Duncan was a quite different thing. What is more it would leave him, Simon, in a very vulnerable position as the only person who had substantial knowledge of The Project.

"I feel sure that we can persuade Duncan to our way of thinking. Clearly I'll need to offer him a considerable sum to encourage him to relinquish his interest."

"You should make him an extremely generous offer," said O'Connell, "but it had better come through Virtual Ventures Ltd. I don't want even a whiff of The Service being involved in this."

"I would also suggest," added Strickland, "that you should make him a yearly income for, say, the next ten years, that would make his current salary look totally insignificant."

"Good thinking, Hugh," said O'Connell. "The trouble is that a lot of these academic types are somewhat unworldly as far as financial arrangements are concerned. They are more interested in status than they are in money. No offence meant, Simon."

"None taken, "said Simon, "Although I have to say that a Nobel Prize is worth an awful lot in kudos as well as being financially beneficial."

"Well you have a very free hand regarding Fielding's compensation," said O'Connell, "just be sure to deliver." He got up out of his seat and moved over towards the middle window that looked out over Green Park. Across the busy road and beyond the park railings lay the usual spectacle of Londoners enjoying their lunchtime break, sitting on the grass. He was not a man given to inner contemplation but if he had been he might have wondered how the successful completion of The Project would impact upon and alter the behaviour of such ordinary people.

Strickland said, "The best outcome would be for us to use Fielding to set up a new ` Project at Lancaster. Not to involve him would be to arouse suspicion, particularly amongst those running the University. Clearly you, Simon, are the person best placed to do this. I would suggest the simplest thing is to take advantage of Lancaster's incubator programme and set up a base on Campus. In the meantime we will, through Virtual Ventures of course, be providing the University with sufficient extra funding to dissuade them from looking too closely at what we are up to."

"What happens if Duncan decides not to cooperate with us?" asked Simon.

Strickland glanced at Brian O'Connell and gave a wry smile. He said that in his opinion Fielding would be happy to go along with them if the money was right. "However if we have to employ an element of coercion in respect of Fielding then we have the option of having you and Joe on the spot to conclude the matter."

"I'll do what I can persuade Duncan to be sensible," said Simon. "If he can be tempted then it'll make things so much easier. I know him quite well but I really have no idea as to which way he'll jump. If only we could rely upon his motivation being money."

"Make him whatever offer you think is necessary."

"I'll do my best."

"That goes without saying," said O'Connell, turning from his contemplation of St James' Park. "In the event of his serious resistance then it'll be up to you to deploy Joe."

"That might be a trifle inconvenient for Fielding," said Strickland.

"I'm sure that Simon will use his powers of persuasion to good effect," said O'Connell, "and that'll remove the necessity of Joe having words with Fielding"

All three of them had a pretty clear idea that the sort of words that Joe would have with the Professor would tend towards being few, monosyllabic and punctuated by long and rather painful non-verbal interludes.

"I do not subscribe to owning a dog and then barking myself," said O'Connell, "however both Strickland and I will make ourselves available to join you up north should it prove necessary."

"Oh, and do be careful," said Strickland by way of a concluding remark. "I'm not talking about your personal safety, but rather the secrecy of the whole operation. What we are proposing must remain in absolute confidence, no leaks. Understood?"

O'Connell turned back to his window with an air of finality, giving the cue to the other two. The meeting was over.

"I'm heading for Whitehall Court, Strickland. Would you care to join me for a spot of lunch?"

"Excellent," said Strickland anticipating that lunch was unlikely to be a meal devoid of liquid refreshment.

"We can take the mole to the Treasury and then carry on above ground from there."

"Glad you know the way, O'Connell, those passages can get a bit confusing around Parliament Square."

O'Connell acted with considerable energy in his efforts to ensure that the room was neutralised. He ripped out the topmost sheet of all three blotters in case any of them had been doodled on. He switched off the radio jammer, and put the chairs back in place. Entering the lobby he unbolted the doors to allow normal access to the boardroom, then signalled for the lift where he joined the other two. He missed spotting the internal communications link that had been quietly monitoring their meeting from the security of the top left-hand scroll of one of the eighteenth century pier glass frames.

Once they gained the main tunnel O'Connell and Strickland strode off in an easterly direction leaving Simon to take the narrower passageway back to the car park. If anyone should chance to see either of the two principals leaving the Treasury then it would not seem an entirely inappropriate location to spot a well-known public figure walking with a senior civil servant. Queen Anne's Gate had really been an excellent place to hold a private meeting.

Simon walked towards the car where he had left Joe. He was a little concerned about the ruthlessness of these people, but he'd already been handsomely rewarded and expected a good deal more of the same. This operation might well be of the greatest importance to The Service, but he had it firmly in mind that once he was the Project leader then he would be in the best possible position to stake his claim on a Nobel Prize

Joe had clearly been patiently awaiting his return. This hulk of a man eased himself from a pillar that he had been leaning against. It was possible to imagine the pillar sighing with relief. "OK Boss?"

Simon rather liked this salutation. "Yes, I think so. You may well be needed up in Lancaster in a day or two. You might have to bring someone with you."

"That'll be the Merc then," said Joe. "Anything I might need?"

"If I give you the call you'll need to get a move on. We need to get this thing wrapped up quickly."

"What will you be doing?"

"Meeting people, looking at places."

"Anything interesting for me?"

"Quite possibly, Joe. It may not come to it, but if I can't persuade this professor to see it our way then we may require your special skills."

Joe cracked a bunch of his special skills with the similar bunch that formed part of his other hand. He was looking forward to the possibility of a little excursion up north.

Nine

The Marylebone office of Room for Business Ltd, Ro-Bus to the cognoscenti, was housed in an elegant property in Devonshire Street. The building did not thrust itself upon the passer by, rather it maintained a spirit of quiet aloofness, an air of detachment that gave it the opportunity to be all things to all men. The solid iron railings and the well-scrubbed front steps ensured that the invitation to enter was one of discretion. It was this quality that had appealed so much to Helen. Her clients' requirements were such that it was best if it were difficult to pinpoint, without nameplates, the exact building that they had used in the past. The whole system was designed to exude anonymity and confidentiality.

Helen was usually the first to arrive at Ro-Bus and today was no exception. She thought that Dr. Reinout Schmidt would have approved of such diligence. When she had sold on her original business in Tooting and moved her venture to this respectable location in the West End she had decided, for the sake of gravitas, to invent a fellow-director, an Austrian emigré, Schmidt. It had given this new up-market enterprise a certain caché within the business circles that she frequented. This totally imaginary character had sustained Helen for the past five years and had become so important a driving force in Ro-Bus that not only did the staff know that he was a real person, but Helen herself was beginning to wonder if that might indeed be the case.

She passed off Schmidt as the financial brains behind Ro-Bus and in many ways it had proven most useful to have this shadowy figure lurking in the background. She had used him to good effect with her bank manager from whom most of her initial funding had been obtained. Now, five years on Ro-Bus was thriving despite, or possibly because of, the recession. Helen had paid off all her debts, and Ro-Bus was making a handsome profit. She let it be known, to her own advantage, that Reinout Schmidt was pocketing the lion's share of this, as was only right as he had put up the initial capital. Lately she had expanded the firm by renting a further set of offices, her Westminster suite, in Queen Anne's Gate so as to better cater for the political lobbyists and others who required an anonymous location convenient to the hub of power. She had chosen the situation for these offices with equal care, settling upon the discrete anonymity of Queen Anne's gate.

Helen had been a little surprised by Duncan not being at home last night, but she would ring him this morning. She thought it best to wait until after eight o'clock. She was aware, from staying with him, that he was not an early riser.

Helen accepted that she could only bring very limited skills to investigating the cause of Miranda's death. She had no idea how to discover whether it really had been cancer, however she was quite prepared to explore the vast online library of instant medical resources on the web. In preparation for further investigation she started to jot down the little she knew about Miranda's symptoms. She was aware that her sister had presented as unconscious, vomiting and with low blood oxygen. She had also suffered loss of hair and had a weak pulse. That would do for now, it seemed to offer a clear enough picture of the dying Miranda.

She pointed her browser at what seemed to be the most relevant symptom sorter and entered the first three symptoms from her notes. She was rewarded with a list of potential diseases that was as numerous and diverse as the stars of the Milky Way. This needed further refinement. She added 'hair loss' and 'co-ordination – lack of' to the list. That was better, only 232 possibilities!

She read through the list. There seemed to be a vast number of disparate conditions that could cause such symptoms. Cancer in its various forms featured prominently, but that was not what she was after. If her unknown correspondent was correct then it had to be something that had much the same symptoms as cancer but was a different disease. This was a good long way beyond her very rudimentary knowledge of things medical. She was getting nowhere and feeling increasingly frustrated.

If Miranda had not died of cancer and had died instead of something with similar symptoms, then so be it. What did it matter? Perhaps the hospital had got it wrong, but her sister was clearly dying and any treatment given would have most likely been purely palliative unless this 'other' disease had been caught in its very early stages. So what on earth was the point of the letter alerting her? Who would bother to upset her in this manner?

Her employees were beginning to drift into the building. She heard their footsteps pass the open door of her room. Some had firm authoritative strides, others walked with rather more timidity. She wondered if she could guess who they were without looking up from her computer. Silly game, she thought to herself and glanced at the wall clock. Five past eight, time to phone that brother in law of hers. She wondered idly if that was what he still was. Could you have a brother in law when you no longer had a sister? She had no idea. Perhaps he was now a brother once in law?

The phone rang for quite a long time before a drowsy voice answered "Hello."

"Duncan, it's Helen"

"Helen?" eventually the slow falling penny crashed downwards, "Oh, Hi Helen, how are you?"

"Where the hell were you at midnight, I tried to call you."

There was a bit of a grunt from the other end of the line "Asleep, I think. Had a bit of a weird dream."

"Never mind your dreams, I'm coming to stay with you."

There was a discernible lack of enthusiasm in Duncan's response to this news, and even less upon his learning that Helen intended to come up by train the next day. No doubt he was wondering why on earth she wanted to come and see him – something to do with George perhaps?

"Are you sure you don't want to hear about my dream?"

"Quite sure, thank you. Perhaps you should go and see a shrink about it."

"I'm not sure it was that bad."

"Well don't see a shrink then. Now do you understand that I'll be with you tomorrow, late afternoon?"

"Of course I do. As ever it will be good to see you. But what's afire that you need to be up here at such short notice?"

Helen thought it best not, at this stage, to tell him about the five word note that she had received. She was not quite sure why, but she felt certain it would be best to judge Duncan's reaction to its contents face to face.

"I could just do with a bit of time, you know, catching up on one or two things, sorry Dunc, must dash, see you tomorrow." She put the phone down slowly. Duncan was not a fool; he would be well aware that she was up to something.

Helen did not have a particularly busy day ahead of her. She had set up a meeting between her Senior Business Manager and a slightly nervous Arabian gentleman. She was aware that this potential client was not likely to do business with her in the room, a mere woman.

So she had left negotiations to her senior assistant. Mind you she would be listening to every word via the in-house video link. All meeting rooms at the two Ro-Bus locations were so equipped. Ostensibly it allowed the staff to keep an eye on their clients to ensure legality of use, however it also gave Helen the opportunity to watch her employees in action. It had become particularly useful now that she'd expanded her empire as that she could now see what was going on in her Westminster suite from the Marylebone office.

She needed some medical expertise. She wasn't going to get any sort of sensible result from following the online symptom sorter. She wondered how people managed to use it if they were ill. She thought about what to do next, to whom she could turn. The answer came to her in a flash. "Aletia, of course."

Aletia worked just around the corner in Wimpole Street at the very exclusive medical practice known as The Whole Clinic. She and Aletia had met at the nearby Langham Hotel Spa and had got to know each other moderately well. Aletia had come to the UK from Spain just a couple of years ago. She was an excellent doctor and, perhaps of even more importance given the clientele of The Whole Clinic, had no problem in charming their well-heeled and mostly middle-aged, patients. She now had a full partnership and was highly valued by her colleagues. Helen dialled her number. She did not beat about the bush.

"Hi. Aletia. I need some help"

"OK what can I do."

"I can explain over lunch – on me of course."

"As long as you don't bore me with your bunions and expect a free prognosis for them then I'm your woman."

"Well, be warned, as the saying goes 'There's no such thing as a Free Lunch'."

"Come over to The Whole Clinic just before one o'clock and I'll meet you at reception."

The morning passed swiftly. The Arabian gentleman turned out not to be such a gentleman after all. Whilst Ro-Bus was happy to indulge in a little subterfuge on behalf of its richer clients Helen drew the line at anything that was totally illegal. The recruitment of rent boys was definitely on the far side of that line.

Helen was at The Whole Clinic shortly before one o'clock and Aletia came down to meet her straight away.

"Hi, Aletia, you're looking good today"

"I'm not too sure about it. I raided Liberty yesterday but I'm not certain that it's quite me."

Helen looked at the slightly racy figure-hugging dark green dress that set off Aletia's gorgeous figure and dusky skin to perfection. "My dear it is divine. If your patients have included any elderly gentlemen this morning you will have improved their heart-rate without having had to wave a single stethoscope at them."

"Perhaps I should be careful, I won't be very popular with my fellow Partners if I start giving our wealthier patients coronaries." laughed Aletia. "Now, do we need a taxi?"

"No." said Helen. "It's only a very short walk, and it'll do us good."

"True, especially as I've not been to the Spa recently."

"Nor me," said Helen as they walked briskly down Weymouth Street.

"Where are you taking us?" asked Aletia.

"You'll see in a moment."

They crossed Portland Place and entered the RIBA building.

"Oh good, great choice."

They walked through the lobby of the Architects emporium. Ahead of them the inviting grand staircase beckoned them up to the first floor where they negotiated their way around the gallery café to the glass doors of the Restaurant. They were ushered to a table for two in the light, airy room.

"Never seems terribly busy," said Aletia. "I don't know why, it's such a lovely place."

"Must be one of the best kept secrets in London," said Helen, "No need to be a Member, you can just stroll in off the street."

There was silence as they both considered the menu with practised eyes.

Some little time later Helen fixed Aletia with a smile, "Well I hope you enjoyed that – now its payback time!"

"Well, it was a decent lunch, so I suppose it's worth it! What can I do?

Helen explained about Miranda's illness and how the hospital had diagnosed a virulent and inoperable brain stem tumour and how she had then died within a week of admission. Aletia made soothing noises. Helen came to the tricky bit. She told Aletia about the strange note she had received and how George had advised her to go to the police. She said that she knew she had to do that, but was putting it off until after the weekend whilst she considered the whole thing a bit further.

Aletia looked a bit puzzled. "So why you want my advice?"

"What I really need to know is could the anonymous writer be on to something. I've no idea why it might matter, and I probably won't unless I find out that Miranda died from something other than cancer. I looked up her symptoms in an online symptom sorter but honestly Aletia, there was just such a deluge of possibilities that I was overwhelmed. I've never seen so many diseases, if I had hypochondriac tendencies I would've diagnosed myself as several times dead. I could hardly understand some of the diagnoses, let alone compare them with the cancer verdict."

"You need to know what might look like cancer but be something different?"

"Well that's what I had in mind."

"Presumably the diagnosis was carried out by the consultant oncologist at the hospital."

"Yes, I think so. I know she had lots of scans and things."

"Then the answer is simple. Nothing!"

"You mean that the hospital couldn't be wrong?"

Alex explained that it was very rare for a hospital to make an incorrect diagnosis of a brain stem tumour. True the symptoms were unspecific and very varied in the early stages. This did mean that the disease was often not diagnosed until well advanced, sometimes, as in this case, too far advanced for more than palliative treatment.

"However, there is a definitive diagnosis. Almost certainly they will have given your sister an MRI scan and, on the assumption that showed a tumour they would have carried out a biopsy. The tissue would have undergone microscopic assessment and the result would be conclusive and irrefutable."

"There's no way that the Hospital could have misinterpreted that?"

"I'm not sure what you are after, Helen, and if it involves suing the NHS you can count me out, but the pathology really is quite conclusive. The hospital must have got it right."

Helen looked somewhat subdued. She'd hoped for more. "Do you think it'd be worth my while going and talking to the consultant at Lancaster?"

"Well, I doubt if you'll get very far at consultant level. No one likes to have their diagnoses questioned, especially in a terminal case and I don't see how you could approach the subject without looking as if you wanted to heap some blame on the hospital. They really do clam up if they think that you're trying to get information that you can use against them in the courts."

"I'll have to find a way," said Helen, "I owe it to my sister."

"My opinion is that is would be a waste of your time. It'd be almost impossible for the hospital to get such a diagnosis wrong. You're just going to upset a lot of people, most of whom will have done their very best in treating your sister during her final days."

"That's almost exactly what George said last night."

"Well. I'd take that as sound advice. Just give the note to the police, as George said, and forget about it."

"I'm not sure I can give it up, just yet." said Helen.

They sat and chatted a while over coffee, agreed to meet in the Spa the following week, and made their way back to their respective workplaces.

Helen was feeling deflated by her meeting with Aletia. She wondered whether she should phone Duncan again and cancel her visit. She could do just what George, and now Aletia, had advised and hand the note over to the police. It would get the whole thing out of her hair. Then she thought of Miranda and how much she owed her, even in death.

She would go to Lancaster and see if she could discover anything. If she found nothing then all she had to do was to hand the note over to the police. In any case she loved the area. The southern Lake District had been home to her and Miranda and as the family home, Deanstones, was now hers she really ought to check it out and decide what she was going to do with the place. She could well use a forty-eight-hour break from city life. She would travel north tomorrow.

Ten

The phone is howling at me. On and on it goes, an unloved intrusion into my privacy screaming 'wake up',' wake up'! With the greatest reluctance I turn over and fumble the instrument up to my ear. "Hello," I say.

It is Helen asking me where I was last night.

'Wow," I sit upright in a rush, "That was some dream." I am shaking slightly at the reality of it, and in particular that final headlong plunge into oblivion. What on earth did I eat last night to encourage a dream like that? Slowly at first, and then with a great rush, the memory of my strange evening returns to me.

What is Helen saying? That she is coming to stay. Does she not have a job to go to? What the hell is she coming back up here for? I try to winkle it out of her but get the typical Helen brush-off. Why the hell is she not telling me what she is up to? Oh well, at least she is not bringing George.

My toast is no more than the anaemic by-product of the steam-cooked sliced white that engendered it, but it perks up quite noticeably when brought into close proximity with chunky marmalade. The coffee is strong, black and sugarless.

But what about that dream? The experience plays back to me as a vivid kaleidoscope of contrasts. Winter and summer, fear and desire, cold and hot. Unlike most dreams I have a very clear memory of each individual scenario, although the order is a jumble. The only haziness is in trying to discern any meaning in it. I recall the journey to the Lakes and that climb in Langdale, but where did the daylight come from? Then I remember with a growing sense of embarrassment and unease that swipe I took at a girl who asked me to call her Starlight. That brings me back to her arrival at Druridge Road and my ordering of the pizza. I ruminate over that for a bit, strange how such mundane things as a pizza delivery lead the mind to such wild flights of fancy. There is the pizza box still stuffed into the bin.

It is the last few moments of my dream that now play back as reality. I rehearse that scene where I am blundering around in the dark, twisting my ankle and stumbling into the beck. Then I re-live stepping out into nothingness and the explosion of fear that drilled down into my soul.

"Hell, what a fool I was, just as well I only do that sort of thing in my dreams! "

It is strange how dreams allow their perpetrator to make sudden drastic changes that seem quite logical at the time. In this case I had no problem in translating the scene from a bright day to a wintry night, vaguely I wonder why. Hell, but that final moment as I plunged over the cliff, now that was real!

I like to think of Tuesday as being an easy day for me, but if truth be told I don't find much of my work at Lancaster particularly demanding. In many ways I regret that. Under normal Tuesday circumstances I would turn up on Campus mid-morning in preparation for my tutorials. Today I have made arrangements to meet Simon at about eleven. 'Thought-Energy - a route to The Parallel Worlds of Dark Matter' is falling behind schedule and I need to tighten things up a bit. I am not so sure that it would be wise to discuss a title change with Simon. Perhaps it might lead him to think that I am weakening over agreeing to his joint authorship of the Paper.

Today I will go in a bit earlier than usual. I need to talk through this dream of mine with someone, possibly Simon, or better still Valerie. I know that Val has written some interesting stuff on the psychology of stress and, whilst she will no doubt turn my overnight experience into a case study for her students, I would welcome her professional insight. Having worked with her in my early years at Lancaster means that I both trust her as a person and value her as a colleague. I suppose I have been under some stress of late, what with Miranda's death and trying to sort out the continuation of the project. It is not that I feel stressed, but no doubt Val would tell me that was irrelevant as my conscious mind would be in stress-denial. Bugger it; I must talk. Touch of the old Freudian dream-analysis, that is what I need to re-adjust the Duncan equanimity balance.

I plonk my plate and mug into the dishwasher, grab a jacket and walk through the utility room to the garage. I push the door open. The garage light flicks on automatically.

I stop dead.

"Shit."

I look again; there is no mistake.

"The bloody hood is down."

The Spider is languishing there in full topless beauty. I do a quick backtrack of the early part of yesterday evening. It was cold. It was dark. I parked the Alfa not far from the Lab and remember how chilly it was just walking the short distance to it. I got into the car and drove straight home. And the hood had been up! I had not lowered the hood for over a month now, the weather was incessantly wet until just a couple of days ago so I just could not take it down. Then on Monday I only used the car to travel the couple of miles or so out to campus first thing in the morning, and straight back home in the evening. I had not liked to raise or lower it in the frost for fear of cracking the rear window in the freezing conditions. I am quite, quite, certain that I did not lower the hood.

But the hood is down.

Although shaken I am determined to be logical.

"The automatic garage door is closed. There is no way anyone could open it from the outside without the key-press.

There are just two electronic fob controls, one on the key ring that was in my jacket pocket; the other that I would have left in the car. Either of them will open the garage door, but you need to turn on the ignition with the car key before the hood mechanism will work. There are no car keys on either of those fobs. I usually leave my car keys on a corner of the kitchen work surface.

I walk slowly around the outside of the house looking for any signs of a break-in. Nothing. The windows are closed and locked and there are no signs of any sort of attempt at a forced entry. I return to the kitchen. I am certain that no one has gained access to the house and found my car keys.

"Anyway, who the hell would take all the trouble to break in just to lower the car hood, then put the keys back where they found them?"

There are only two conclusions that I can come to. Either I lowered the hood when I came home last night and am experiencing some sort of mental lapse, or that dream was closer to reality than I dare imagine. I do not like either possibility very much.

"So, let's assume that 'The Dream' is real – or at least partially real. What other definite and indisputable things actually happened to me that were part of it?"

I stare glumly at the waste bin thinking of Starlight; the bread knife; the Old Dungeon Ghyll car park. Why the hell had I not kept the receipt from the ticket machine? Such things could so easily be figments of my imagination, there is no corroboration, they probably did not happen. I continue to glare angrily at the kitchen bin.

"Of course, that's it!" I jump to my feet. There in front of me is the answer. "The pizza." That was real, the packaging was physical proof of that.

The garage doors open to my touch. The Alfa growls its way backwards out of its cage. I pause for a moment whilst the hood mechanism winches itself into action, cocooning me into the car, then I am bowling down Druridge Street in the direction of the Pizza Palace.

The market for hot pizzas at 10 o'clock in the morning is, necessarily, a limited one. A year or two back the Palace therefore branched out from its hot pizza business to include the selling of 'ready to cook' pizza products. This means that they open at nine o'clock in the morning thereby increasing their staffing costs, if not their turnover. True to form it is thus open, but without custom, when I arrive. I shove back the glass door and am relieved to see that Donna is standing behind the counter. She knows me as a regular customer and it will be so much easier to talk to someone who recognizes me.

"Hello, Professor Fielding. Not often we see you in here at this time of day."

"No," I reply.

"What brings you here. You going to start cooking your own now?" Donna is of Italian extraction but English birth. She has jet-black hair, cut fairly short, large brown eyes and what is described in kind terms as an ample form.

"Heaven forbid," I say acknowledging the very low limit of my cooking skills.

"Well you get first rate service today, whatever you've come for."

"That's because I'm your only customer!"

"Don't I just know it."

"Well sad to say I'm not here this morning to swell your vast profits."

"Shame on you!" says Donna. "Nor is anyone else. What are you here for?"

"Information."

"Well you've come to the right place." Donna is a renowned gossip. Her friendly, indeed downright cuddly, nature encourages everyone to confide in her, and those confidences are as swiftly dispersed as they are given. She and her husband Luigi know everyone in the neighbourhood and Donna in particular loves nothing better than a good old chinwag.

I press on. "Yesterday evening I phoned you with an order, yes?

Donna looks a bit doubtful. "I don't remember that," she says, "and I'd always remember a phone call from you, my love." And then in a rather worried way as a thought strikes her "Was there something wrong with it?"

"Oh no. "I say, "I'm not here to complain. But are you sure you don't remember a phone call from me?"

"I think I did all the late phone orders last night. Luigi managed on his own up to about eight o'clock. I suppose it would have been after that?"

"Oh yes," I say, "about half nine or a quarter to ten. It was definitely a female voice that I spoke to, I assumed it was you although you weren't quite your normal chatty self."

"Now that doesn't sound like me at all, I'd never let you get away without your filling me in on all latest and spiciest bits of University gossip."

"Well you were pretty short with me last night. No conversation at all."

"I really can't remember it," says Donna, "and I'm quite sure that I would. What was the order for?"

"Hawaiian, with Nachos."

"Hang on a moment," says Donna. She goes out the back of the shop calling "Luigi. Luigi." She reappears muttering things about cloth ears.

A voice from the back yells back, "What do want, I'm busy out here."

"Busy! I'll give you 'busy'. You've got your nose stuffed into in that smutty magazine again."

"O.K. I'm coming, what is it?"

"Luigi, I've got Professor Fielding here."

"In the shop? At this time of the morning?"

"Yes, he's in the shop."

"What's the problem?"

"No, no problem, but he wants to know if you remember him ordering a Hawaiian last night."

Luigi comes through from the back rubbing his hands on a cloth, making out that he has been indulging in hours of hard physical labour. He is a short dark man, almost as plump as his wife and with an equally cheery smile. "No, I don't think so," he says. "We only did about half a dozen Hawaiian's last night, and I'm sure that there were none for delivery."

"Any with nachos?" I ask.

"Let me think," says Luigi, "yes there was, just one I think, must have been sometime just after ten."

I start to feel strangely excited. "Can you remember anything about the customer?"

"Yes, I think I can. At first I thought it was one of the young Hoodies from around here. They don't mean any real harm, but you have to keep a bit of an eye on them. Had a bit of vandalism a few months ago, quite minor really, but you can't let that sort of thing get out of hand. Anyway I remember thinking, 'best watch this one'. But then I got a closer look and realised it was a lass of about twenty or so. Not really a Hoodie, just someone with their coat hood pulled up if you see what I mean."

"What was she like?" I ask.

"I didn't really see her at all well, but she was well spoken and seemed a confident sort of person."

"Does she live around here?"

"Never seen her before."

"Hey," says Donna "The Proff's got a girl-friend. Come on, do tell, who is she?"

"That's just it," I say. "I really haven't got a clue."

"Oh, come off it," says Donna, "you know I'll find out soon enough, so you might as well tell me yourself!"

"I really haven't a clue," I repeat, "but it does sound very like the girl who delivered my pizza."

"Bit of cheek," says Luigi, "sounds as if she's cutting in on our business,"

"Oh, I don't think so, "I say, "she was just trying to do me a favour."

"Oh, Professor Fielding," says Donna, with a twinkle in her eye "we knew that right from the start!"

I leave the Pizza Palace with my face a slightly redder shade than when I arrived and with the certain knowledge that Donna's un-doubted talent will ensure that the whole of the neighbourhood will know within a very few hours that I have a live-in girlfriend who col-lects my pizzas for me.

I slide into the Spider and sit there to think things through.

I have got to assume that the girl who collected the pizza is Starlight. That seems certain. But how is it that she managed to take my order? How did she know about me? I suppose she could get my address from the phone call, after all I told the person that I spoke to both what my name was and where I wanted the pizza to be delivered. The more I look at the situation the less sense it makes. There seem to be two or three possibilities.

It is certainly arguable that someone is engaged in a very sophisticated bit of planning and interception so that this girl, probably as a front for some larger organisation, can target me, although goodness knows why. Or possibly it is not something aimed at me but a sort of random exercise that I just happen to be the victim of. The other possibility is that the whole thing is going on entirely within my own head and, I try to find a nicer way to put it and fail, "and I'm going stark staring Bonkers!"

None of these scenarios particularly appeal to me, but given the sequences that made up the 'Dream' I am beginning to favour the Bonkers theory.

"The trouble," I say to myself, "is that I just can't see why any person or organization would want to play what appears to be an elaborate practical joke on me. What could they achieve by so doing? It is not as if anyone has anything to gain from screwing me up."

My personal circumstances hardly warrant me becoming a target for some gang. I have no close relatives, a reasonable salary but not much capital, and a line of work that whilst intriguing is not worth anything much to the corporate world – as the vice chancellor never tires of reminding me.

I revisit the idea that I should talk it over it over with Val. As a psychotherapist she runs the human interaction course at University. She is damn good on sorting out hang-ups, and this one qualifies as one hell of a hang up.

If I am going barmy then it must be due to something in my psyche, possibly to do with not yet having fully come to terms with the loss of Miranda.

There is a bit of a downside to seeing Val. I am a private sort of person and, following a slightly strange childhood, have a very strong aversion to being analysed by anyone. I therefor have always strongly resisted opening myself up to any form of personal psychological intrusion. It is of course a problem that is entirely individual to me, but I have learned to live with it by avoiding too much contact with psychotherapy and those who practise it. Val is a good friend, and probably knows as much about me as anyone else in the world, but I really do not want to open up certain bits of me to anyone, even Val. It might be best to remain wary and steer clear of her and her profession.

That said why should I keep hearing a voice inside my head that tells me it would be best to talk it through with Val, rather than Simon? Part of me wants to run like hell, but I have got to discuss it with someone or it will be off to the funny farm for me. I rather like the idea of a Funny Farm. I see cows roaring their heads off and chickens with a fit of the giggles. There is a donkey wearing a stupid hat with flowers on, and a pig telling silly stories to its piglets. "Bloody childish," I mutter.

Decision made I twist the chunky ignition key. 3.2 litres of V6 power bursts into life with a low rumble that throbs through the small car. Ridiculous really the chassis just is not up to the power of the engine. I am not entirely sure that I am either. With a flourish not normally associated with middle aged Professors of Philosophy I hand brake turn the machine in a one-eighty and head south towards the Campus.

Eleven

Dr Simon Pennick was in full flow. He had been working at Lancaster for just over a couple of years and fitted in well with the small scientific community. He was admired for his energy and his enthusiasm and for tackling any undertaking that was put his way, even though it was well understood that he would be doing so almost entirely to enhance his profile and further his career. This willingness to get involved with things prompted his participation in the research being carried out by Duncan and the late Miranda. He was sociable and generous and it would take a very perceptive person to see through this extrovert charm.

Simon, in his light West Country lilt, was holding forth on the subject of the Flat Universe to anyone in the Senior Common Room who would listen to him, which was not many.

"Yes," he pontificated, "but with this type of Universe triangles do indeed conform to what you might call normality, and have 180 degrees."

"Well of course triangles contain 180 degrees," said one of his listeners, a recent entrant to the SCR, who should have known better than to encourage him.

"Ah, but you are wrong," said Simon, "As I was saying, in this particular type of Universe they do, but only because in a Flat Universe all lines are parallel. Now if you take the Closed Universe theory then lines in space do not run parallel so triangles do indeed have angles adding up to more than 180 degrees. It is much the same in the Open Universe hypothesis that has been recently postulated."

"But that's counter-intuitive. I don't see how you can have a triangle of more than 180 degrees."

"OK let's take a two dimensional example, "Simon was clearly enjoying himself, "consider for a moment a triangle that has its apex at the North Pole and its two base angles exactly opposite each other on the equator. Now, what have we got? Huh? Yes, exactly – a triangle with each of its three angles making a right angle of 90 degrees – a total of 270 degrees!"

"But that's not a true triangle."

"Oh yes, it is. If you view it from anywhere outside this planet then you would see that it most certainly is," said Simon.

"Is this flat Universe of yours in a state of expansion?" Asked another of Simon's colleagues.

"That's right," he said," infinite expansion, but the rate of expansion may be slowing down, and if that is the case it'll slow to almost zero – the maths can't cope with it finally ceasing to expand though, so it'll never actually attain zero expansion."

I push through the small group of people standing by the door and, arriving behind Simon, clap my hand on his shoulder. "This man is a charlatan!" I say. "He is a Mathematician trespassing in the realms of Physics. Get the hence, Pennick, back to your lands of Chaos and Fractals."

"Philosophers are even worse than all you quantum physicists," he says to his fast waning audience, "you never know what state of existence they're in."

"Still boring the pant's off everyone!" I say by way of further greeting.

"You're early, Dunc," says Simon, "what 's dragged you in at this time of day?"

"Need a bit of a chat with Val before you and I get together".

"You are going to have to wait a bit then," says Simon. "I bumped into her earlier and she was just off to talk to some folk over at Info-lab."

"Blast," I reply.

"Anything that I can help with?"

"I was going to pick her professional brains about a very peculiar thing that happened to me last night. It might've been a dream, then again I rather doubt that."

"Hmmm. Perhaps you'd better talk to Uncle Simon about it first. Exposure of your night time fantasies might just prove too embarrassing for our dear Valarie." So-saying Simon catches me by the arm and propels me towards the door.

As I leave I turn back to the small circle of puzzled acolytes that Simon has been regaling, "Sorry, folks, I must drag what remains of his mind away from you." I don't seem to meet with much resistance to this intention.

Simon and I make our way out of the SCR. My room is the nearer, but by mutual consent we walk across to the further corner of the same floor to where Simon's much tidier, although slightly smaller, study is situated. The room shows very few signs of being the den of a research scientist. There are no books piled high on battered looking desks, no sign of papers and articles littering the floor. His neat desk bears only a rather fancy computer and some associated equipment that is connected to a vast plasma screen that dominates one wall. There are two very modern easy chairs into which we settle ourselves.

I really did not intend to confide in Simon, but I need to talk this 'dream experience' through with somebody to get it off my chest. In Val's absence Simon will just have to do. When I first met him I did not really take to the man, he struck me as slightly arrogant and extremely pushy. He is however extremely good company and ,whilst we are unlikely to become close friends, we have lately taken to spending a bit of time in each other's company, usually at the Kings Head.

"OK Dunc – what's to do then?" says Simon, introducing slightly more vernacular into his voice, thereby trying his best to adopt the mantle of a psychiatric caseworker, "you look pretty shaken up about whatever it is."

"Yes. I suppose I am a bit. Something rather strange has happened to me. I'm not at all sure what is going on. I need a bit of a mind scan from that analytical brain of yours!"

With great care I describe the events of the last twelve hours. I try to recall everything that I have said, done and felt so that when I eventually finish telling the tale by recounting my visit to the Pizza Palace I am pretty certain that Simon has the whole picture.

As I retell the story I get a strange sensation of reliving it through my own words, it is almost as if I am there again, facing an intruder, driving to the Lakes, falling off a crag. It is as if the telling of it reinforces the event, making it more certain, giving it greater substance. If I speak of it to more people will it gain even greater credibility?

"So that's it," I say, coming to the end of the adventure, "I can't explain it. There do seem to be solutions to bits of the puzzle, but no one explanation seems to cover everything that happened."

Simon sits thinking for some time with a slight frown of his face. He likes puzzles, no doubt that is what makes him a good mathematician, although philosophers are also problem solvers. It is the endless search to explain the inexplicable.

"I think," he says at last, "that you have two different problems, both of which have rational explanations."

"Go on."

He says that in his opinion there is the 'pizza trick' and the 'Langdale experience'. The latter he thinks could fairly easily induced by drugs. Something a bit wild introduced into my portion of the pizza and then just enhanced by appropriate suggestions whispered into my ear.

"It wouldn't be that accurate," says Simon, "whoever did this to you would not know exactly where your imagination would take you, but with the right drug and with careful suggestion I think it could be done, after all exactly where your mind took you and what you imagined yourself doing would not matter in the least, the important thing would be that you had a weird, intellectually challenging, and slightly frightening hallucinatory experience."

"But what would they get out of it?"

"Not sure at this stage, but we'll need to explore the Why's later, let's stick with the How's for the moment."

"O.K., Si, I'm with you so far, what about the pizza thing then?"

"Well I reckon that's fairly easy, if a bit more technical. The thing is though that I can't see it being done in any way that does not mean that you were the intended target for this whole operation. This means that it wasn't a 'joke', or some sort of experiment that happened upon you by chance. You were the one they were after so it was aimed specifically at you, Duncan Fielding."

"I'm not very happy about that," I say, "but how could it have been done?"

"Well it's dead easy really. There are two explanations that I can see immediately. Do you have the Pizza Palace number stored in your landline phone memory?"

"I use it two or three times a week nowadays."

"Exactly! There would be no real need for any technical knowledge at all. If someone could have gained access to your house it would be but the work of a moment to change the stored number to one that they controlled. So when you hit the button for the Pizza Palace they took the order from you."

"That must have been it," I cry. "Not only does it explain why Donna never got the call, but also the rather cool conversation that I had when I placed the order. I assumed that it was Donna, but she wasn't her normal friendly self. I thought there was something odd going on at the time."

"The other way it could have been done would require a rather higher degree of sophistication. It would involve hacking your phone signal and could have been achieved without entering your house. This wouldn't have been a job for an amateur."

"Not much point if you can do it the easy way."

"Now for the bit that I can't explain," says Simon," the Why. I cannot for the life of me see why anyone should want to play what amounts to an elaborate practical joke on you. And I certainly don't see why they should specifically target you."

"Well at least we seem to have ruled out the third explanation," I say, "that I'm going totally off my rocker!"

Simon gives me a serious look. "I'm not so sure", he says.

I start to grin, but realize that Simon is being serious. "Hey! You look as if you really mean that."

"Well it is a reasonable possibility," says Simon," and one that I'm not really qualified to pursue. But there is at least one other explanation."

There is a pause during which I expect Simon to carry on, and Simon appears to consider the subject closed.

"What other explanation?" I ask.

"Not sure I want to say at this stage", says Simon. "If you want to follow up the 'Loopy' theory I would suggest you go and have a decent chat with Val, otherwise I would think it best to do nothing for a bit."

"I'm not that keen on doing nothing. If I'm going discover the truth about what's happening to me I need to follow it up now."

"Look," says Simon," if someone did target you then it was done for a purpose. If so, and we do nothing, they will have to follow up on that purpose."

"Not sure I like the sound of that."

"Well apart from making you think that you hurt your ankle and fell off the side of a mountain no one has done any harm to you as yet, have they?"

I have to admit that to be true. Perhaps things are becoming a bit clearer, but I am far from totally convinced about the use of drugs to guide me into this Langdale adventure. The more I think about it the more I rather like the idea of talking it through with Val. Mind you, if I am going a bit mental then I am not sure that I want to have it confirmed, and certainly not broadcast amongst all my colleagues.

It seems a bit weak, but I can see no alternative but to go along with Simon's suggestion that I do nothing further for the time being. I say as much and we agree to drop the subject for now.

Simon and I discuss the need for a review of the Project and make plans to spend an hour or two in the afternoon catching up on how things stand and identifying what further work is needed to establish Miranda's theories and bring the Project to a conclusion. He seems keen to talk me into transferring The Project into the University's 'Incubator Programme'. This is a step between pure research and development of such research for business purposes. I tell him that I will consider it, but that I doubt if The Project is capable of being developed into a business model.

Thinking about Simon's advice on my strange evening experience I decide that it would be best not to bother Val with my ramblings. Fate however takes a hand. As I'm leaving Simon's room we exchange a few words at the door:

"Well," I conclude," you've taken something of a weight off my mind – unless I really am going barmy of course. And don't forget that you suggested that!"

It is just then that Professor Valerie Staples wafts down the corridor towards her room that is nearly opposite Simon's. She is tall with short, light brown hair. She will be about 40 years old but manages to look almost a decade younger. Her face is unlined, her eyes coloured a very light brown and her manner almost professionally unruffled. She is dressed in a stylish, if slightly hippie, fashion.

"Hey Ho!" she says." Those words are but music to my ears. Do I detect a 'cause celebre' for my next seminar?"

"No! No!" I protest.

It is too late. Val has me by the left arm and I am being seduced in no uncertain manner into her 'parlour'. My mind leaps uncontrollably to thoughts of spiders and flies.

"That is not what I meant," I wail pitifully. "Barmy was just a figure of speech." As I am thus propelled I cogitate upon wailing in that it seems to me that it would be extremely awkward to wail in an un-pitiful manner. Wailing is, I think, pitiful per se, so the adverb is tautological.

Realizing there is no escape I decide it best to play the situation for laughs. "I'm sane! I'm sane!" I cry out in the manner of a madman at a lunatic asylum. "Simon, my only friend, my last friend," I implore," don't let them take me away!"

"Best place for you, old boy", says Simon and, winking at Val, "definitely a padded cell job."

I am soon sitting in Val's comfortably appointed room holding not an uncivilized mug, but a welcome cup, of coffee and trying to explain the situation I find myself in. Her room is almost exactly the same size as Simon's but any similarity ends there. This den exudes calm and refinement. It is a sanctuary into which one can enter to immerse oneself in peace. There is no desk, but a beautiful rosewood regency writing table. The walls are hung with reproductions of eighteenth and early nineteenth century landscape paintings including a Crome and a Cotman from the Norwich school. The chairs are elegant, upright and surprisingly comfortable.

I am keen not to reveal every part of the story, but Val has a probing mind and I fear that it is unlikely that I will get away without most of it coming out. I decide to concentrate on the 'Langdale episode'. I explain that I was enticed by a strange girl into driving her to the Lake District and that we walked up a fell in what, then, seemed to be a glorious warm sunny afternoon. I tell Val about the row that we had about personal perception and how the girl then disappeared. I leave out the bit where I tried to strike Starlight. Finally I recount the inrush of the winter's night, my reckless stumble over the fells, and my final plunge over Pavey Ark.

Val listens to me quietly throughout. She will be only too aware that I have missed bits out, but that might not matter.

"So, what do you think?" I end, rather lamely.

There is a long pause. Eventually Val speaks. "First of all, I believe everything that you've told me. That is not to say that all or any of it actually happened, but I do think that everything that you've said is the truth as you see it."

I feel encouraged by this. It is a vote of confidence in me, coming at just at the moment when I was beginning to doubt myself.

"However, Duncan, I know you have kept some stuff back from me, and we may want explore that in a moment."

"Simon said that I could have been drugged with something in the pizza," I say.

"And I daresay he also said there were other possibilities," says Val.

"Well, yes, I suppose he did."

"Come on, Duncan, stop pussyfooting about and talk to me! What is the worst thing that could be happening to you?"

"I suppose that I might have rather lost the plot." I admit with considerable reluctance.

"OK" says Val, "so you're worried that your mind is playing tricks on you? That you are, in the vernacular, 'going mad'. That's hardly surprising is it? Now I know you've left out a good deal at the start of this story, and you may well have good enough reasons for that, but what I must know is why the girl left you."

"I can't tell you that", I say.

" Can't or won't?"

"Well I really would prefer not to."

"Come on, Duncan, I'm trying to help you."

"I err, sort of took a bit of a swing at her"

"That bad, eh? What exactly did she say?"

"She told me that I was behaving badly."

"Sexually?"

"Well, yes, sort of."

"That's OK then", says Val." It would be perfectly reasonable for you to 'disappear' an imaginary girl if, in your fantasy, she taunted you into taking a swipe at her and then you felt really guilty about it."

I am feeling really uncomfortable about this. I really wish it had not happened as it did. I suppose the only positive thing to come out of it is that Val seems to think that it would be a rational thing to do. "You don't think that I'm going Bonkers?"

"Oh that!" says Val "I have no idea what 'Bonkers' is. We all have our moments of dysfunction, it is just a matter of scale really, the term is largely irrelevant."

"What do you think happened to me? Do you think it probable that this was all a drug induced hallucination, or that, just possibly, it might have been something else?"

"Logic points to the former, but I think you may be more comfortable with the latter."

"I'm not sure about that."

"Well there's no certainty, but let's suppose that you were not drugged. Let's also suppose that you may be a little off-beam, but certainly not certifiable."

"That sounds just a little bit better than 'bonkers', but what then?"

"I should think that that was rather more in your field than mine," says Val.

"Hmmm, so we are talking about dreams creeping into reality? We are touching that which I am always propounding to my students, that thin veil between reality and illusion?"

"Well you're right, certainly in our dreams the two merge, there are no boundaries."

"Talking of dreams," I say, "I keep hearing a voice inside my head. I'm imagining that Miranda is talking to me. Do you think that's strange?"

"No. It's perfectly normal. After a death, particularly a sudden death, you can often hear the voice, sometimes even see a vivid image, of the dead person. Does it seem as if she is actually telling you anything?"

"I don't know really; it is difficult to make out."

"Well let's be clear. We are not looking at a ghostly Miranda trying to send messages to you. It is your subconscious that is using your memories of her, and of her ideas, to make it seem that Miranda is saying something to you."

"No wonder it's is a bit of a jumble."

"Just let it happen, it'll do no harm. Given time it'll disappear of its own accord."

I sit still for a while, still worried about whether I am under any form of threat. "Simon said that if we were looking at the fiddling with the phone scenario then there would be someone out there who is targeting me for a specific purpose. Not just anyone, but the aim would be to affect me. I just wonder whether it could possibly have anything to do with my field of research, and more specifically the Project?."

Val is watching me closely. "I should tread just a little carefully," she says," I've no idea how much of this is down to external forces and how much is coming from within you. What I do know is that the mind is a tough old thing, but it can become pretty fragile if you push it beyond its natural limits."

"And you think I'm pushing mine a bit?"

"I know you must be under a lot of stress. Not only have you had to cope with Miranda's death, but also your research project has been pretty severely knocked off course. No wonder you are experiencing weird things."

There is little I can do about it at this stage. It is really kind of Val to have given me her time and professional advice. I thank her profusely and she says it is what Miranda would have wanted her to do. That's a slightly odd thing to say, but I let it pass.

"Keep talking about your experiences, Duncan, it'll help you. You know you can come and see me any time you want to."

"Thanks, Val, it's all rather worrying, more because of the uncertainty than anything else. I reckon that as long as I stay focussed on The Project then my life will have a clear objective and things will work out just fine."

I quietly close Val's door and walk slowly along the corridor to my own room, wondering how I can possibly resolve matters. Simon has told me to wait and do nothing. Val has told me not to get involved in anything that might be mentally stressful. I feel uncannily addicted to that experience in Langdale. I want to revisit it, play it again, and ideally have it end very differently. In the meantime I have little option but to heed the words of my two advisors and, for now at least, do nothing.

Twelve

George had taken less than 24 hours to resume his occupancy of the house in Bewdley Street. Toothbrush and razor had settled back into their accustomed places and suits, shoes and sundry garments had reoccupied the spaces that they had so recently vacated. George himself seemed rather less evident, although he had put in a guest appearance just before midnight. He had still been stretched out under the duvet the following morning when Helen, packed, orange-juiced and mueslied had left the house at seven fifteen.

She had hoped to catch a mid-morning train to Lancaster, but work, as it so often did, had claimed her. She spent a large part of the morning sorting the fall-out from the rent-boy situation. She had endured the pleasure of no less than three abusive phone calls from her would-be client who had been so upset at having his plans to molest small boys thwarted that he had screamed down the phone that she, the Filthy Whore of Babylon, should do something impossibly intricate to a very graphically described part of her anatomy.

She had tried, and failed, to find time to run through yesterday's tapes for both office suites. She doubted whether there would be much of interest although she wondered rather vaguely why such small group of men were prepared to pay so much for their straightforward meeting at her Westminster suite. She had not dealt with this firm before, but they seemed just the sort of clients that she needed. They had used the tunnel lift, which was unusual.

She had managed to persuade a rather reluctant Buildings Manager at Marylebone that he would be able to create, by Friday, an office interior that resembled an eighteenth-century gaming den. It was gone twelve fifteen before she managed to hail a taxi that by dint of squeezing and blasting its way through the traffic along Euston Road had deposited her in time to catch the twelve thirty train.

In fact the timing was not too bad, she had arrived at Lancaster before four o'clock giving her sufficient time during the later part of the afternoon to carry out a bit of investigation at the hospital to see if she could unearth anything. The rail service had improved dramatically over the last few years, knocking nearly an hour off the journey time. Mind you it was still not possible for her to consider travelling standard class, these Pendolino trains were all very well but unless you travelled First you were squashed into what were rather strangely referred to as 'aircraft' type seats without the chance of reading your paper or using your laptop. This train was crowded enough; what a Standard class journey might be like on a Friday evening Helen could scarcely imagine. It seemed so stupid that Virgin, or whoever was responsible, could not run trains with more carriages.

Helen considered her forthcoming 'shotgun' nuptials dispassionately. She supposed that most 'forced' marriages were still the mournful result of an unplanned pregnancy, destined to stagger through a few wilderness years of mutual indifference and end with a release slip of legal gibberish. How much more suitable, she thought, for marriages of convenience to be rooted firmly upon the solid ground of mortgage repayments. Yesterday she and George had talked briefly about a pre-nup agreement. He was not so keen on the idea, but she had insisted, being damned if he would walk away in a couple of years owning a large chunk of her house. It was not uppermost in her mind that in the meantime he would have paid for at least half of it! She was not sure that she wanted to be a married woman, there was something terribly final about 'Mrs', but if that was what it took to ensure financial stability then she would bear up under such novelty of title. Anyway it would be George's third bash at the wedding stakes so it would not be much of a life-changer for him.

Virgin Rail had swept her through the West Midlands and into northern England. There had been a major exodus at Preston and now the train manager (why didn't they call themselves Guards still?) was telling her in insistent mechanical tones that she was approaching Lancaster. Furthermore, he went on, would she please be sure to take all her belongings with her as she left the train. She stowed her iPad in her small, but exquisitely priced, Prada Beige overnight bag, slipped into her black suede Toscana Shearling coat and, as her steed bore her into the station and drew up obligingly at the platform, she was ready to take on the world.

Helen had given some consideration about the best way of approaching the hospital. She needed to speak to someone who had been with Miranda during that last week and, following Aletia's advice, thought that little would be achieved in 'getting heavy' with the Chief Executive at this stage. She admitted to a fleeting sense of disappointment at this decision. She normally operated at the highest level, and would have enjoyed deploying a verbal pin to deflate some Administrator, puffed up with his own sense of self-importance. Instead she realised that she would achieve a good deal more if she went in rather lower down the batting order and played the 'grieving relative' card.

"In any case", she thought, "such is the truth, Miranda was my only sister and I loved her."

The taxi brought her to the main hospital entrance. During the short journey she had adjusted her make-up with care so that it was now a less sophisticated looking Helen that walked into the medical unit. She did not look dowdy, but her whole demeanour had altered, she had lost that air of haughtiness. She was now a quiet, ordinary, and concerned person, the type than posed no threat at all to anyone at the hospital. She took care to ensure that the coat, label well hidden, that was draped over her arm was all but covering her over-opulent bag.

She made her way to the ward where only a month ago she had squirmed at visiting the dying Miranda. She remembered the way quite clearly but was surprised to discover that the harsh corridors brought back such sad memories of her sister. There were several uniformed women clustered around the nurses' station. She was in search of any nurse who had known Miranda, and hit lucky the first time.

"Excuse me," she said," I wonder if anyone could possibly help me." She explained that her sister had died in the ward just a few weeks ago, that she lived in London and that although she had of course come to Lancaster for the funeral, she had not had time to have a word with the staff who had cared for Miranda and talk to them about her last few days.

"You would like to come with me?" said a young nurse whom she took to be Polish, "I know who you should be speaking to." She deposited Helen in a small, sparsely furnished room, brought her a cup of tea, and went off in search of her colleague.

Moments later Helen was talking to staff nurse Elizabeth Barnes. A pleasant rather rounded woman in her early fifties with a shock of brown hair, a slightly harassed look and a gentle manner.

"I understand that you nursed my poor sister. I only managed to get here from London on a day visit during that week and it's so good to know that during her last few days she was in such good hands," gushed Helen.

"If there is anything I can help you with, or tell you about, do just ask me, Miss Marston."

"When I came to see her she was very drowsy but seemed to be in good spirits. I suppose she must have suffered quite a bit at the end?"

"Well there are so many ways that we can help patients cope with pain nowadays," said Nurse Elizabeth. "It is all a matter of using the right drug in the correct dosage and at the appropriate time."

"Was she on many drugs?"

Nurse Elizabeth had brought with her Miranda's Patient Record, which she now consulted "Well towards the end the main painkiller was Oromorph, but with Mrs Fielding we used it sparingly as she was hardly with us anyway. Oromorph is a pretty heavy sedative with hallucinogenic properties and, whilst it suits many patients, they do rather lose touch with reality; especially in the sort of dose that we use in the last few days of terminal care."

"Presumably the consultant saw her regularly?"

"Well actually Mr Fremantle made rather a special case of her. He visited her at least twice a day, which is unusual and just shows what a caring doctor he is. I think she deserved that extra attention. I know it was agreed by Mr Freemantle that we should carry out a recently authorized clinical trial, with her husband's consent of course. Sadly, but not unexpectedly, it did not do her much good."

"Does it say much about that trial in her records?" asked Helen.

"Not much, it was an experimental drugs treatment, as I understand it, that had been trialled on patients elsewhere and Mr Freemantle got the consent of the Senior Medical Team to involve Miranda in the process."

"I suppose that's normal?"

"Well I wouldn't say 'normal'. From time to time we do use new drugs as part of clinical trials, and these trials will occasionally take place with terminal patients. The thing is though that I've never known Mr Freemantle carry out such a trial with a dying patient.

"Was my sister able to say anything about what was happening to her?"

"She had moments that were almost lucid," said Nurse Elizabeth. "It seemed to me that your sister had reached a state of accepting her fate at a very early stage – perhaps even before she was admitted."

"You kept her here for the full week. I suppose that is normal in the case of a very advanced stage patient, the alternative being that she might have spent her last few days in a hospice?"

"There really wasn't the time to consider hospice care. She was gravely ill and quite honestly beyond the sort of care that a hospice can give. Somehow everybody regarded your sister as a special case. What's more she was trialling the new treatment for the team and needed to be here so that she could be kept under surveillance at all times."

"I know this sounds a little odd," said Helen, "but she was diagnosed as having a malignant brain tumour. Did you ever see anything that might suggest to you that she was suffering from anything other that?"

Elizabeth Barnes looked a little startled at this and thought for a while before saying with great care "I'm not sure why you are asking me all these questions. Is there something that I ought to know?"

Helen knew she must tread carefully. "It was just that she was my only real relative and it matters so much to me that she was at peace when she died. I just wondered if there might have been anything that made her feel better or worse, or seemed unsettling to you?"

"It's not so much that there was anything strange about the symptoms themselves. I've seen people dying of such tumours before and the symptoms that your sister had were exactly those that I would have expected. No, it's just that they did not seem quite connected. I haven't put that very well, what I mean is that although the symptoms were exactly those that are consistent with a brain tumour, they didn't presentr in quite the manner or the timing that I would've expected."

"I'm not sure I follow you."

"No? Well I'm sure that I'm mistaken, it just seemed very slightly odd at the time. Best forget I said anything at all. You'd be so much better talking to Mr Freemantle about the medical matters relating to your sister's death; and he could tell you all about the drugs trial. I really am not the best person to talk about such things. Sorry."

And with that Nurse Elizabeth got to her feet; the meeting was over.

"Thank you so much," said Helen, "You have been really helpful."

"Well I'm glad you came and that we had this little chat. You don't need to worry about anything that happened to your sister here. She had the very best treatment, and the end was really very peaceful."

They shook hands and Helen made her way out of the ward.

It was a very different Helen that emerged from the ladies lavatory and arrived back at the main entrance. Gone was the sympathetic relative. She was fully coated and bagged. She demanded that the security staff find her a taxi, which to their own surprise they did with alacrity.

"Aha," she thought as she sat in the back of the large saloon car, "There was something different about Miranda's disease, and the treatment of it." Not much, but enough to confirm that the accusation of her anonymous correspondent might not have been totally misplaced.

It was early evening. There was some snow in the air and the traffic was struggling to cope with it, slithering around in the frenzied manner that only the English can offer when faced with the horrors of a full half inch of slush. She directed the taxi to Duncan's house. Time to have a serious talk with her brother in law.

Thirteen

Simon is already in the Lab, busying himself with some maths on the whiteboard when I join him at just gone three o'clock.

Although known as the 'Lab' this room that was the hub of Miranda's practical work it is hardly a laboratory other than in name. It comprises two rooms, the larger of which contains one piece of bulky electrical equipment. It looks like a combination of a laser generator and a brain scanner. The rest of the room appears to be devoted to the pursuit of mathematics rather than physical experimentation, although there is a collection of varied and rather old apparatus stored on some benches lined up along the rear wall. The smaller room is just a glass-fronted cubbyhole carved out of the main area. At some stage it must have served as a retreat for those conducting hazardous experiments, but its use now is limited to brewing a cup of tea, or taking a quick rest.

Miranda had become obsessed with particle physics at an early age. She showed great aptitude and it was no surprise that she acquired a First in the subject. Her enquiring mind however then took her into medicine, and thence into neuroscience. It was a combination of her extraordinary skills in this obscure collecrion of disciplines that opened up this Project for her. She had brought herself up to date with the latest thinking in particle physics and was intensely interested in the results being obtained from the Large Hadron Collider. She was as frustrated as everyone else at the early setbacks suffered at this experimental site and immediately dismissive when some experimental data seemed to imply that neutrinos travel faster than light.

Whilst Miranda was taking her particular theoretical route in physics and neurobiology, I turned my philosophical thinking towards recent developments in quantum theory. I am no quantum physicist and could never get my head around some of the hypotheses that were being propounded by those much better qualified in that field than I. Nevertheless there was, and indeed remains, a great deal of work to do on the manner in which quantum theory acts upon us as rational human beings. I contributed to a paper on this subject that also explored the impact upon mankind of a universe that had two dimensions in time, as well as the three or more dimensions of space

Miranda and I had combined our expertise and had postulated that there were very sound reasons to accept the existence of parallel worlds. We looked at ways in which we might access such worlds and considered that this might be achieved through the application of thought-energy. It was the practical proving of this hypothesis that Miranda had been working on at the time of her death.

"See you've managed to escape from Val's clutches at last," says Simon.

"No thanks to you, Si. Where was the cavalry when I needed it!"

"Did she help?"

"To be fair she was very good. Between the two of you I reckon I can close the door on the whole experience. If nothing happens from now on there will be no need to ever bring it up again."

"And if something does?"

"I think we'd better just take it as it comes."

"Good man, that's just what I advised."

The Project was very nearly dealt a deathblow by Miranda's loss. It was fortunate that she and I agreed, some weeks before her accident, that we should employ Simon to help her out with some of the mathematics involved. It means that he has a fairly good grasp of Miranda's technical thinking and will be in an excellent position to write up her notes and complete her analysis.

We settle down to discuss progress to date. I have really got to rein Simon in a bit, but I need to do so without upsetting him too much. I am grateful to him for agreeing to increase his involvement, but that does not put us on an equal footing. I am now left as the sole team leader whilst Simon is my deputy. The basic intellectual leap that forms the basis of the Paper has already been made. The problem lies only in ensuring that we have full documentation of Miranda's proof of our hypothesis.

"Simon, we need to sort some stuff out. I know that it's been a bit difficult of late with Miranda's death and all that, but we've got to put that behind us now. We're in danger of going off at tangents, and this probably comes from our working recently in a somewhat haphazard way."

Despite my efforts Simon is immediately on the defensive "You mean that I'm working in a haphazard way?"

"It may be partly my fault," I say, trying to calm the situation, "but perhaps we need a clearer sense of direction."

"Come off it, Dunc, this is me, Simon, your mate that you are talking to. With my involvement now I reckon that we can get this Paper finalised. In fact I was going to have a word with you about my authorship of it."

"Authorship?"

"When I was working with Miranda she told me very clearly that she valued my work as being extremely professional."

"I'm sure she really appreciated everything that you did for her. Your efforts took a lot of the strain off her. And I know it allowed her to concentrate on developing the experimental side."

"Well that's just it. Shortly before she was hospitalised Miranda was kind enough to ask me how I would feel about becoming a co-author with the two of you. As you can imagine I was really chuffed about that."

This is outrageous. Miranda never mentioned anything about this to me. I am quite certain that she would have spoken to me first before mentioning the matter to Simon. I am equally certain that she would not have considered Simon to be of a sufficient standard to warrant such formal recognition. The man is lying through his teeth.

"Simon, are you sure about this?"

"She said she'd have a word with you about it. Perhaps she didn't get a chance."

"Look, Simon, well over half the impetus for this work was Miranda's. When the Paper is published I want Miranda's name on it with my own. No one else, not even you. Do you understand?

"Perfectly, thank you. But I do have a claim now to be co-author, you cannot finish this project on your own, you need me to analyse Miranda's notes."

"Yes, I do need you. You are now a very important part of this project, and that will be duly acknowledged. But I have a duty to Miranda to ensure that the end result seen as being her work."

"Dunc, things have moved on. Not only is Miranda no longer with us, but there are exciting new possibilities that will give this research a much higher profile than Miranda could have possibly imagined."

"I'm not sure that I follow you."

"What we are doing is of the most immense interest to some very powerful people," says Simon.

"How do you know that? Have you been talking out of turn?"

"No, far from it, but I did have a quiet word with a chap I met at a conference in London the other week and he, and his people, are most interested in what we are up to."

"Why's that?"

"Well as I understand it they invest in research projects that have far-reaching social possibilities, just like this one has. They have a great deal of money, and in these difficult financial times I imagine that such backing is incredibly important to struggling Universities."

"They want to invest in us, do they?"

" They want to buy into the Project," says Simon, "but in no way do they want to take it over. We would still be in charge."

I am not sure that I like his use of 'we', but decide to overlook that for the time being. "You said something about an 'incubator scheme'?"

"That might be one way to move things forward."

"Who are these people?"

"Virtual Ventures are an international company with a small but impressive list of directors."

"Never heard of them."

"I think they like to keep a low profile."

"Hmmm. It all sounds a bit iffy to me."

I look rather bleakly out the window trying to evaluate what Simon is saying. I just wish that Miranda were still here and able to help me consider this unexpected financial offer. I know well enough not to trust this man, but I am also aware that he has the ear of the Vice-Chancellor and could easily make political waves within the University corridors of power.

I look continue looking out of the window. There is a very light sprinkling of snow drifting gently to the land. A transformation is underway, that which was green is being turned to white. No longer is it a scene of end-of-season growth, but one of finality. This white suffocation is upon us, either to hold us in its frosty jaws, or to vanish back into the ether as a warm front thwarts its wintery plan.

Simon, in his real universe, continues. "These people are really keen to take on and develop our line of research. They realize that we don't have the expertise, following Miranda's death, to take things further. If we can move to 'arms length' status with the University then they would be happy to fund new lab, obviously with us in charge."

I nod. "OK, so they know what Miranda was up to. You must have been talking to them in some depth. How much more do they know?"

"I was just sounding them out really," says Simon. "They seemed interested and I thought it might be a really good way to ensure a great future of The Project."

"Go on then."

"Well they know that Miranda was following up on thought-energy transference before she died."

"Did you tell them about the accident?"

"They seemed suspicious about her death. I told them that an experiment had very nearly succeeded. I suppose they might have put two and two together. They were also aware that further R & D would require some very hefty funding, and this they are in a position to provide."

"Miranda needed further information from CERN."

"Just so, and these investors would be happy to expedite that, they really do have the most immense resources and such excellent contacts," says Simon. "I explained to these guys that the research had led Miranda to look at two related strands. The formation of 'hidden' worlds using dark matter and then the neuroscience of thought-energy."

"Clearly they suggested that this research might be taken further?"

"That's what really excited them," says Simon. "The notion that a specific form of energy is generated by thinking and that thought-energy might therefore be as valid as any conventional energy. They were really interested in expanding Miranda's work on the basis of thought-energy."

"But what I don't understand is why they should be so excited about this. What's the point of them investing a few thousand pounds in this Project unless there is a pretty generous pay-back for them?"

"Duncan, we are not talking a few thousand pounds here. These guys are talking of hundreds of thousands!"

"What on earth are they going to do with that sort of money?"

"Amongst other things, pay you! They really do have very deep pockets and I think that if you decide to go with them you could just about name your own price."

"I still don't see why they're so interested. What are they going to get out of the project for that sort of investment?"

I am getting more than a little worried that Simon has no idea about this quagmire he is leading us into. Like many academics my interest is in the theory rather than any resulting technology and I have never given a vast amount of thought as to whether there would be any exploitable opportunities as a result of the work that Miranda and I were doing.

"Look," says Simon, "We're setting out to establish that thought-energy is a way to access parallel worlds. The next step is to confirm Miranda's experiments and so prove this in practice. If this is successful then we will be very famous. The thing is though that we simply don't have the resources here at the moment to carry out this work effectively."

"What would my role be?"

"They want you to head up the team and are very keen to keep your theoretical involvement. They would pay you handsomely for that. They would want to set up this 'incubator' company here under the aegis of the University so that the research could be taken further."

This is not good. I feel a rising sense of panic at the possibility of being swept along by this torrent of sense. "I can see that there is some merit in this, Si, but I need a bit of time to think about it."

"That's the problem," says Simon. "They want us to give them an answer within the next couple of days."

Deadlines such as this make me feel really queasy. I like to ponder things for a while letting decisions emerge, rather than rushing to snap judgments. I am also concerned about the effect it would have on the way Miranda's work will be viewed by posterity. I am very keen to see my late wife's name on a serious academic Paper that might revolutionize thinking. Somehow I very much doubt if that would be possible under Simon's proposal.

"I am a bit worried about it, Si, I'm far from sure that I can see where it will lead us, it'll be like jumping onto a never-ending fairground ride."

"Look Dunc," says Simon, "give it some thought overnight. These people are offering you a very large pot of gold for this. We can have another chat about the idea tomorrow or the day after. I'm sure that will be time enough to give them an answer."

"OK," I say, "Let's go into this very cautiously, but for now we had better call it a day."

Simon and I close the Lab and make our way towards the entrance lobby, quite surprised to find that it is getting on for seven o'clock.

"Many folk around this evening?" I say to a security guard.

"Dead as a Dodo", says the man. "You two are the first souls in or out of here since I came on duty four hours ago. Oh no," he corrects himself," there was a young lady came in a bit back, pretty young thing with spikey blonde hair, but she's left now."

"Oh well, try to stay awake. Goodnight."

Fourteen

The snow has turned to a light drizzle and that which was turning white has now bethought itself and is returning to its gang-mower hue. Simon and I bid a cordial farewell to each other and ten minutes later my red Alfa is approaching home.

"Same routine," I say as I sweep into the garage and hit the 'close' button for the garage doors.

I stare glumly out of the windscreen focusing on a brown urn placed on the shelf in front of the car. Miranda's ashes. What the hell am I supposed to do with that thing? I swing myself out of the car, go over to the receptacle and pick it up. It is more of a screw-top bottle than an urn. I wonder if this rather slippery plastic canister would have impressed The Ancients. On one of its four sides there is a label bearing Miranda's name and date of cremation. Not much to record a life past.

I stand looking at the urn for a moment then, rather gingerly try to unscrew the top. It's stiff. I try again, harder, but without effect. I put the urn on the workbench and find an oil filter removal chain. This I wrap around the lid of the urn. I apply a spanner to the nut on the chain and twist it tight. Holding onto the bottom of the urn I put a bit more weight on the spanner. The lid spins off. The chain and spanner fall to the ground with a clatter and the canister slips from my grip falling to the garage floor with a dull thud. Miranda spills out in the form of a coarse grey powder.

I stare disbelievingly at my wife. There is a surprisingly large quantity of her. Surely she was not that big? Perhaps they mixed up the ashes at the crematorium. It could be that this is the way that they dispose of unwanted remains – just shove a few in everyone else's urn.

I kneel down on the floor and scoop up as much of Miranda as I can by pushing the neck of the open bottle into her. I look around for a suitable tool and grab a pointing trowel. I catch myself grinning at the thought that with my help Miranda is getting plastered. Once most of her is safely back in the container I screw the lid on again. Using a small paintbrush I usher the last few bits of Miranda underneath the workbench. I doubt if she will be very happy there. I dust the remains of my wife from my hands and head towards the utility room.

"What the Hell." I say taking a pace backwards. There is light showing from under the door. It is not coming not from the utility room, but apparently from the kitchen beyond. I wonder if I could have left the kitchen light turned on when I went to work this morning. I am not sure that I ever turned it on, for it was broad daylight before I got to the coffee and toast stage. I am sure I did not touch it. Someone must be in there.

Very carefully I inch the door open. There is a radio playing something vaguely classical. I open the door a bit further and slip into the utility room. There is a woman in the kitchen humming along to the music. I move, almost cat-like through the utility room trying not to make a sound, trying to control my breathing, trying to stop my heart from pumping so loudly.

I peer around the doorway.

Standing at the sink, with her back to me, is Miranda.

"Miranda!" I exclaim. But no sooner are the words out of my mouth than I realize my mistake. The figure by the sink wheels round; it is Helen. I have forgotten all about her. I feel foolish and embarrassed.

"Oh, Duncan, I've startled you. I'm so sorry. I got here nearly two hours ago and let myself in with the key from behind the shed door."

"I thought, just for one moment, that you were Miranda. You do have very similar figures you know."

"Did." she corrects me.

Helen and I have got on reasonably well in the past, although we would hardly have considered ourselves as great friends. I suppose her outlook on life is different from mine. Of late she had taken to coming to see us accompanied by George, who is a prick of the first water. I did not enjoy those visits. It comes as a slight surprise therefore to feel a sudden glow of pleasure that Helen is here.

I am confused by the offer that Simon was speaking to me about. It does not seem to make much sense, and I find Simon's keenness towards it to it somewhat odd. In any case he should have discussed it with me before talking in such detail to this contact of his. I need to discuss it with someone who is not so involved or as biased as Simon is. Helen will do just fine.

"Let's have a glass of something," I say, walking through to the Living Room, "what'll you have?"

"G&T thanks," says Helen following me through.

I pour out a couple of fairly stiff Tanquerays, add a little Fever Tree tonic and a slice of lemon to each and hand one of them to my sister-in-law.

"Helen, I need to talk. I've had a really rather unsettling afternoon and could do with running something passed you. Also, what the hell are you doing here?"

Oh blast, that sounds awfully ungallant. I hope I have not upset her. Quickly I add. "Not that I am anything but delighted to see you."

"I came because of a note."

"I never sent you a note!"

"No, I'm not sure who it came from. Any ideas?" Helen passes me a letter. It says very simply:

'FROM WHAT DID MIRANDA DIE'

I can sense that she is watching me closely, although I have no idea as to why. I read the thing a couple of times and pass it slowly back to her. "I find that more than a little worrying."

Helen tells me that George has urged her to go to the police, and that she intends to do just that, but not immediately. That is good. I need to try to wean her from such an idea, goodness knows what would happen if the authorities started to take a close interest in the last week of Miranda's life.

"I rather got the impression that you and George were no longer an item," I venture, trying not to sound pleased about this.

"Duncan, you are talking about the man whom I'm about to wed!"

"Good heavens, he won't marry you!" Everything I say this evening seems to come out the wrong way.

"Hey thanks for that! But actually he will. Even as I speak he is buying me an obscenely expensive ring and engrossing the pre-nup."

"Not at this time of night he won't be."

"I speak figuratively. Anyway he's not going to take up that fantastic job in Paris and will from now on have to pay half my mortgage – how are the mighty fallen."

I keep further remarks to myself to avoid any acrimony, but such thoughts as I have on how best to deal with this man might result in George receiving a few 'Get Well Soon' cards.

Helen tells me about her visit to the Lancaster Infirmary and the very faint hints that she picked up from the Charge Nurse that there was indeed something a little odd about Miranda's treatment.

"It doesn't seem to amount to much," I say. It is essential that I try to dispel this doubt that she has picked up on "I know all about that clinical trial. Miranda was an ideal 'guinea pig'. I was only too happy to give the hospital consent on her behalf. Good scientist that she was she would have been really pleased to have been used to try to improve things for other people in the future."

"Do you know what was involved in such treatment?"

"Not really, apart from the trial the hospital was attempting to treat her symptoms in a variety of ways. I do know that at one stage her faeces turned blue."

"Blue?"

"Yes, but it was only for a couple of days, right at the start of that week I think."

"Was there nothing else?"

"No. It was all very quick, as you know. Lots of friends came to visit her. Towards the end I rather discouraged visitors, more for their sakes than Miranda's. She was out of it of course, but I wanted her friends to remember her as she had been before she was hospitalised. Really it was just Simon, Val and myself who saw her in those final few days."

"I vaguely remember a Simon from the funeral, was he very involved with you two?"

"Of late he had been working closely with Miranda,"

"Who's Val?"

"Oh, she's a friend of both Miranda and myself, perhaps I should say 'was' in the case of my wife. She's a lovely person. She's on the University staff and lectures in Psychology. I know that she does some private practice psychotherapy as well"

"Are you speaking from experience?"

"Well, as a matter of fact I am. Recent experience too. Val caught me earlier today and before I could say 'Carl Gustav Jung' I'm lying on her couch relating my deep childhood desire to have carnal relations with a goldfish!"

"Don't be so stupid, Duncan! What's she like, this Val?"

I give Helen an acutely observed run-down of my would-be shrink.

"Well she must be about ten years younger than me, but looks a decade younger than that. She's fairly tall, tousled light brown hair, and good-looking in a slightly boyish sort of way. She wears loose, flowing dresses and bracelets and things that give her a slightly 'flower power' look if you follow me."

"What's she like as a person"

"Well I've known her for some time, and as I say she was a friend to both of us. She can appear a bit vague, but that's just a front. She's actually pretty acute, and although she has a slightly brusque way with her when you first meet her, she's a really kind, caring person."

"Do she and Simon get on?"

"Oh yes," I say, and then think a bit more about it. "Well I don't know really. They have a sort of jokey attitude towards each other, but that's probably a bit of a front. Now that I think about it I am pretty sure they don't really chime with each other."

"So why did you see her this morning?"

I carefully relate the essential points of my dream culminating in my discussion with Simon about the possible explanation of what might be happening. I explain that I then had a similar discussion with Val.

"Hmmm, I'm not surprised you are a bit worried about going nuts", says Helen. "That is a pretty wild dream. I suppose you just imagined this Starlight girl so that you could give full rein to your sexual prowess."

"Look Helen, my sexual prowess is quite happy as it is, without being enhanced by screwing pizza delivery girls."

"Did you screw her?"

"No, I bloody well didn't."

In retrospect I just cannot think why I did not take Starlight up on her offer. Perhaps there is something wrong with me? It now seems that the most natural thing would have been to say 'yes', and yet when in the dream-state I managed to convince myself that by not shagging the girl I was going to find some 'absolute meaning'. I was intent upon discovering some 'hidden truth' either about her or about something that she wanted to tell me. I fear that I was deluding myself.

This self-delusion thing seems to be at the crux of what I am experiencing. It must be that I have over-stressed my mind and it is taking its revenge upon me by hallucinating. There is little of my recent strange experience that cannot be explained by the realisation that deep within me there is a different 'self' working away to its own agenda. Such things were responsible for stuffing nineteenth century loony bins.

I need to focus on the immediate, and most particularly the purpose of Helen's visit. She has it in her to blow apart the whole hospital charade that culminated in Miranda's death. This I need to avoid.

"So, Helen, presumably that is the end of your investigation, there's not much point in taking it any further is there?"

"I'm really not at all sure," says Helen, "I thought I was onto something when I was talking to Nurse Elizabeth, but from what you say it all seems to have been above board."

"Well, all I can tell you is that firstly the hospital made it quite clear to everyone that Miranda was dying from cancer, and secondly her consultant let it be known how important he thought it was that she should to be undergoing a drugs trial in the final stages of her life."

"I suppose I might as well call in on the Police tomorrow then and hand them the note. I don't expect they will do much with it, but they might as well have it, you never know," says Helen.

This is not good. I had forgotten that Helen was merely put off taking the note to the authorities until she had followed up on any leads that she might find. I have got to stop her. Getting the police involved would, fairly swiftly, result in The Project being cancelled.

"I don't know about that," I say, "if you involve the police aren't you just going to stir up an awful lot of concerns and worries? If you could tell them that there was reasonable doubt about the diagnosis then it might be different. I can see nothing but trouble coming from any form of official interest into Miranda's death. Just imagine the interviews, the evidence gathering, the endless amount of bumph involved."

I have really got to persuade Helen to drop her interest in the whole thing before it goes critical.

"Possibly, I'll think about it." says Helen. "One other thing though. Nurse Elizabeth did say something about Miranda's symptoms occurring in the wrong order, I wonder what she meant by that."

"Probably nothing. Her consultant, Jimmy Freemantle, told everyone that Miranda's symptoms were classic pointers to a brain tumour. He also said that this was confirmed by the MRI scan and biopsy. I doubt if there is a 'correct order' for the symptoms anyway."

"The only thing I can think of," says Helen "is the hair loss. When I came to see her on the second day Miranda had only just started on her chemo, but she was wearing that funny woolly hat, you know the brown and red knitted thing that came down over her ears."

"She liked that hat."

"Yes, I know. But had she already lost some of her hair?"

For reasons that are beyond me I am a rotten liar. I do not mean that I am a 'filthy rotten liar', what I am trying to convey is that whenever I try to tell a lie everyone seems to be aware that it is a falsehood! My work as a moral philosopher has given me a naïve belief in the sanctity of truth so I suppose I am just not convincing enough as a liar. That said I have got to try and stop Helen from opening things up and making difficulties that would cause problems for everyone involved in the cover-up.

"Look, Helen, I'm getting worried about what you're up to. The thing is that if you keep on wriggling your knife into this thing then there is bound to be trouble. The hospital authorities will get wind of your, probably baseless, concerns and then they will come down on that nice nurse that you chatted with, she might even lose her job. Also I am not at all sure that it is such a good idea to take that letter to the police. All you are going to do is to create ill-will and upset people."

"Duncan, you are holding something back, I know you are. You're such a terrible liar, always have been. Now tell me what is it that I'm missing?"

I really don't want to go on with this discussion. I wish that Helen had never come. I wish that she would go away. Now!

As if she is reading my thoughts Helen continues, "Dunc, I'm not going to let this rest. Miranda was my only sister. If I have loved anyone in this life, I loved her. I loved her, admired her and looked up to her. There never was and never will be anyone that could take her place for me. I know she's dead, and that has left a great open wound that I suppose must heal one day, but I want to know how she died. When it was definitely cancer I could pigeonhole that in my mind. People die of cancer. Young people die of cancer, and cancer can be a quick killer. But I think you know something more about whatever it was that Miranda died from, or that something was not quite right about it. I don't do begging, it's not my style, but Dunc I'm begging you now. Please tell me the truth."

"I appreciate your honesty, Helen, and I do know that Miranda meant a lot to you. It was of course mutual. You're right. I have been keeping some of this back from you. I didn't want to, believe me, but it's out of my control. I just cannot tell you any more without talking it through with someone."

"Who?"

I really do not want to go there. Eventually I admit, "Simon."

"Simon! What on earth has he got to do with diagnosing Miranda's illness incorrectly?"

"Well it isn't quite like that."

"What is it like for Christ's sake?"

I explain to Helen that I really cannot discuss it with her. I tell her that I will ring Simon, tell him that she has grave suspicions about her sister's death and, if Simon agrees, go to the campus with her in the morning so that all three of us can talk it through.

Although clearly annoyed that I will tell her no more Helen goes off to see if she can rustle up some sort of supper. I head for the phone.

Half an hour later food having been consumed along with a bottle of wine, I tell her that I have arranged a meeting with Simon for the morrow.

I turn to Helen. "There's something else. I could really do with your advice. Simon tackled me this afternoon about a strange offer that he's had regarding the Project."

"You're not giving up on that project are you? Duncan, you can't, it was the most important thing in Miranda's life."

"Oh no, not at all. In fact these people who Simon has been talking to want to carry on and expand the work."

"Is there a problem in that?"

"They want to pay me an awful lot of money."

"This 'problem' gets better and better."

"The trouble is that I know nothing whatsoever about this firm and what they really want to do with our research. It appears that their longer-term aim is to take it out of academia and put it on some sort of private technological footing."

"What do you mean you know nothing about them? Who did Simon say they are? We can look them up in the Companies House register."

"Well that's just it. Simon says that the people he was in touch with are called Virtual Ventures, but I am pretty certain that they are just intermediaries, perhaps some kind of international business angels."

"And you have no idea who are behind them."

"All this is conjecture, but I cannot help thinking about Simon working for the military a few years back. I just wonder if there is some kind of connection here."

"I think you are right to be cautious. The important thing is what is best for The Project."

"I am very uncertain about whether it is. But having said that Simon appears to be totally smitten by the idea."

"Did he say that these people had made any definite offer?"

"He said that they would pay me a lot of money, both to take over the project and then to keep me on as at least titular head, more likely a sort of consultant. He did say that things would still be based here in Lancaster."

Helen thinks about it. She is a shrewd and experienced businesswoman. She recognises my concern, and will want to take account of that.

"How have you left it then, Dunc?"

"They have given us just a couple of days. Simon is pretty keen that I should throw in our lot with them, but I have just about convinced myself that it would be a mistake."

"Why is Simon so interested?"

"Good point. I'm not sure really. He is a bit of a glory boy, but he won't get much kudos. There might not even be a Paper if we go with these people. Perhaps he just wants the money."

"I shall ask him when we see him tomorrow," says Helen.

Fifteen

Another day, and I am due to be at the University by nine thirty. I have arranged with Helen that she will come up to my room at about midday. When I spoke with Simon on the phone yesterday evening he agreed, with considerable reluctance, to meet with Helen so that we could talk through Miranda's death. I am uneasy about this, but apart from it being only fair to explain things to Helen we have to take her into our confidence. If we do not do so she may well blow the whole thing wide open.

Things are unravelling. My cosy life is being torn apart and I resent it. I like my problems to be ordered – in rows. No perhaps not so much in rows but in rows on shelves. I can then pick each one up, turn it over, inspect it, contemplate and, eventually, return it to the shelf, perhaps in a slightly changed location. This is not what is happening. Asunder, that's the word, my whole life. Chaos, it has been, ever since that fateful phone call from Simon summoning me to witness the death-throes of my wife. Now Simon is pressing me to surrender The Project and Helen is poking her nose into that whole hospital thing. No wonder I am inventing weather-changing girls that supply me with pizzas.

One on one tutorials first thing; I breeze through a couple. They are usually one hell of a grind. Unless the undergraduate involved is very bright my mind inevitably wanders towards more interesting things. Usually the blasted little layabouts just lack motivation, and that of course provides me with a great opportunity to lay into them, letting them know just how profoundly disinterested I am in their work. This morning however I am in good form giving some sound and insightful advice to both of my students. Each leaves my room in the certain knowledge that they are going to make excellent philosophers, which expectation is of dubious veracity.

At ten fifteen I stroll over to the main teaching block and to the smaller of the two lecture halls. I really do not expect a big turnout, morning lectures are not popular and my subject is of specialist interest. I am therefore pleasurably surprised to discover some thirty people sitting in the tiered theatre waiting for me. If any lecture theatre can be described as intimate then this one can be. It is only designed to hold about eighty people; the seats are comfortable and very steeply raked. The décor is overwhelmingly blue.

As if filling church pews the majority of early arrivals have occupied the rows towards the top of the room thus, because of the small size of the theatre, later entrants have perforce to settle into seats near the front, quite close to me. I am hoping for some serious response to this lecture, it was a bit of a tour de force when Miranda and I used to do a joint presentation. I originally conceived it, some two years ago, and was inordinately proud of the way this talk bridged the gap between Philosophy and Science. With recent advances, most particularly within the latter discipline, I have made quite a few changes, especially this last year. It will not be so good without Miranda, but I feel confident that I can cope with the level of physics required. I will leave out any reference to neurobiology. That is beyond my comfort zone.

For the first half hour I slam into the relationship between moral philosophy and physics, then I move up a gear into the scientific part of the talk, getting into the history and development of quantum mechanics. I run through the original experiments made with waves and/or particles passing through pinholes. This is new stuff to most of the non-physicists in the audience so I am pleased that it seems to be going down well. I go on to talk about Max Planke, taking them up to Niels Bohr and the Copenhagen Interpretation. I explain Einstein's reluctance to adopt the latest thinking, especially his concerns about the nature of causality and, as he saw it, the problems of entanglement. This is getting a bit dry so I let Schrodinger's Cat loose upon them, which is always fun. As ever it goes down well. I relate this to Man's perception of himself within the universe and his obsession with a deistic world.

I usually allow questions during my talks and am quite pleased today to be interrupted, and slightly waylaid, by pertinent questions that take me off at a tangent. I am side-tracked into a prolonged discussion about the Arrow of Time and whether that is reality or just a human perception. It is therefore getting towards the end of my allotted ninety minutes when I introduce the Anthropic Principle. I can see that my audience is wilting slightly and wonder if I should skip on a bit, so I plough swiftly through Levels One to Four Multiverses and thence to the Ultiverse. I stop short of getting over-involved in Parallel Universes. That subject warrants a lecture all of its own.

I am not really expecting a question at this late stage, but a female student at the back is trying to attract my attention.

"So if, in an Ultiverse everything exists without need for a reason, why can we not look at the obverse where nothing exists without a reason?"

"Just so" I say. This is good, the input is first rate and neatly bridges my Phil-Phys dichotomy, either my questioner has carefully researched this exact subject line, or she is possessed of an outstanding intellect. I cannot quite see who my interlocutor is, but her voice is slightly familiar so I presume that she must be one of my final year or postgraduate students,

"You have reached the endpoint," I say in reply. "We have now created what is rather menacingly called the Nultiverse. In this scenario only those objects that could create themselves could come into existence, which, if you take it to its logical conclusion, asks the question 'could our own Universe have created itself?' "

I let them go on that note – it is as good an ending as they are going to get.

As the house lights come up to full power I glance curiously up at the departing students, wondering which of them it was who asked that last question.

And my heart skips a beat. There, seated near the back of the hall, is Starlight.

Without doubt it is she who posed that question about the Ultiverse. I would like to talk further with her about that, and indeed about a great many things that are preying upon my mind.

I start to run up the auditorium steps to make sure that I catch her before she disappears, but the Starlight is not exiting the lecture hall with the last few students. She just stands up at the top of the steps with a slight smile on her face. I now move slowly up towards her, not rushing, taking my time. She is dressed in a light, loose-fitting russet coloured blouse and dark jeans. Her close-cropped blonde hair seems a little less spiky than I remember from a couple of days ago. She seems very composed.

"Hello!" I say rather stiffly "you came?"

"Perhaps you called," she replies, and the enigmatic character of her response brings back just a trace of the irritation that I felt on that mountain.

"There are things that we need to talk about." I say

I really feel uncomfortable, both physically and mentally. Whilst Starlight is not one of my students I am conscious that as a matter of professional responsibility I must keep my distance from her at a personal level. Furthermore I am standing perched on the steeply raked floor, one step lower than she is, holding on to the back of a seat and feeling more than a little awkward.

She appears to sense my discomfort. "I think we should do so, but off Campus," she says. "How about we get some coffee in town?"

"Not now, I have to meet someone, but I'll be free this afternoon. Can you make it then?"

"Starbucks; two o'clock. See you."

And with that she turns and is gone.

I walk slowly back to my room, my mind whirling with ideas. So she does exist. I had almost convinced myself that I must have conjured this girl up out of my imagination. I have spoken about my experience with her to Simon, Val, and Helen, and they all at least considered it a probability that she was a figment of my imagination. As I am the only person to have seen Starlight their scepticism is entirely understandable. No, that is not right, someone else has seen her, who? I carry out a quick mental audit. Yes, that's it, Luigi at the Pizza Palace, he served her; Starlight must have been the person that he described, mind you he did not get a good look at her. And what about that security guard? The girl that he described could well have been Starlight.

I am not sure if I should talk to Simon and Helen about this latest appearance of Starlight when we meet to discuss the Accident. It is a sort of vindication of the weird tale that I told both of them. I decide against the idea, we will have enough to sort out without my subjecting them to this alternative world of mine, which is now clearly inhabited by a girl called Starlight.

Arriving at my room I find that Simon is already here, looking slightly flushed. He is worried and clearly bursting to talk to me. "This is very bad, Dunc, what does Helen know, what have you told her?"

"Nothing of consequence yet," I say, "sit down and I'll talk you through it."

Rather reluctantly Simon occupies one of my better chairs, I think about offering him a whisky, but I only have a bottle Glen Garry and consider that it would be wasted on him. In the state that he is in I might as well feed him with industrial grade alcohol, not that I have any.

"The trouble is, Si, that she suspects something isn't right about Miranda's death. She is pretty much on the right track in terms of medical anomalies, and she's not going to let it drop."

"How on earth did she discover anything about this?"

"Someone sent her a note saying that there was a cover-up. Then she came up here and had a word with the nursing staff at the Infirmary."

"But she doesn't know anything for certain?"

"I think it is going to be best if we make a clean breast of it, Si. She won't leave it alone, I know my sister-in-law."

"We can't do that, we agreed not to."

I explain to Simon that Helen is set upon going to the police. That she will take them the anonymous note saying that Miranda may have died from something other than cancer. If she gives them that and tells them of the suspicions that her conversation with the nursing staff have raised then the police are likely to take the matter seriously enough to start a thorough investigation.

"If I hadn't agreed that she could talk with us then that note would already be in the hands of the police and we would be in a much worse position."

"Well we must be certain that it will go no further than Helen. Seriously, Dunc, it must not get out that we rigged the manner of Miranda's death for the sake of The Project. If that ever gets out you and I are in deep shit."

He is of course right, and although he looks a bit dubious I finally convince him that unless we tell Helen the whole truth she has the energy and the contacts to turn this small suspicion of hers into something that would, in the hands of the media, expand out of control. Helen is due to join us any moment so I make three mugs of coffee using good old instant. I am not a de-caff man.

Helen arrives at just the right moment to say that she wants milk but no sugar and the three of us settle down, just a trifle nervously.

"Thanks for being so understanding, Helen," I say, trying to break the ice.

"I haven't been – yet. But I've done the decent thing and waited to hear whatever it is that the two of you have to tell me."

The ice-maiden shows no sign of thawing.

"Well, it's really Simon's story rather than mine, but let me go over the background."

I explain that about six weeks ago the research that Miranda was doing had reached an exciting, critical, and very intensive stage. Miranda needed to carry out further experiments that involved isolating and then stimulating certain discrete areas of the brain. It was becoming impossible for her to do this by herself, and I was no practical help at all.

"The basis of these experiments was related to thought processes as an energy source, and the only way forward that Miranda could see was the time-honoured scientific tradition of self-experimentation. The work was painstakingly difficult and because the project was growing in importance it was essential that the results should be kept entirely confidential."

"Is that why you were involved, Simon?" asks Helen.

I replied for him, saying that whilst Miranda used assistants during the course of her work they were mainly postgraduate students, bright but not entirely reliable. They were eager to make their way in their scientific careers and would be most unlikely to respect the confidences of their leader. Miranda and I had talked the problem through at length and decided that because Simon was helping Miranda with the theoretical side it would make sense to involve him in this practical work.

"We both considered Simon to be capable and trustworthy and should join the team," I explain, "so Miranda approached him to see if he would be willing to help."

"You appreciate that neurobiology is a bit tangential to the main thrust of my work," interjects Simon. "And practical experiments with thought energy are trampling a path into the unknown."

I acknowledge this saying that Miranda was well aware that Simon would not be able to contribute very much to the theoretical side but this was experimental research and he was a very methodical worker well able to properly document the resulting data.

"She was entirely happy to have him working with her to assist with the practical stuff that she was doing. Above all she trusted him with the very sensitive findings that were just beginning to emerge from the project."

Simon takes up the story. "For the first time, after a very long absence, I was back to being a proper Researcher, and working with physical things. It was good because I wasn't really up to speed with what Miranda, was doing and I was able gain a much clearer idea of the direction that The Project was taking. That in turn allowed me to contribute to the best of my ability some of my own ideas. I was a little uneasy about assisting with the practical side, but I could understand why I was needed."

"But what was this project all about?" asks Helen.

I look over at Simon. "I cannot explain all of it," I say, "because it really is very sensitive indeed. Basically we are exploring the concept of the interaction of thought-energy between our own world and one, possibly two, parallel worlds."

"Are we talking about parallel universes, I have read a bit about that in press articles?"

"No this is different, we are talking about worlds within our universe," says Simon.

"What does this interaction involve?"

"Look, Helen," I interject, "we're getting a bit too close to the sensitive part of the programme, but in essence we're exploring a connection between the quantity of dark matter in our universe and the existence of parallel worlds. This quantification involves using anti-matter as a sort of marker. We're then looking to access these worlds by the transference of thought-energy."

"Wow," says Helen, "If I understood what the hell you are talking about I'd be working at this University as well! What's all this got to do with Miranda's death?"

Simon takes up the story again. "We worked together on the experimental side for some two weeks. This could not be a full-time project for me, I couldn't just drop the bulk of my other work, but it did begin to take up more and more of my time so that Miranda and I were working late into the evenings, and twice we went right through until the next morning."

I explain how tired Miranda was and how I became more and more worried that both she and Simon were suffering mentally and physically from sleep deprivation. I acknowledge that, in retrospect, I should have done something about this, but explain that my work was also taking up a lot of time, and the Project was becoming so exciting that the last thing that Miranda wanted was to slow it down.

Simon continues, "Now we come to the difficult bit. As Duncan says, Miranda and I were working a string of late nights. We were in close contact with CERN regarding the results they were getting from the Large Hadron Collider and the extraordinary thing was that our hypotheses in relation to anti-matter were being confirmed by CERN on an almost daily basis as they got the LHC up to speed. Obviously we were not creating anti-matter particles as they were doing, but we were beginning to see how it was possible to use anti-matter to quantify dark matter."

"Again you are getting too technical for me," says Helen.

"OK" Simon says. "The point is that what we were doing demanded the utmost concentration, and Miranda and I were really getting to the end of our respective tethers. At least I was able to grab the occasional catnap, but Miranda did not seem to sleep at all. On occasion she just went into a sort of trance, not really registering any outside stimulus, but still looking as if she was fully awake."

"She would do so at home as well," I add, "not that she managed to get home that often."

"Did something happen to her?" asks Helen.

"Well that's just it," replies Simon, "we'd worked through the previous night and when I joined her in the lab that afternoon she looked tired, although she told me that she had managed to get home and grab a couple of hours sleep. We were working on the biological source of thought-energy and this latest of a series of experiments involved Miranda using a brain scanner coupled with minute amounts of radiation to detect brain activity of a specific kind. She was setting every thing up and I was processing some figures that we'd obtained the previous day.

I heard Miranda say that everything was ready to go. I'd just gone into the cuddy to make us both a coffee when there was a sudden commotion. She let out a startled "Oh!" and slumped down.

I rushed over to find her sitting on the floor, her mouth open and hands shaking. Clearly something awful had happened."

"What did you do?"

"I laid her flat on the floor. There was some activity on the monitor so the next thing I did was to make the whole area safe, that must have taken me at least a couple of minutes, but I couldn't do anything to help poor Miranda until we were fully secured.

When I did get to her she was pretty incoherent and lapsing in and out of consciousness. She was mumbling about brain energy fusion and saying it had proved itself. Her head was very hot and she was complaining that she was thirsty so I gave her water to drink and poured more water over her. I called the medical unit and said we needed an ambulance, then I got in touch with Dunc."

I tell Helen that I was just about to leave the faculty when Simon got me on my mobile.

"I rushed down to the Lab and realized the gravity of the situation. Miranda had been seriously, if not mortally, injured and the project was about to be totally compromised. By that stage Miranda had regained consciousness and was almost entirely lucid. It was then that she hatched this plan. She was determined that the three of us were to tell everyone that she was terminally ill from cancer rather than that she had an accident."

"But why", asks Helen.

"So that the work could be concluded by Simon and myself," I say, "that's what Miranda wanted above everything else. She knew that she was in a very bad way, and certain to die. She made Simon and me agree that we would do everything we could to protect The Project and the University."

I tell Helen how when the ambulance people arrived Simon explained that Miranda had collapsed. He had gone on to reveal that she had been working despite knowing that she was suffering from terminal cancer. This seemed to satisfy the immediate concerns of the medics. Miranda was still at least partly conscious at that stage and never once suggested that an accident had occurred. They took her to Lancaster Infirmary.

"But once she was there then surely the doctors would have realized that she didn't have cancer but had been injured as a result of the accident?" says Helen.

"We started sorting that out straight away," says Simon. "I went to see the pro vice chancellor, who is a bit of a mate of mine. I told him that there'd been this accident, that it had been fully contained and that it couldn't happen again. He was aware of the nature of our work so it was quite easy to explain to him how far advanced we were and how the reputation of University would be enhanced as a result of publication of our academic Paper. He could well see that conversely the University would suffer if the press got wind of the, probably fatal, accident to Miranda. In the end it was a no-brainer. He agreed to help and rang the chief medic at the Infirmary."

"In the meantime," I say, "I followed the ambulance to the Hospital and, as her husband, managed to stay with Miranda through her initial assessment process. I was able to ensure that our cover story of a brain tumour was well to the fore. Things did not move fast and it must have been an hour or so before the consultant joined us."

I explain that Mr Freemantle must have been approaching sixty years of age. "A pleasant man with snow-white hair he has a rather deeply lined face. You know I remember that his white coat was several sizes too large for his small frame. Funny the little things you remember in a time of crisis."

"I never got to meet him when I was at the hospital," says Helen.

I explain that Freemantle had agreed against his own better judgement, as senior consulting oncologist, to take on this case as if it were a suspected malignant brain stem tumour in the inoperable phase. He carefully went through how the hospital could be duped into carrying out this deception thereby avoiding the need to implicate any other staff.

"Freemantle suggested that Miranda should be seen to take part in a new clinical trial. That would allow for some 'extra' treatments and procedures to be performed without arousing suspicion, and it would also be a very good way of ensuring that Miranda was kept in the care of the hospital rather than being removed to a hospice."

"I'm beginning to get the picture," says Helen.

"So," I say. "That's how we played it. It was exactly what Miranda asked us to do and, as you can understand, we really did not want anyone else to know what was going on. There was a difficult moment when Miranda's hair started to fall out. Freemantle put her on Chemo that day, but I'm not surprised that the more experienced nursing staff became a little uneasy."

Helen looks from Simon to myself.

"Duncan, I do think you might have said a little more to me, don't you?"

"I thought you wouldn't suspect. Or if you did you would not care much."

"She was my sister, for Christ's sake, of course I was going to care."

"What I don't understand," says Simon, "is who wrote that note to you. It couldn't have been the nursing staff or Nurse Elizabeth would surely have dropped you a hint."

"Bit of a mystery, I'm afraid, but I don't think it much matters," says Helen. "Anyway I am grateful to you Simon for telling me exactly what happened. You can be sure that I will not be blabbing off about it to anyone."

It's clearly a dismissal. Simon gets up to go, shakes Helen by the hand again, and asks me to give him a shout sometime soon. I know that he wants to talk to me about the Virtual Ventures offer but doesn't want to say anything about it with Helen in the room.

Once the door has shut behind Simon, I turn to Helen. "You were a bit brutal giving him the heave-ho like that."

"Sorry, Dunc, it's just that I had an idea that I wanted to share with you, but not with Simon."

"Go on."

"It's about the letter. You know you told me about that psychologist woman, the one that was friendly with Miranda?

"Yes, that's right Valerie Staples."

"Do you think you could introduce us? I just need half an hour with her."

Five minutes later Helen and Val are in deep conversation in the latter's room, from which I have tactfully withdrawn.

Sixteen

It would have been hard, Helen thought, to find two professional women, approaching middle age, with such different working lives. She, Helen, had been driven from an early age by the necessity to compete, to do better, to outshine everyone else. She had therefore from the very first flung herself into a largely male-dominated business environment and taken it by storm. Her compulsion to succeed had become an obsession to make money, lots of money. Money had become almost the sole measure of her success and this she advertised by her lifestyle. Not only did she have a house in one of the most sort-after parts of London she also wore top label designer clothes and enjoyed having her hair styled by one of the more outrageous of young male stylists at a very up-market establishment. She made money and she spent it. She had succeeded.

Sitting next to her, by contrast, was a naturally graceful woman, possibly slightly older than her who, despite her almost total lack of make up and a hairstyle that might have been the result of an unfortunate entanglement with a thick bramble hedge, still looked a good five years younger than she did. Helen was intrigued by Val's weird dress sense, or lack of it. She was wearing the sort of things that Helen's mother might have been proud of being seen in at Woodstock. Helen was certain that whatever Val's goal was in life it was not money. Yet this interesting and slightly off-beam woman was clearly not the sort of person who drifted through life, she seemed to have bags of motivation and her energy was well focussed.

Duncan had guided Helen to Val's room. When they got there Val had asked him if he was still on for tomorrow.

"Oh yes, Cartmel," said Duncan. "I'll pick you up at ten o'clock at your spot if that's OK?"

They had agreed a few days ago that they would both like to visit Cartmel Priory, where Miranda's funeral service had been held. Helen wondered whether she should stay on for another day. She needed to go and see Deanstones so had every good reason to join them in visiting Cartmel. She made a mental note to talk to Duncan about it later.

Helen was delighted to find that Val was so friendly and helpful and once Duncan had seen that they were going to get along fine together was pleased that he had cleared off as fast as he decently could. Now she was happily seated on a long sofa, with Val next to her, chatting about the very different lives that they led.

"Do you practice psychology as well as teach it?" asked Helen.

"Well I teach clinical psychology here at the University, but I also have my own private practice working as a consulting psychotherapist."

"Is that in Lancaster?"

'No, I work from home. Just at the moment I'm renting a house near Milnthorpe, and I see clients there, but it is not really that easy. I need a place of my own where I can set up with a proper consulting room, Using the dining room is far from satisfactory."

"It must be very different, living up here in the North," said Helen, "my life in London is just one long rush; mind you I thrive on that."

"You are a very different person from your sister." It was a statement rather than a question.

"Oh I hope not. Miranda meant so much to me, especially when we were younger. Try as I might I could never live up to her standards." She paused for a moment. "I suppose that's why I am so competitive now?"

"As is so often the case with younger siblings."

"Ah, the professional judgement.

"No, Helen, I don't judge people, I observe and, if it's helpful, comment."

Helen turned back to Val. "I'm not sure if Duncan has explained to you that I'm up here to find out a little more about Miranda's death?"

"No, he didn't, but I surmised that."

Helen explained what she had been doing. How she had received the anonymous note and how that had set her off in the direction of Lancaster. She described her visit to the hospital and her meeting with Nurse Elizabeth. She told Val how she had become almost certain that all was not right with Miranda's treatment. She explained how she had confronted Duncan with this as being a very real possibility.

"I'm glad you came." said Val.

"Why is that?

"I was very fond of your sister."

"Had you known each other for long?"

"One year, eighteen weeks and six days," replied Val.

Helen looked at her and saw with a sudden clarity a woman who was suppressing a great grief.

"You knew her that well?"

"I knew her that well," said Val, looking straight at her.

It all made sense. She knew why Miranda and Duncan's marriage had never been entirely fulfilling. She understood why, even after their wedding, their deep friendship had never developed into love.

She realized with a sudden certainty that she knew more about Miranda now than she had ever known, and it all seemed just fine. It was a thing of contentment and peace and beauty.

"Of course," said Helen." I should have known."

"It was something that lay very deep within Miranda," said Val. "She didn't know about it, or rather she would not allow herself to acknowledge it, until this last year or so. Even when she did accept herself as she was she would not go public with the revelation. She didn't want to hurt Duncan. Love was not the most important thing in her life, without any doubt that was her work, but if circumstances had been different . . ." her voice trailed off.

"Val, you must have been devastated when she died?"

"Yes."

"And you didn't tell Duncan about the two of you?" said Helen.

"What was the point? Miranda was gone, we were all so sad about it. Why should I stir up things that didn't need to be brought into the open and might only serve to confuse and upset him?"

"But you did write that note to me."

"I had to. I was at my wits' end, and I was so pleased when I learned that you had bothered to come. The thing is that there was a bit of talk, not here on campus, but amongst my medical colleagues in the area. We have all known Jimmy Freemantle for years, and a sounder man you couldn't wish for, but he never in all his professional life, got involved in drugs trials on terminal patients. He had a deep suspicion, bordering on loathing, for the big drugs companies, and he just wouldn't let them near his patients, especially if they were nearing death.'

"So it was thought a bit odd when he agreed that Miranda should become a 'guinea-pig'?"

"It wasn't just odd, it was unbelievable. And not just that, but no one had ever heard about this clinical trial and there was no input from whatever company was supposed to be sponsoring it."

"So why did you involve me?"

"Well I needed someone who wasn't connected with either the hospital or the University. You won't remember but we did have just the briefest of words at Miranda's funeral, and you gave me your business card in case I wanted to use your Companies Hosting service at any time."

"But your letter was delivered to my home address."

"I just rang your people and said that I was a friend of your late sister. I said that I wanted to write a note of condolence. They were kind enough to give me your home address."

"Hmm," said Helen, making a mental note to sort that out when she returned to London. That sort of kindness, she thought, had no place in her well-run business.

Val got up and to make them both a cup of tea. Helen looked closely at her and tried to imagine her together with Miranda, physically with Miranda. It was not a difficult picture to bring to mind and not one that was in any way offensive to her. She felt an overwhelming sense of joy that Miranda had found a measure of emotional and physical fulfilment with this graceful and intelligent woman.

Val had made tea from a caddy using a proper teapot and poured it through a strainer held over the cups. Helen was not surprised to see that she was using a bone china tea set.

As Val passed her the tea Helen said, "So you didn't know then about the Miranda's accident?"

"Accident?"

So they hadn't told her. A momentary pang of guilt passed swiftly across Helen's train of thought. Duncan and Simon had sworn her to silence and here she was chatting about their secret to the very first person she had met since learning of it. That she was about to betray this confidence did not cause her a great deal of anxiety.

Taking great care as to its accuracy, she related the conversation that she had just had with Duncan and Simon. She told Val about the need Miranda had for help in the Lab, about the workload that she, and to a lesser extent Simon, had suffered, about the tiredness and about the accident itself. She explained how the University and the Hospital conspired to cover things up and how only a very few people were privy to this whole deception.

Val was still standing, holding her own cup and saucer. She was very still.

Helen, sitting, reached for Val's hand and held it. 'I'm so very sorry," she said. "I thought you knew."

Almost reluctantly Val slowly subsided onto the sofa. She said, very quietly, "There was no way that she could tell me." There was no hint reproach in her voice, just a quiet statement.

"I think," said Helen, "that she was incredibly brave. From that first moment when she knew that she was going to die all she wanted to do was ensure that the research Project was not compromised by the accident. Later she was unconscious most of the time."

"Yes, I can see that. It was just like her; she wouldn't care for herself. She wasn't like that."

Helen started talking, going back over those childhood days that she had shared with that wonderful big sister of hers. She talked to Val about the Miranda that she had grown up with. She tried to tell her of all the things that made Miranda the person she had been.

She recalled the time when she had been smoking behind the science block at school and Miranda had found her there and had pleaded with her to stop. How the Games Mistress had happened on them and how Miranda had taken the ciggy from her and, the next morning, told their housemistress that it was she that had been smoking, and Helen that had been attempting to stop her.

She remembered the day that their parents took them to that small fishing port on the island in Scotland. How they had gone down to the harbour together and how she had tried to stop Helen from pulling the boats in towards the beach on their adjustable moorings. She described how, when they were spotted, it was Miranda who owned up to doing the deed and who made it clear that Helen had nothing to do with it.

She related the story of their mother finding her bra behind the sofa cushions the morning after a bit of a wild party, and how Miranda had said that it belonged to her, not Helen.

All this she told to Val, and Val listened quietly.

"She was my idol," said Helen, "she was the best big sister in the world. She cared for me, she protected me, she encouraged me, and she loved me. For the first time since Miranda's death Helen felt tears welling up in her eyes. She fumbled for a tissue and dabbed her eyes. "I'm so sorry Val," said Helen, "it just all came out."

"No, don't be sorry. These are the things that matter in our lives. I'm so glad that Miranda meant this much to you. I know it hurts, but how very much worse it would be if her life had meant nothing to you."

"I never make a fuss. I am just not like that." Helen, still the sophisticate, had managed to not quite shed a tear. She raised herself to her feet just a trifle unsteadily. "Val, I am so grateful to you for listening, and it's really you who must be grieving more than I am."

"We both need to grieve."

Val seemed to be lost in thought. She was clearly moved by Helen's recollections, but she was also interested in them as well. "So she always took the blame, whatever the circumstances?"

"Oh yes, she was totally selfless, as well as showing no fear for the consequences."

"That's very interesting," said Val, "very interesting indeed. I knew she would always think of others before herself, but I'd no idea that this behaviour was so deeply rooted in her childhood."

"You are looking at it from a professional point of view?"

"I suppose I am, at least in part, but then she was just such a marvellous person, dedicated to her work and to others."

"You have summed her up to perfection," said Helen.

With some reluctance Helen said, "I think I have done all I came to do. There is nothing more for me. I'm off back to London. My partner, well fiancée really, warned me that I might stir things up if I tried to discover the truth, and I see now what he meant. He was right."

Val was deep in thought.

"What are you thinking about?" asked Helen.

"I am thinking," said Val," that Simon has got more than a few questions to answer."

"You don't believe him?"

"Do you?"

Helen thought again about the conversation she had just had with Duncan and Simon. Yes, Simon's explanation had seemed a bit glib. She felt anger rising up within her. "I don't think I do."

"Helen, listen to me. Miranda let him get away with whatever he did to her by letting the blame for the accident fall upon her; behaving as she always had. She did so because for her it was the right thing. It still is the right thing. Don't let the situation get the better of you."

Helen looked into Val's eyes. There was real concern there. Concern for her. It had been a long time since anyone had really cared.

The two very different women hugged each other warmly, then kissed cheeks for perhaps a fraction of a second longer than necessity demanded.

Helen departed in search of Duncan.

Seventeen

It is just after two o'clock. Starlight and I are sitting in Starbucks each of us cradling a latte and warming chilled hands. There is an air of relaxed intimacy that is hardly warranted by our encounters to date. I look carefully at the girl, trying to take her in quietly and calmly. Her skin is pale with just a few freckles on her nose. She has well formed eyebrows that are just a shade darker than her hair. Her lips are fairly full and her mouth somewhat large. If she is wearing make-up at all it is applied with considerable restraint. She is wearing rings on her left hand, on the little finger and the index finger, this former bearing a small blue stone that even with my limited experience of jewellery I know to be outstanding. She is not beautiful in any conventional sense; although she was certainly quite pretty. She exudes an inner vitality that sparkles from her deep blue eyes and turns heads towards her.

It would be interesting to know what Starlight makes of me. Tall, certainly, thin, brown hair worn quite long, rather sharp features but a broad mouth with 'smile' lines that are a tell-tale of happier times. I am hardly a snappy dresser tending towards a 'retro 60s' look; with black roll neck sweaters worn under rather well-used jackets. I enjoy cultivating a slightly off-beat image although image is all that it is. Occasionally, as is the case today I go for a slight variation in style, wearing a black open-necked shirt with a neckerchief, not a purpose made thing but rather a woman's headscarf wrapped around my neck and tied with a loose knot so that the ends dangle free. My jacket is comfortable, with patches at the elbows.

She would be hard put to know much about me from that lot. She must have done some homework on me, not difficult really, just a matter of looking up my name on the University Staff List – or perhaps Googling to bring up a potted biography, which would include my academic Papers and other achievements over the past fifteen years.

Both she and I are staring through the windows. Outside in the December afternoon people are hurrying to complete their Christmas purchases. Harassed figures dip into shops with increasing desperation attempting to find something – anything - that could be given with impunity to expectant loved ones, and not so loved ones. Food shops are doing brisk trade selling at vast profit the excessive trappings and over-rich trimmings of festive fare that will lead, inevitably, to the honking of guts in the wee small hours. All witness to one of the strangest rituals that western civilization has devised. A mawkish quasi-religious sentimentality combined with gluttony of both stomach and wallet.

I am hardly registering this passing and re-passing, this forlorn quest for material satiation, exemplified by large carrier bags containing rich food and poor presents. Instead I consider the divergence between the real, grounded, practical world that I live in for all physical things, and the rarefied intellectual one that I inhabit only in my, humanly limited, imagining.

"This is what I call my Real Life", I blurt out, speaking my train of thought. I feel a twinge of embarrassment. "What I mean is that I spend much of my time in abstraction, looking at the things that make us tick, and the morality of that. There is a huge jump between such musings and ordinary living. I have to make a considerable mental effort to bring myself back to the here and now!"

"You have to live," says Starlight "but you need to live in the mind as well as the body."

Up to this point I am not sure if I had noticed the timbre of her voice. She speaks with in a deep but not husky register and her accent is what is called 'Received Pronunciation' and some might describe as 'posh'. I am also aware that she said 'you' and I am not sure if that meant me, or people in general. It is clear however that she is not really including herself in the observation.

There is another long pause. Silence seems to be our thing.

I try again to start a conversation with this girl who calls herself Starlight. "We physically inhabit only this world, this reality. We can also use our thoughts to project real-world things. So, I can think 'This is a great cup of coffee'. But we can also use our minds, our thoughts, to take us well beyond our physical limitations. I can, in my mind only, toy with the concept of space-time warping around mass thereby giving rise to the phenomenon that we perceive as gravitational attraction."

"I think that you are trying to tell me something more subtle than that."

"True. It is not the concepts themselves that I'm stumbling over, as a philosopher I am well used to trying to imagine things that our minds just do not have the capability of imagining, such as our living in multi-dimensional space-time. No, what I am trying to get to grips with is the power, the energy, of thought itself."

"This of course was the nature of the research Project that you and your wife were involved with."

"That was part of it and is the direction we have been exploring for some time. Mind you I'm not sure how you know that. The nub of this latest twist to the project is that scientists have, for a century now, accepted that there is mutual changeability between Mass and Energy. So far energy has been perceived as being of a physical nature, such things as motion, sound, heat and other sources like potential kinetic. Now where Miranda and I were going out on a limb was to suggest that our thoughts could also be considered as a type of energy. We were postulating that if that were provable then we could explore the use of such energy to access the parallel world or worlds that we think are most likely to account for the majority of dark matter"

Just for a moment I get the distinct impression that Starlight is really quite upset by what I am saying, but the shadow passes. "You may be heading into trouble, Duncan, do you think that you can prove this?"

"We can imagine, we can hypothesise, and I think we can do the maths. Proof requires experimentation and that is both dangerous and uncertain." I begin to worry that I am going into too much detail about The Project to this girl, but despite my earlier experiences with her I am of the firm belief that she is trustworthy. She is also intelligent and interested. I try to convince myself that the undeniable truth of her also being extremely desirable is supremely irrelevant.

"Sometimes it is easier to take a sideways look at things," says the girl who calls herself Starlight.

"That makes sense, but what are you suggesting?"

"I know that you have a good understanding of science, which is unusual for a philosopher, but you, as a philosopher, will be aware that the human brain demands other forms of stimulation besides the scientific and logical."

"To be truly human," I say.

"In your case I think you also enjoy art?" she says.

"Yes, with reservations. But I'm not sure how you know that?"

"And you prefer modern art, I think?" says Starlight, ignoring my question"

"In the main, yes. I can appreciate most periods but if pressed I would say that, like many people of my generation, I really enjoy the post-impressionists, and some of the inter-wars' movements."

"Know anything about Dada?" she asks.

"Well not much, but I happened to be in New York a few years ago and a colleague of mine took me to the Dada exhibition that was at the National Gallery of Art, I think it went on to MoMA later, but am not sure."

"Did it do anything for you?"

"'I'm not sure that I liked it very much, I certainly felt uncomfortable with it. The images were so 'in your face' as were the sounds, and as for the poetry - well. I really enjoy many of the modern poets but this was really beyond me - having three poets all reading their different works in the same place at the same time."

"That's Dada for you."

"Well, there are limits."

"Not in Dada. But the movement did lead in a lot of interesting directions."

"What, Dadaism? Yes, I think it did."

I am fairly easy on most of the 'modern art' scene, although lack an in-depth knowledge of some aspects of its history. I resolve not to bluff it out "What have you in mind?"

"Well," says the girl who asked me to call her Starlight," although, as you know, Dada started as a protest about the horrors of the First World War it developed into a fully fledged anti-art movement, mocking and decrying the Establishment and all it stood for."

"Sounds like to me like a recipe for anarchy."

"Well you are dead right, in that its resurgence many years later in post Berlin Wall Germany was as an anarchistic movement. But that's not what I was talking about, it was its influence on some of the later 'isms, such as Social Realism, and in particular Surrealism."

"I'm not too sure about Surrealism," I tell her," It appeals, but the message that it attempts to portray often seems too obvious, too contrived, too trite. I think that's why I don't really rate Salvador Dali."

"True, in many instances. I fear that is particularly so of much of The Great Wanker's work. But there were others, painters, poets and writers who seized the moment and ran with this new idea. It had the tremendous attraction of liberating people from the stylised and the conventional."

I am trying to figure out what is going on here. I am sitting in a coffee house discussing modern art with this enigmatic woman who has either taken me on an incredible dance over the Langdale fells or has drugged me in my own home. What is she doing? What does she want of me? All I can do is stay in her company and see where this conversation is leading. Already it has moved well away from where we started, with the science of the thinking process. "OK, suggest an artwork."

Starlight hesitates for a moment." Magritte," she says, "you'll know some of his work?"

"Oh yes," I say, thinking quickly, "wasn't there something by him that showed a train coming out of a fireplace, with a mirror above depicting the reflections all wrong?"

"You've got him! Yes, 'La Durée Poignardée'."

"And something about pipes?"

"Again you are right, but I was thinking of a different work by him. Do you know 'La Magie Noir'?"

I am fairly certain I have not seen that, I shake my head

"A naked woman," she says," standing against a classical column. The top half of her body, nearly to her waist, and including her upper arms, is painted as if she were made of marble, as if sculpted. The rest of her is rendered as flesh and blood, warmly painted."

"I think I've seen something rather similar to that, half woman half fish. Presumably that was Magritte as well?"

"That's right," she says," on a beach, but to my mind that just doesn't work anything like as well as La Magie Noir. It comes across to me in a similar way as your comments about Dali, it is an image of the absurd, and as such does not particularly shock, nor does it make you want to delve deeper into the anomaly that it presents you with."

"Rather like that guy, what was his name, you know, the photographer chap who came second for the Taylor Wessing prize in 2010."

"Lamprou", says Starlight, "Panayiotis Lamprou with 'My British Wife'."

"That's it," I reply, rather surprised by the depth of knowledge that Starlight possesses, "it really shocks everyone who sees it, not because it's pornographic, although to my mind it certainly borders on that, but because an element of what might be pornographic is juxtaposed with what is an almost totally banal holiday snapshot. And yet it is not even that, she has the most enigmatic expression on her face that makes the whole composition so difficult to read."

Starlight says, 'that's exactly what Magritte was doing, although in a rather less crude manner. He was contrasting the same body as seen from two totally different aspects. Possibly by two different people, or the same person looking at it in two different ways. And that of course is what happens to all of us, your reality and my reality, your illusion and my illusion, perhaps even your reality and my illusion."

"Is that what you are, an illusion? A form of energy generated by my thought process?"

"Well you are just beginning to ask sensible questions," says Starlight. "But don't expect instant answers. The knights of old would search for the Holy Grail, but in many ways it was the quest itself that brought them fulfilment, not the finding of the answer. Cavafy had it thus in his Ithaka. In some old books it was stated that knowledge of the Grail itself would lead to death."

"Because it was too much for human understanding?"

"Yes, but be clear it was not the Grail that was the threat, it was knowledge of the Grail."

"I am half-following you."

"What I'm saying is that there are certain things in this existence that you can see, conjure up, imagine, play with, if you like. But if you try to fully understand them, or ground them in any form of reality then you could be putting yourself into mortal danger."

"I think you are trying to tell me something that I'm not quite getting. Are we talking about my work? Or possibly you?"

Starlight looks at me in what I could only describe as a fond way. "We need to keep you out of this danger."

"Then is that what are you doing here?" I ask.

"Possibly."

"It's obviously reasonable for me to, on one plane at least, question your reality. And yet you are here, talking, drinking coffee and just being human. I really do have to try to make some sense out of it you know."

I tell Starlight that I went to see Toni at the Pizza Palace and that from his description of her it was clear that she was the person who had ordered the pizza that they had shared the night before last. I tell Starlight that I reckon there is a strong possibility that she drugged me and suggested most of the Langdale experience to me whilst 'under the influence', and that metaphorically, in my drugged state, she finally abandoned me to fall from a crag to my doom.

Starlight does not deny or confirm anything, she neither says I am correct nor takes me to task for creating a fairy tale. She persists with her enigmatic responses, but I am getting used to this treatment by now and am determined not to let it annoy me.

"I do need you to explain at least some of this to me." I say.

But she is off on a different tack. "I think you had a proposition from someone yesterday."

This flusters me; I am not sure what to say. "Really?"

"Yes," says the girl who had asked me to call her Starlight "In your laboratory"

"Oh, that." I acknowledge, deciding I should be very cautious about what I say. "Simon was telling me about a pretty outlandish offer from some people who wanted to become involved with the work that Miranda was doing."

"And you told him that you wanted to give it some thought?"

"It seemed the best thing to say at the time"

"Have you thought about it?"

How the hell does she know about this strange offer, and what business of hers is it anyway. It is all very well, but this is my career and I am not going to have it discussed and probably trampled over by some slightly fey stranger. "Yes, I have. But it's none of your bloody business."

As soon as I say this I realize that I have hurt her. She looks taken aback by my rudeness and turns away to stare again at the Christmas shoppers.

"Damn. Sorry, I really didn't mean it like that," I stammer.

"I'm trying to help you," she says, and I can just make out a tear in her eye.

"I'm so sorry. I didn't mean to be that rude and I appreciate what you are doing. I must be a bit touchy about this research project, and really don't know what to do about the offer. I've never been approached with anything like this before. I've no idea if it is genuine, but from what Simon told me I'd be incredibly well paid for letting them have control of The Project."

"If you buy me another coffee and promise not to shout at me again I'll talk with you about it."

I go to the counter and order the coffees. I need to know more about the organisation that is putting up the money to buy into The Project, but how does Starlight know about them, and how did she know that Simon had put that offer to me yesterday? I walk back to the table slowly. The girl is sitting in a composed manner. It is my experience that anyone sitting on his or her own in a café or restaurant likes to indulge in some sort of displacement activity to avoid feeling embarrassed. Some people read, or take an exaggerated interest in pictures on walls, or play with their smart-phones, or rummage in their bags or wallets. Starlight does none of these things. She just sits, quietly, waiting for my return. There is nothing anxious or nervous about her.

"I rather suspect that you know something about these people whom Simon wants me to turn over The Project to," I say.

"In a manner of speaking I do. I know their type."

"Do you know anything much about them, what they are working towards? Simon said something about social responsibility."

"Duncan, you need to be aware that the work that Miranda was carrying out, and which is now your sole responsibility, is of the very greatest interest to some organisations. I know that you see it as a fascinating piece of academic research, but there are others, very powerful government organisations, who can see that it could either strip away their existing power, or add to it. You really have no idea of the forces that you might unleash."

"Hey, steady on. I know the work is a bit special and as a piece of academic research it is really exciting. But I think you are letting it go to your head."

"You must believe me." She is very calm, very firm.

"Well what about these people then. Can you give me any good reason why I shouldn't throw in my lot with them, gain every facility that I could possibly need, and in the process do pretty well for myself."

"Your first duty is to respect Miranda's wishes, she wanted you to finish this work here at Lancaster. From a perspective of morals, both personal and universal, I must warn you that you would be supping with the Devil if you were to take Simon's offer."

"Simon may have been taken in by a rather dubious outfit," I say, "but I'm hardly about to sell my immortal soul. If I tell them to stuff their offer they may well get quite a bit of what they need from Simon and go ahead without me."

"Simon?" says Starlight, "I didn't realize that he was capable of handling The Project. Have they made him an offer to work for them?"

"I have absolutely no idea. He never mentioned it, but clearly there must be something in it for him or he wouldn't be so keen that I follow his advice."

"Do you think he would be prepared to work for them?"

"I am almost certain he would agree to it, if he's not already done so."

"Can he complete The Project on his own?"

"Most probably not. He is not an original thinker and could never have done the initial stuff that Miranda did, but that is behind us now. He has full access to her notes and has done quite a bit of the maths. So he's a good long way along the road. Understanding another's work is one thing, interpreting it and taking it forward is altogether different."

"Does he have access to your thinking?

"Well he does really, not in detail you understand, but in principle."

Starlight is looking more and more concerned. "So he could pull the whole thing together?"

"No, not yet. There's still quite a bit of stuff that needs to be done before I can be sure that we have things sorted out."

"Good," says Starlight. For the first time since I met her she looks a little rattled. "Look I've got heaps to do, it was lovely seeing you and thanks for the coffee, but I must go."

"Will I see you again?"

'Oh, yes," says the girl, "you can be quite sure of theat."

"Where are you going?"

"You can come with me for just a few steps of the way."

As we emerge into the afternoon crowds Starlight pulls the hood of her jacket over her head. It has started, very gently, to snow again and whilst it is not yet a problem it does seem to have some serious intent to become one before long. I parked the car near the Castle so am quite relieved when we turn left towards the one-way thoroughfare of King Street.

Starlight put her hand on my arm "You carry on and get your car out of here before the snow gets too thick," she says. "I must leave you now." And with that she turns and disappears into the crowd.

"Hey!" I exclaim, but she is gone. I look for her expecting to see her bobbing through the throng of people, but there is no sign of her.

I make my way to the Alfa and head back to the campus.

Eighteen

A few minutes later and Helen is sitting comfortably in my den. The room exudes an air of affable and casual masculinity. Old leather chairs fraying at the edges, books teetering like miniature tower blocks, papers stuffed into bookshelves. I love the feel of this room, it is a place to think, where it is possible for me to imagine a world so different from the day-to-day one that we all have to cope in order to live.

Helen had popped her head around the door, and asked if she could have a word.

"But of course," I had replied and cleared away some periodicals from one of the easy chairs, "how did it go with Val."

"She's so helpful, so insightful. And she knew Miranda very well."

"She was more Miranda's friend than mine really."

"Yes, so I understand." Very gently Helen explains what she has learned of Val's relationship with Miranda. This comes as a big shock to me. I really had no idea that Val was Miranda's lover. I think back about the sort of life that Miranda and I lived together and it all begins to make so much more sense.

"I knew she had a lover," I say, "but she never said who it was and, naturally I suppose, I assumed that it was a man."

"Does it worry you that it was not?"

"No. Or rather, Yes! I don't have a problem with her having a lesbian relationship; I do just wish that she had told me. It explains everything. I'm sure I could have made her life easier if I'd known."

"I wonder if she kept quiet because Val is someone that you both knew?"

"You mean she didn't want me to go off and shout at Val!"

"No, not exactly. I just wonder if she wanted to keep the marriage going, either for your sake, or possibly for the sake of both of you. If you'd known it to be Val then you might have encouraged her to leave you?"

"I suppose that's possible."

Helen then goes on to tell me that she discussed Miranda's accident with Val. "She took it pretty well, although she seemed to think Simon knew more than he was telling anybody."

"Well I did wonder about that," I say, "You see I just can't believe that Miranda would make such a fundamental error. We only have Simon's word that he was not directly involved. He could have, indeed should have, been working with Miranda at the time of the accident."

"He seems very ambitious. I wonder if he's ruthless as well."

I have known Simon for some years now, not well, just someone I met at various conferences. Then, about a couple of years ago, he was appointed to the faculty and we sort of drifted into a convenient, if not very close, friendship. I find him an amiable sort of fellow to have a pint with at the end of a difficult day, and useful as a sounding board.

"I'm not sure. I haven't known him that long. It was rumoured that he was connected with something funny when he was working on a Government thing a few years back, I can't remember much about it now, but I seem to recall it caused a bit of a stir at the time, but I think that was more because of the way it was hushed up."

"I think we're within the realms of his having deliberately killed Miranda," says Helen, "and I know that Val considers that to be a possibility."

"That's pretty horrible."

"Would he have any reason to do such a thing?"

I start to wonder about Simon's insistence, following Miranda's death, that he should take over the work that would lead to the academic Paper. I remember Miranda saying, after Simon had been working for her for a month or so, that whilst he was useful in tying the maths together, she did not rate him at all as a scientist, at least not in the field that they were working in. Then of course there is Simon's almost obsessive interest in the Nobel Prize.

"I really don't know. He's ambitious, and certainly has a ruthless streak, but what makes Val think that Miranda's death was anything more than an accident?"

"Well it's more to do with Miranda's actions than with Simon's. I told Val a lot about my sister and how she was always ready to take the blame for me when we were children. It would, according to Val, be well within Miranda's personal profile to take the blame for this accident, saying that it was all her fault, partly to protect Simon, but probably more importantly in her eyes, to make sure that The Project wasn't compromised. Even if she had not been protecting your research I think she would have taken the blame for what she might well have thought was a simple mistake."

"But you think it might have been deliberate?"

"Yes, I rather think that I do."

"I wonder if Miranda thought that? The thing is that there is absolutely no proof, it is all suspicion based on both Miranda's and Simon's personality traits. Whatever you and Val may think, and I'm not disagreeing with you, I really need Simon just now to get this research tied up. I know it's selfish, but at the end of the day it is what Miranda wanted. She kept quiet about Simon for the sake of the Project. I just cannot imagine why he let her take the rap."

"I am afraid I can," says Helen. "Miranda had that sort of effect on people. She took the blame for me more times than I can remember. The strange thing is that every time she did it she totally convinced me to let her do so."

"I really don't see how we can do anything other than just keep it to ourselves right now," I say.

It crosses my mind that I could confront Simon with our suspicions, but there really seems little point, and in any case that would be going contrary to Miranda's wishes. If she went through the last few days of her life knowing that Simon caused the accident then she did so to make sure that the research was not compromised. I can hardly jeopardise the whole thing now. My job is to ensure that the work that Miranda started is brought to a proper conclusion.

Thinking about Miranda turns my attention towards that urn sitting on the garage shelf.

"Helen, what are we going to do with your sister's ashes?"

"Have you still got them? How ghoulish."

"They're at home. I should've done something with them by now, but I really don't know what Miranda would've wanted."

"Difficult. She wasn't very religious."

"No. Like many of us she would put 'C of E' on any form that demanded protestation of Faith, but it was a label, not a belief."

"Then I suppose scattering them in a churchyard would be out."

"I don't think she would have minded, it's just that it doesn't seem very appropriate, what do you think?"

"I don't know really. Some people like to scatter ashes at well-known beauty spots, but I rather think there are laws against that."

"Not so much laws against scattering ashes as taking liberties with other people's land – even if that land belongs to large Authorities. Mind you I bet lots of people do it anyway," I say.

"I don't really know why, but I am rather against the idea of scattering her around a stately home, or even a beauty spot like Tarn Hows. Really we want to find her a proper home."

"I'm not sure where we can find that."

"Yes we can! Of course we can," says Helen, "what about Deanstones?"

"But I thought you were going to sell your house at Cartmel"

"Funny really, I spent a year pestering Miranda to sell it, and now that it's mine I really want to hang on to it."

"But what are you going to do with it?"

"Let it I suppose. Oh, Duncan, I've just had a marvellous idea. Val was telling me that she is looking for somewhere rather better than the place she has at present. I just wonder if Deanstones might be ideal for her, there's a ground-floor garden room that could easily be used as a consulting room. I must talk to her about it."

"Well we are both going to Cartmel tomorrow, why don't you come along with us. We can take Miranda's ashes."

We leave it at that, both feeling good about several problems solved, and hoping that Val will see it the same way.

"Dunc, I need to go into town, can I borrow the Alfa?"

"Yes of course," say I, "Why don't you take it back to my spot when you are done, I can always beg a lift home from someone in an hour or two."

"Great, I just want to find somewhere with a health spa, do you know anywhere good? I also need to get my hair seen to"

"Use the gym on the campus," I suggest, "I've got a free pass somewhere, hang on."

I scrabble around in a couple of drawers and find the freebie, giving it to Helen together with the keys for the Alfa. I take her to the outside door, point the way to the sports facility and tell her where I have parked the car.

Just as I arrive back at my room I run into Val.

"Hi," she says, "I was just coming to see you."

"Oh yes, taking a second stab at the poor wounded beast!"

"Come off it Duncan! No, I was wanting to have a word with Helen really."

I tell Val that she has just missed Helen, but get the impression that she wants to chat and that I will do as a substitute. Within a couple of minutes she is ensconced in the chair so recently vacated by my sister in law.

Val looks at me closely. "Helen did tell you, didn't she?"

"Yes," I say.

Good, I was not sure how to bring the subject up. Val has done the very best thing by tackling it head on. The trouble is that I really do not know how I now feel about her. It really is a very strange situation that we find ourselves in.

"If you'd been a man," I say, "I could do a sort of Man-Thing and either physically assault you, verbally abuse you, or both."

"Would you have done that even now that she's dead?"

"Oh yes," I say. "You see the Man-Thing is not really about recovering a straying wife, it's all about showing who is the head of the harem and the driving off of Young Pretenders."

"Like a stag?

"Exactly like a stag!"

"So what would a stag do in our case?"

"I don't think he would be in the least concerned about the situation. Another hind would not be a threat to him; he would just include her in his herd. I think it's all to do with passing on genes, and as hind do not pass on their genes to other hind then there's no threat."

'Well I am not sure about being part of your herd", laughs Val, "But how do you feel about me now?"

"Well it's difficult. You see when I thought you were male I resented you."

"Even though you did not love Miranda?"

"Yes, you see it's a possession thing really, and to the male that's probably more important than love."

"So was I not a threat to possession?" says Val

"Well had I known about you and Miranda then I suppose you would have been. After all she might well have left me and gone to live with you. The thing is though that our animal analogy rather breaks down at this point because we are human, we think as well as feel. I might have resented you a bit, but it wouldn't have been a ball-wrenching, horns crashing sort of resentment.'

"Wow," says Val, "I'm supposed to be the Psychologist!"

We both laugh.

"You loved her." I say. It is not really a question.

"Yes, very much, probably more than she loved me. You see Miranda's real love was her work. I enjoy my work, but it's not all consuming. For Miranda work was her passion."

"She'll have told you that we did not have much of a marriage?

"No, she didn't put it like that at all. She was very fond of you Duncan; she enjoyed your company and your intellect. It was only physical sex with men that she found so difficult. It really wasn't about you so please don't feel that she rejected you as a person." Val pats me on my knee. "Anyway she told me that you managed to find a bit of sex when you needed it."

"Not that much fun, though." I say. "A quick bonk may be OK to relieve a bit of physical tension, but it is only satisfying for a very short period. I am totally selfish and want the best of all worlds, sex and love together."

"Ah," says Val, with a slight huskiness in her voice, "You and me both."

We sit in companionable silence for a while. I want to allow the emotional temperature to drop just a bit and Val seems lost in her own world. My thoughts turn towards Starlight. The mystery surrounding her seems even more impenetrable.

"Val, you know we talked yesterday about this strange experience that I had."

"Yes, all that stuff that you most probably dreamed as happened to you the evening you visited Langdale? I do indeed."

'Well the plot has been thickening!" I tell her about meeting Starlight again. I tell Val about Starlight coming to one of my lectures and of the agreement to meet in town. I recount much of the conversation that Starlight and I had, including the bit about Dada, and about Surrealism and René Magritte.

Val is clearly interested in what I am saying. It is very odd, and I cannot put my finger on it, but following our discussion about Val's relationship with Miranda I find that I am much more relaxed talking with her; especially discussing Starlight.

"Do you fancy this girl?" she asks.

"Well at times I do, but it's becoming less and less sexual. I can't really explain why."

"What do you think she's doing?"

"I don't know, but I think it has got something to do with power. No, I don't mean power, I mean energy."

"Can you describe it?"

"She was using imagery to tell me about herself and, I think, a bit about me. It seemed to have a good deal to do with the research Project."

"Why's she so interested in this painting by Magritte?" muses Val. "If I remember correctly he actually produced a series of such paintings of women, half human, half stone. At least two of them involve a dove, and think there's also one where the woman is holding a cupid."

"But it is the simplest picture that she originally referred to, the one with just the female figure, half stone and half flesh."

"So is she telling you that she is partly human and partly something else?"

"You might be right, but I think it was more to do with my perception of what she was rather than what she actually is."

"So it could be to do with you thinking that part of her is soft and approachable, and part is as hard and unfeeling?"

"Again I just don't think so, it wasn't as personal as that. She seemed to be pushing me forward along the lines of thought-energy. She knew that was what Miranda was working on and where I have a great interest. I wonder if she was trying to say that thoughts could alter one's perception of people, that they could change from stone to flesh, or visa versa?"

"That sounds plausible, "says Val. "She's certainly trying to get you to understand some concepts that aren't easy to grasp when you look straight at them."

"She said that to me at one stage, I think it was when we were on Sergeant Man."

"So what can we make of Magritte?" says Val. "Is it the power to change perception?"

I am a bit doubtful about that, "Not exactly. But just perhaps it might be energy. She could be talking about thought-energy in its purest form. I think she may have been showing me, demonstrating, something about the way that thought-energy interacts with physical life."

"And you think that is related to Miranda's accident?"

"Yes, I'm almost sure of it. She was pushing the boundaries, trying to find the biological source of this energy."

"And she so nearly succeeded," said Val.

"I don't know how aware Simon was of what he was doing. He may not have understood the process or why it was so powerful, but I do think that he realized that it was lethal."

"So in a way it was success for Miranda?"

"Yes, it was. She only made the briefest mention of it to me, just after the accident, but before that she was certain she was on the right track. That is why in her mind the research project couldn't be jeopardized by what had happened to her."

Val stands up to go. "Duncan, thank you for being so understanding, I am so sorry that I just couldn't bring myself to tell you about Miranda."

I feel a sudden wave of empathy for this emotionally aware woman. I find her utterly charming and rather surprisingly find myself musing that I would have been not just willing, but privileged to have openly shared Miranda with her.

"You know that we are off Cartmel tomorrow, would you mind if Helen were to join us?"

"Not at all. I would love it. I know that Helen is very much a woman of the world, but she is still very like her sister you know."

"She wants to go and see Deanstones, and I had better warn you that she has designs on you living there."

"That's worth a thought. Perhaps I could have a look at it whilst we are in Cartmel?"

"Well the other thing we thought we might do is to scatter Miranda's ashes at Deanstones. Do you think that would be a good idea?"

"I wondered what you were going to do about them. Yes, I do. I understood from Miranda that the place was very much part of her childhood."

"I'll bring the urn."

'Perhaps we could plant a tree there as well?" says Val.

"Yes, I think she might have liked that very much. We'll ask Helen."

"Are you going to make a day of it at Cartmel?"

"We thought we might leave first thing and have lunch there. I would quite like to be back here by mid-afternoon if I can."

"Tell you what, why don't you two come up to Milnthorpe and leave your car at my spot. Then we can all three of us travel on together in mine? We can hardly squeeze all of us into your boy-racer."

"It's not a boy-racer!"

"Have it your way – boys toys for the sexually frustrated. We psychotherapists know a thing or two."

"Shoo – get out, three hundred years ago they would have put you on a ducking stool."

"Bye then, see you about ten thirty tomorrow."

"Oh, hang on a moment," I say. "Helen's got the Alfa, any chance of dropping me off at home. I could bribe you with a glass of wine?"

"No problem. Just give me five minutes."

Nineteen

Helen had enjoyed her visit to the gym but had failed to find a hair stylist. They must have a decent one somewhere, she thought, but despite her efforts she could not find anything that came up to her, admittedly high, standards.

She had driven back to Duncan's house; found a gin bottle and tonic water. Where the Fielding lemons hid themselves she had failed to discover so she contended herself with a squeeze of 'instant lime' in the dubious hope that it might add something piquant to her drink.

She had phoned her Marylebone office and instructed her PA to upload the recordings from both offices for this week to the company intranet. She then settled down with her iPad connected to Duncan's WiFi to run through the information from both suites. She normally did this on a daily basis, but what with one thing and another she had not caught up with this week's sessions. She would have to do so now.

For some time she browsed the files with only passing interest. Yesterday and today had been fairly busy at Westminster, a couple of meetings with junior ministers talking to lobbyists, and a couple of rogues presenting themselves to some Americans as representing an art auction house.

At Marylebone there had only been one client and they had taken the suite for all three days, they were causing her a bit of concern. She was fairly sure that they were legal, but they were arms dealers and it was important to her that this did not stray the wrong side of the law. She listened to the sound recording for a bit, made a mental note to have a word with their principal when they next used her services, and turned to the previous day.

It was really rather too late for her to be checking the recordings for Monday, she knew she should have looked at them yesterday. She was interested in that letting at her Westminster suite that seemed so innocuous and for which a lot of money had been paid. She pulled up the file and started the playback. First up were just two of guys from the new client. They appeared to be chatting away casually to each other. Shortly they were joined by a third person, fairly short with red hair.

"Wait a tick!" she exclaimed. "That can't be right, surely that's Simon?"

She tracked back and started the recording again. Yes, it certainly was Simon. The picture was really very clear and there could be no doubt that it was he. She tracked back once more and added the sound.

For some time she listened attentively. When the recording showed that the three men had left she went back to the very beginning and listened to it all once more. Her whole body was rigid throughout. Her facial muscles did not move. It was clear that both Barry O'Connell and Hugh Strickland had been behind Simon in arranging the 'accident' in the lab. This was concrete evidence of their intention to remove Miranda from The Project. They had planned to kill her and were now intending either to take over The Project, or to trash it.

Val and I stop at the 'Chip on the Block' on our way back to my house and arrive bearing three very hot and rather smelly packages of traditional English take-away food.

"I'll put them out onto plates," volunteers Helen.

"No," says Val," they never taste as good if you do that, we'll eat them out of the paper.

As a compromise and in deference to my furniture we put the wrapped fish and chips onto plates and then eat them with our fingers, raiding the kitchen cupboards for salt and vinegar that I am rather surprised to discover I possess.

I have been hanging on to a rather drab little Chardonnay that I could not quite face drinking, even with a pizza. It would do very well for fish and chips and had obviously been waiting for just such an occasion as this. My wine snobbery makes me give serious consideration to decanting it to hide its origin, but in the end I own up and leave the half empty bottle on the table. It is quite palatable.

Helen has been unusually silent during the consumption of this most British of takeaways. She now sits next to Val on my comfortable sofa whilst, good host that I am, I finish putting the plates away in the kitchen. She starts to tell Val about the recording arrangements at her offices.

"It's not that we do it to pry into our client's affairs," she says, "but we do have to keep a bit of an eye on some of them. In law we are responsible for what happens on our premises, so every couple of days or so I just whizz through the videos to see if anything looks odd and catches my eye."

"What happens if you do see something?" asks Val

"Well I can go over it again, and we also have sound recording, so I can usually pick up what's being said."

"I bet you get some weird stuff sometimes," I venture, coming in from the kitchen with a second bottle of wine. This one boasts a rather more respectable heritage so I will be happy leave its label in full view without a qualm.

"Well that's just it," says Helen, holding out her empty glass for me to replenish, "That's what I must talk to the two of you about."

"You mean that we are involved somehow?"

'Well yes, and in a very worrying way."

"Come on then, tell all," says Val as I fill her empty glass as well.

"It's quite serious really," says Helen. "You see I let our Westminster boardroom on Monday to a firm that I know as Virtual Ventures."

"Hmm, they're the same people that approached Simon." I say.

"Exactly. Initially there were just two guys there. I recognized one as Hugh Strickland who is a senior civil servant. I think he heads up one of the more hush-hush of the services. I don't think I know the other one. Anyway the point is that a little later they were joined by a third person, and I got one hell of a shock when I found myself looking at Simon."

"Wow!" says Val. "That's fairly compromising isn't it Duncan? Academia would not like one of its own to be caught with his pants down talking to the Secret Service."

"Too true, especially without a long spoon" I say a little uneasily, it seems that Helen has not finished yet.

"Listen, you two, can you please get sensible. It becomes a lot worse. I replayed the video and it was absolutely and irrefutably Simon. I then found the sound clip. They were talking in some detail about your project Duncan."

"Bloody little worm!"

"Yes, but here is the really bad bit. It was quite clear from what they said that they all conspired together to deliberately kill Miranda."

"Oh No!" says Val "I suppose I should be surprised but that's what we suspected isn't it."

"I know, but to have it as recorded evidence. That's quite a shock, and a pretty sickening one."

"Are you really one hundred percent sure about this," I say, clutching at straws Why would you want to clutch at straws? I suppose it has something to do with drowning, but why would anyone leave straws around for a drowning person to clutch at. Sometimes this language of ours is a complete mystery to me.

"I can play it back for you if you like," Helen is saying.

Helen has only seen it on her iPad. Although the resolution is excellent the device is a bit on the small side. I boot up my twenty-seven inch iMac and then Val and I cluster around Helen as she logs onto her intranet and pulls up the recording. The screen is large and the images clear. The sound is slightly crackly, but more than good enough for us to follow the conversation between the three men with ease.

We watch it in silence. Helen re-plays it, twice. As one we move away from the computer and sit down again. For quite a while no one speaks.

"Jeez," I say at last. "I mean we suspected it, but this is so – so cold-blooded. There's no doubt about it at all, this is evidence of conspiracy to murder, and of murder itself"

"They are of a type, these people," says Val. "They may be government employees, but they can only see their own side of the story, it's the only thing that matters to them and if anything or anyone should get in the way of their ultimate goal then they will remove it."

"Christ, how horrible," says Helen.

"Yes, you see they don't really think that they are doing anything wrong. It's as if they pull up a sort of 'shield of righteousness' around them. They think that they're always right, always invincible."

"And killing Miranda was little more than unfortunate?" I say.

"Yes, that is about it. She was in their way, or at least in Simon's way, and she certainly would never have sold out to anyone," says Helen. "They must have thought that they have at least a better chance with you, Dunc."

The realization that my friend and colleague, Simon is, without a shred of doubt, responsible for Miranda's death hits me really hard. I find it almost impossible to imagine this rotund little man with his West Country lilt as a hardened criminal. That said Simon is undoubtedly ambitious. Not for the Project, but for himself. Others assumed that he was joking when he talked about receiving a Nobel Prize, but I now realize that Simon is in deadly earnest. He really does think that he is of that standard.

"Quite apart from the way it affects all three of us," Helen is saying, "I'm a little worried about the ramifications regarding my business. If I know that my premises are being used to discuss a crime, then I'm pretty sure that it makes me an accessory, or whatever it is that they call it, to that crime."

"I suppose that applies to each of us," says Val.

"I think we have to do some very careful thinking," I say. "By implication we are now party to the killing of Miranda. We've got to decide now. We need to agree what we are going to do about it."

"There is the Hospital to consider," says Helen, "and the University. If we go public with this then heads are going to roll, including yours, Dunc."

"You mean because of the cover up? But that wasn't the cause of Miranda's death"

"But it will come out, you won't be able to stop it, am I not right Val?"

"Yes, I am sure that's the case. The trouble is that you, Duncan, are as guilty as hell of pretending that Miranda's death was an accident. I know the top people at the Uni and the Hospital are implicated, but like the good Administrators that they are they'll wriggle out of it somehow. They'll heap the blame squarely on your shoulders, and those of poor old Jimmy Freemantle. And it won't stop at that. They'll say that you conspired with Simon to carry out the murder, and that you then covered it up."

Shit, this isn't good. As a bit of distraction therapy I open another bottle of wine. We are all in this together and a bit of alcoholic bonding will do no harm. I look at the two women and a glow of appreciation almost overwhelms me. There is so much talk of glass ceilings and male prejudice, and yet here, in my home, are two women from very different backgrounds. They are both successful and immensely capable. Just a centaury ago neither of them would even have had the vote. I hate the idea of seeming complacent, but surely the resentment and jealousy against women in the workplace is at an end now? Oh well, I am only a man, and a philosopher at that. I am almost certainly not well enough equipped to understand these things.

"I think we'd better make some decisions," Helen is saying. "And we'd better stick together on it whatever we decide."

Somewhere inside my head a voice is trying to make itself heard. It is as if a desperate Miranda is trying to speak to me, to make me listen, to make me understand. She is pleading for me to keep quiet about Simon and his actions. She is determined that the thing that really matters, The Project, should carry on until it is finished. It seems as if she is telling me that if anyone can sort out the theory behind the thought-energy thing then I can. That it is best to leave until later any idea of exposing Simon and his disgusting colleagues.

I am unnerved by the insistence of this voice within me. I am not usually given to such imaginative musings. It rings true, whether they are Miranda's thoughts or my own. There is little choice for me, but what about the others?

"Hey Dunc, where have you gone?" Helen is reaching across to my arm and looking at me with some concern.

"Oh, sorry, too much wine probably. What were you saying?"

"We were just trying to look at the pros and cons of keeping this whole thing under wraps for a bit," says Helen. "What do you think?"

"Well I'm in the thick of it whatever is decided," I say, "so I'll go along with whatever you two decide. I can't in all conscience ask you to break the law."

"Oh I think you can," says Val "I'm out of the immediate firing line if things get rough. But I think that my role is to support whatever Miranda was trying to do."

"You mean by trying to keep it quiet?" I ask.

"Yes. You see we are pretty sure now that Miranda was aware of Simon's engineering of that accident. So what did Miranda do about Simon? She did nothing, absolutely nothing. She was determined that you, Duncan, along with Simon should persuade the hospital authorities to cover up the accident and convince the rest of the world, including you and me, Helen, that nothing in the least suspicious had happened."

"This is all true," I say.

Val continues, "So why did she do it? So that Duncan could ensure the completion of this work that was so important to her. During her fleeting bouts of consciousness for that last week she kept her silence and said nothing that might derail the Project. What Simon thought about why she was doing this goodness only knows, but that really doesn't matter. Nothing material has changed, just our knowledge of what happened."

"Val, I agree with you," says Helen. "The problem is that knowing something to be true is very different from suspecting it. It throws upon the three of us one hell of a responsibility."

"I think we just have to live with that," I say. "I know it won't be easy, but it shouldn't be for very long. I reckon it should take me a couple of months, three at the most, and then, once the Paper is published, we can discuss what we do about Simon and his dubious colleagues."

"So we're agreed?" says Helen.

'Perhaps we should all sign something in blood!" I say, trying to lighten the tone.

"Honestly, Dunc," says Helen," you have been reading too much Swallows and Amazons."

"Guilty as charged!"

"Now we need to decide about tomorrow," says Helen, ever the practical one. "Val, I know that you and Duncan are off to Cartmel to revisit the Priory, do you want to kill two birds with one stone and have a look at this house of mine whilst we're there?"

"It'll be my first visit to the Priory, I didn't come to the family funeral, just to Miranda's memorial service at Lancaster."

"Oh, of course, sorry."

"But yes. I'd love to see Deanstones. Duncan mentioned your ideas to me, and, it might suit me very well. So if the two of you come up to Milnthorpe tomorrow morning I can drive us all to Cartmel."

"Val," says Helen, "You can't go home to Milnthorpe tonight. You are in no state to drive. We must have had a bottle of wine each haven't we Dunc?"

"Yes, Val. Helen's right. You shouldn't drive."

"I suppose I must be a bit over the limit, I just wasn't thinking."

I try to think of practical things," You are welcome to the small spare room, I'll see if I can rustle you up a duvet from somewhere."

"Oh, there is one in the cupboard in my room," says Helen "I'll get it for you Val."

Val looks relieved "That's really kind of you both." she says.

"Come on then or we'll be in no fit state in the morning," says Helen.

Helen leads Val upstairs in search of bedding, beds and sleep.

I stand and look at my departing friends for a moment or two, then switch off the downstairs lights and make my way upstairs to my own room. It is a funny old life. For the past month or so there has been no one but me in this house, and all at once I seem to be becoming quite sociable. I am not sure how well it will suit my temperament in the long run.

Twenty

Val turns the car down the narrow Priest Lane into Cavendish Street then, through the grey stone arch of the medieval gatehouse, the road opens out into Cartmel Square. Helen has been sharing the back seat of Val's VW Golf with six foot of fruit tree ever since we stopped at Beetham Nurseries. It took a bit of time to decide upon a Damson as being the most appropriate for both Miranda and the garden.

"If you two want to do your thing in the Priory," says Helen "I'll take my arboreal chum round to Deanstones. Come over when you are done, and I'll show you around the place. I've got one or two things to sort out so no need to hurry."

Clasping the tree to her chest she sets off across the square whilst Val and I head towards the Priory.

Standing again at the gate into the old churchyard I feel more of a sense of loss than I did at the funeral. Then I was kept busy coping with the formalities of it all. I was tied up with undertakers and coffin bearers, the subsequent cremation, the vicar, the order of service, and all the very necessary but essentially practical arrangements. There was not really any time for thinking, or perhaps it simply was not the right moment to do so.

Val and I walk into the Priory grounds together and stand in silent contemplation. The magnificent old building squats, hunched up against the centuries of pain it has witnessed. We passed no one in the village and now this place is as silent as if it were death itself.

Beside me Val is standing very upright and very still. A tear trickles slowly down her left cheek. I put my arm around her and discover that she is quivering.

"This cannot be it," she says, "there must be something more."

I understand what she is saying, and I would like for that as well. However the panacea of religion has slipped past me like a lady of the night, promising so much, but its charms barely masking its obscenity of purpose, and its price tag all too evident.

"Not to believe puts us in a minority, even in this post-Christian age."

"But love does not die," says Val.

"It slips away quietly, leaving the living with its companion - grief."

"And that we both feel."

Despite the lack of a proper marriage in the conventional sense I was very fond of Miranda. She was a very good friend to me even if we were hardly Man and Wife. I realize how much more she was to Valerie and recognize the emptiness that she must be feeling.

"We're not good at death," she says.

"In the West, no, we're not. We don't wail, or light funeral pyres, or beat our breasts. The most any westerner would accept would be a quiet vigil."

"And then only if they were devoutly religious."

We walk together, in emotional equilibrium, towards the building, entering by the southern porch. There is the sound of music playing very gently within the building. It is recognizably Gregorian Chant presumably emanating from a sophisticated sound system. It seems very appropriate for a religious building of this age.

There is a small bookstall on the left but no one is manning it. We move together to the centre of the nave and look towards the great East window. The Priory is one of the very few that escaped total demolition under the dissolutions of Henry VIII. It was a parish church as well as an Augustine Priory and so was, in part, spared for the use of the villagers. That said most of the Canons were hanged at Lancaster for asserting themselves and resisting the will of the king. The Priory is still a place of Christian worship, a huge ecclesiastical house of glory now humbled for its use by just a handful of twenty-first century parishioners.

"I didn't take you for a religious person," I say.

"Nor I am, at least not in any formal sense. And you?"

"Not I, although I am certainly not atheist."

We walk towards the crossing and the Chant becomes just a little louder. Whoever is in charge of this great space has worked wonders with the sound system. We pass on through the beautiful screen to admire the famed Misericords.

"We're so different in our spirituality to the people who worshipped here eight hundred years ago," says Val, "they were so confident, so convinced that everything in life belonged to an established order of things."

"Perhaps we are just arrogant. We think we can pick out bits of morality from all religions or none and adopt that as our personal creed."

"So we're the ultimate 'pick and mix' generation when it comes to moral purpose."

"I don't like it that much either, but at least we're given the chance to make ourselves responsible for our own morality. To your people of eight hundred years ago such freethinking would be a capital crime against both Church and State."

"Which was repressive and cruel." Says Val. "We've moved on since then and developed a different sort of public and private morality."

"That is surely just a way of saying that these days you live in a moral vacuum where you can do anything you like?" says a deep voice behind us.

We both spin around to discover a tall man standing no more that a couple of yards from us. He wears a dark tunic over a white vestment. He has thinning hair and is clean-shaven. His brown eyes have a merry twinkle to them and he is smiling broadly.

"Sorry," says this man, "eavesdropping, a terrible habit of mine. May I introduce myself, Canon Bryan Willan, at your service. And who, may I ask are you?"

"Duncan Fielding and, . . "

" . . . , and your lovely wife, I presume?" finishes Bryan.

I look at Val and we both burst out laughing. "No. No." we both splutter at the same time.

"Oh, my silly mistake. So you are?"

"Valerie Staples, spinster of the parish of Lancaster, and most willing to stay that way."

"Hmmm," says Bryan looking at me, "You don't seem top have made much impression on the lady."

"That wasn't exactly my intention," I reply, a trifle ungallantly. Realizing the import of my words I add, "Val is a good friend of mine and was exceptionally close to my late wife."

"Duncan is the widower of Miranda Fielding whose funeral was held here in September", says Val, adding, "Miranda and I shared so much."

"Tut, tut," says Bryan. "My condolences to you both. Mrs. Fielding grew up in these parts I think?"

"Her parents were the Marstons ," I say, "you may remember that they were killed out in India a couple of years ago."

"Yes, yes. I do remember something about that. A terrible loss, and now followed so quickly by their daughter. I seem to recall that there is a sister, younger I think?"

"That's right, "I say, "Helen, she's with us today, but has just gone off to have a look at her house, Deanstones."

Bryan is looking at Val's tear-stained face. "I can see that you are both upset. Perhaps you would care to come over here and sit down."

He shepherds us gently through into the Town Choir. It is now used as a side chapel but was the original Parish Church of the old Priory. About one third of it is filled with the enormous church organ.

At the entrance to the chapel is the most beautiful modern sculpture by Josefina de Vasconcellos; a depiction of St Michael battling his way through the jaws of the dragon. I stand and look at it, mesmerized by its power and its simple lines.

"It's very modern," says Bryan.

"It has such a sense of urgency," I say. "It's as if the dragon, which I assume is Satan, is about to devour our hero."

"And so it is. Josephina captured this modern age perfectly. However I have no idea who our St Michael is."

"Everyman," says Val.

"Now that is an interesting thougt," says Bryan, "did you know that the concept of Everyman has changed over the centuries. In the fifteenth century it was an ideal, devoid of individuality, used often in morality plays to create a universality that was understood by all. The present-day Everyman is an individual, also used in plays, but with whom we may either agree or disagree according to our own convictions."

"So the change in Everyman echoes the development of freedom of speech and freedom of expression that Duncan and I were discussing when you joined us."

The three of us sit together in this quiet and fairly private retreat; the cleric dressed in a dark habit, the sad widower, and the grieving lover. Bryan engages us both in talking fully and frankly about our feelings for Miranda, He discovers that we are both professors attached to Lancaster University. He winkles out of Val that she is a psychiatrist He shows considerable interest in my work, and rather more in Miranda's.

"So she was exploring the theory that you could just possibly communicate between your two or three worlds that exist on a different plane to our own then?"

"That's right," I say. "Theoretically we can measure the mass of these hidden worlds, and my wife was working on the possibility of communicating between one world and another through the medium of thought-energy. Miranda was looking to prove that thought is a unique but quantifiable form of energy."

"So are you still pursuing her work?"

"Yes, I am indeed," I say in a rush, "My problem is that I'm a philosopher, not a physicist. Miranda sought to prove that there is a correlation between energy and thought. If I can delve deep enough into her experimental data and gain an understanding of her theorems then I should be able to find the right connection. We'll be able to show that certain energy forms can move between worlds."

"Now," replies Bryan, "You are straying into my field. Welcome.'

Val picks up on it straight away. "Of course, that is what religion has been professing to do for millennia, enabling the transmission of thoughts from one space-time to a different space-time."

"But what's the mechanism?" I say, still slightly perplexed.

"Prayer," says Bryan." It really is that simple."

"But hang on," interjects Val, "Although you may pray we can't prove that it works. Prayer strikes me as being a reassuring delusion. Not that I mean to deride it, but I'm not sure that it is much more than a spiritual comfort blanket."

"Are you talking professionally or personally?" asks Bryan.

"Well both. I am not sure all practitioners in my profession would be quite that dismissive of it, but I see no concrete proof of prayer actually working,"

"I wonder, "says Bryan. "You see you have to have Faith."

"But that takes you around in circles," I say, "If you have to have Faith to accept that prayer works then you are just saying that you have to believe in prayer to make it real."

"People in these modern times," says Bryan, "have a tendency to think that they know it all, that their intellect is superior to that of previous generations. They dismiss all things spiritual, including prayer, unless that happens to accord with what they like to term their personal morality."

"But surely it's better to rely upon our own inner conviction than to be strapped into a straightjacket prepared by the Church?" I say.

"You could be correct, but only in the smallest minority of cases," says the cleric, "The vast majority of people who like to imagine that they are free-thinkers are what I would describe as sloppy-thinkers. If they find a sudden yearning for the spiritual then they think that it's entirely in order for them to just conjure up a neat little package of beliefs that suits their emotional and spiritual needs of the moment."

"That's a bit harsh," says Val," you've made quite a few points there. Firstly we may not be intellectually superior to those that have gone before us, but we do have the opportunity and the moral freedom to express that intellect, to nurture it and to give it rein. Secondly, . . ."

"Hang on, let's deal with that one first. What you say is flawed. Let's take the analogy of poetry. Are you saying that because the poets of today write blank verse that they have greater intellectual capacity that those who wrote in a more structured format, such as the sonnet?"

Val is becoming just a little unsure of her argument, "I am not sure that is a fair analogy. It is like comparing apples and pears."

"Exactly. So it is not intellectual ability that we're considering, but the modern attitude by which we judge our predecessors. So, your second point is?"

"You implied that we are not free-thinkers, but sloppy-thinkers. I'm certain that we have the opportunity these days to think what would have been unthinkable even a hundred years ago, let alone when this Priory was founded."

"I agree with you in part," says Bryan, "in the past there was much more by way of spiritual or moral restriction. But those are not the only restrictions that we are faced with. You only have to look at the way western civilization behaves today and you realize that it's a politically motivated myth to think that you possess your own free will. You and your morality are subservient to the morality of the State and, rather more covertly, to that of Big Business. Did you have free will when the UK went to war in Iraq? No. Even if you had the nerve, the energy and the time to join street protests against the war you would still in the end have had to shrug your shoulders and admit it was out of your hands. There was no chance for you to exercise your free will. Even Parliament would not have stopped it had they had the balls to vote against the war. Much the same with big business, just look at the bankers – need I say more?"

"We still have a great deal of personal free will," says Val. "But what about your third point, that we have a tendency to manufacture little spiritual bolt-holes just to suit the circumstances of the moment. That may to some extent be true, but those beliefs normally include acceptance of the moral absolutes. And I still believe in those absolutes; goodness, beauty, courage."

"I am very pleased to hear that, but I think that you own profession admirably exemplifies my point," says Bryan. "I am not saying that psychoanalysis is wrong, or bad, but to some, notably the rich and the famous, it has become their 'bolt-hole' religion. They find religiosity within their own minds. Celebrity spiritual wankers."

"Hmmm," I say. "I rather agree with you, although that is a somewhat risqué turn of phrase for a man of the cloth. But we were talking about prayer and the ability of prayer to actually do or change things."

"This Priory was founded by a very rich man. He did not build this magnificent structure for its architectural merit, nor did he import thirteen Augustine monks from Wiltshire and maintain them year in year out just to enhance the papal employment statistics. No, he did so because he believed in the power of prayer. He decreed that these Canons would say daily prayers for him and his family in perpetuity."

"That doesn't mean it did any good."

"No, but he was one of millions of people who thought it would, and put their money where their mouths were."

"So what is this power of prayer? Where do prayers come from? How are they made? "How do they get delivered?"

"Now I hear the philosopher talking," smiles Bryan. "The answers are within you. Prayer can be incredibly powerful; it knows no bounds. It can travel instantly and it can move seamlessly between heaven and earth."

"That's an interesting concept, but difficult to accept as reality without some experimental proof," I say. "But two things that you have just said are of great interest to me. If we consider 'heaven' to be a parallel world then we could be talking about the communication of thought-energy between different worlds."

"And your 'hell' would just be another such parallel world," interjects Val.

I continue. 'And I can rationalize prayer transfer as being instant across long distances, or even worlds. Miranda would have told us how quantum mechanics can prove that alterations to the state of a wave/particle in one location can alter the same attribute in a similar particle many millions of miles away – and that it does so instantly, no cosmic speed limit involved."

"So in many ways we are seeing this as one," says Bryan.

"I agree," says Val. "The task is to define and quantify this power that you see as prayer, and we have been calling thought-energy, in such a way as it can be harnessed."

Bryan looks very concerned. He fixes first Val and then me with a long stare. Finally he says, "You must stop this now; at once. It's very, very dangerous. You have no idea of the sort of power that you are working with. Not just for your own sake, but for the sake of others I must beg you to stop."

This startles me. Why should this priest be moved to utter such a stark warning? Do I have anything to fear? He obviously thinks that my attempt to bring some rational and philosophical basis to his long-held belief in prayer is going to cause great harm. I can't see why. Surely it's right for mankind to push boundaries, to expand our knowledge base?

We all get to our feet and start moving towards the South door, Val is a little way ahead of Bryan and myself. I turn to him, "I know what you are saying is from deeply held conviction, but I'm concerned that it's just a reaction from the Church. Over the millennia it has fought to keep its mysteries under its own control. The time has come when our secular society is going to change that."

"I can do no more than plead with you from the bottom of my heart to drop this line of research. I'm not trying to protect the Church, it's far more universal than that. My plea to you is so as to protect the whole of mankind."

"Bryan," I say, "please believe me it's all going to turn out just fine."

So-saying I stride on to catch up with Val, leaving Bryan Willan standing in quiet contemplation in the South Transept. I can't pretend that his words are not worrying to me. Those that initially worked on splitting the atom were doing it in the pursuit of knowledge rather than the construction of an evil weapon. Even if The Project does lead to some harm I do not, as a philosopher, think that I can pull back from seeking after truth.

Together Val and I walk through the Priory and out into the southern porch.

"I think I'll have a bit of a look around the churchyard," I say.

'OK, I'll go and give Helen a hand at Deanstones. See you there in a bit."

Val walks off towards the Square and I make my way, still in some perplexity, around the southeast end of the building. As I round the corner I find myself almost knocked flat by a hurrying figure dressed in a sports jacket and wearing a dog collar.

"Ooops! Sorry", says the perpetrator in some disarray, "always colliding with people. Must be in too much of a rush."

"No problem," I say. I look more closely at the man and recognize him, "It's John Somerville it not?"

"Ah, yes. Oh, I remember, sorry not to recognize you immediately. You're Duncan, Miranda's widower, I've got that right, haven't I?"

"Yes indeed. We just wanted to come and have a little bit of peace here, now that there are fewer people than there were at the funeral."

"Quite understand. Good thing to do. Chance to say your personal goodbyes."

That's right," I say. "You just missed my companion, Valerie Staples, she was a very dear friend of Miranda's. She thought she would come up here with me because she didn't get to the funeral service, although she did of course come to the memorial in Lancaster."

"I'm sorry I missed her."

"What a beautiful place this is," I say, "and surely at its best in this low winter light. Even the gravestones seem to be sitting up and sunning themselves in it."

"It is one of the few Priories that did not get sacked at the Dissolution."

"Yes, we were talking about that just before we met your colleague," I say.

The vicar looks at me with an intense curiosity. "Colleague?" he says.

"Yes, really knowledgeable chap. You must count yourselves fortunate to have him on your team ministry, said his name was Bryan Willan.'

"We have no Bryan Willan here. I do hope this isn't some sort of joke? If so it's in rather poor taste."

"Honestly," I say. "That's what he said his name was. A large slightly balding man in a dark cloak."

The Rev. Somerville looks just a little disturbed. Speaking rather slowly he says, "there was a Bryan Willan in this parish. He was the Canon Cellarer at the time of the Dissolution, one of only two

Canons to be acquitted of treason at Lancaster Assizes. His fellow Canons were executed. He came back here, you know, and was re-installed as the priest in charge of the parish. He died in 1585."

I am astounded.

"But we left our Bryan Willan inside the building only a moment ago," I say. "He cannot be the man you are telling me about. Look, John, would you just come in and meet him with me?"

We walk briskly back into the Priory. I am not sure if I really expect to see Bryan there. If I did I am disappointed. There is no sign of the large black-clad figure.

"It does happen, you know," says John.

"You mean he has been seen before?"

"Not to my knowledge, what I meant is that people do see or imagine that they are visited by figures from the past. They have to be in a receptive state. One in which they can release their imagination."

"I'm loathe to suggest it was a figment of my imagination," I say, "perhaps if it had just been me, but for two of us to have had the same imaginary experience would surely be very unlikely?"

"It's probably best not to try to fully understand an experience like this. It may be better just to accept that there are things outside our normal everyday lives and that these experiences, however they arise, should be treasured for what they are, but not dissected."

"You're probably right. I doubt if it's what is known as 'Group Hallucination' where the resonance of emotional images conjured up by one individual can be received by others."

"Yes," says John, "There certainly are associations with specific places that seem to lead people into having what might be termed 'ghost' experiences. But that's probably more to do with personal sensitivity and association with particular locations than any type of spirit manifestation."

"I think it's probably best to admit that we had an inexplicable experience and leave it at that."

"Ah, but can you?" says John. "Once you start to admit the inexplicable you're invoking the supernatural. Then you're starting down the road of Faith. Not necessarily Christian Faith, but Faith nevertheless."

"Strange," I say, "that's just about where we got to in our discussion with Bryan."

It begins to dawn on me that it is strangely quiet in here, and I realize that the music system must have switched itself off.

"I really like the sound system that you've installed," I say "it works very well. The Gregorian Chant is just perfect in this setting."

For the second time in as many minutes John Somerville gives me a very odd look. His answer seems almost inevitable. "We've no such sound system installed here."

We look at each other. There does not seem to be much more to be said.

"Look Duncan, I really must dash. I was already late for a meeting when I, quite literally, bumped into you and I shall be doubly late now. Stay as long as you like, and do contact me if you should find the need to."

John Somerville dashes out of the Priory. It is almost as if I've been accosted by a minor whirlwind. But the physical disturbance is as nothing to the mental turmoil that he leaves behind.

I walk slowly up the nave into the Choir. Here are the renowned Misericords. I would love to try one out for size, but they are roped off and although there is no one around I would feel guilty about taking such a liberty. The Canons must have been quite small to use them to good effect; they seem pretty low. For myself I am in need of slightly greater comfort than a misericord and am therefore pleased to be able to sit down quietly in one of the choir stalls.

I shut my eyes and let myself imagine what this place was like four hundred and fifty years ago. The Canons and their Prior have been routed. A large part of the Priory and virtually all of the domestic and administrative buildings are razed to the ground and the people of the parish are trying to come to terms with this new Anglicanism that is sweeping the country. They must have welcomed the familiar figure of Bryan Willan back as their Vicar with feelings of the greatest relief. He would offer them some sense of stability in those troubled times. I can see Bryan growing old in physique but young in spirit ministering to the parish but remembering the glory days of his youth when the Priory was the centre of trade, travel and power as well as spiritual authority.

Twenty One

I'm aware that I am not alone. There is someone sitting just a short distance away from me in the same choir stall. I did not notice them when I sat down, and am more than a little embarrassed to discover that I'm encroaching on their private space.

I clear my throat, ready to apologise and remove myself. The slight figure turns towards me.

It's Starlight.

"What are you doing here?" I blurt out.

"Hello Starlight, how nice to see you – is a more usual form of greeting," says the girl.

"Well of course I'm pleased to see you," I say. "What I mean is that I would like to know why you are here and whether you came specifically to speak to me."

"You have just seen what you think is a ghost."

"Yes, at least that's what seems most likely."

"According to the Christian faith a ghost is a spirit that's tied to the earth but does not live on the material plane. It's considered that souls are allowed by God to return to earth to bring warnings to the living."

"You seem to know a lot about religion"

"My point is that according to Christian theology the Bryanghost of this place must have been here to warn you about something."

"Well he didn't issue any dire threats, or tell us to repent our sins, or anything like that."

"Go on"

"What he did was to talk about faith and prayer."

"Well those are his stock in trade. Didn't you talk about anything else?"

"We started to discuss The Project in relation to religious faith, and yes, now I come to think of it he did give me a pretty firm warning."

"Do you remember what he said?"

"It was when Val said something about harnessing thought-energy and targeting it to access other worlds. Up to then he'd been accepting that our interest in thought was similar to his belief in the power of prayer. Once he realised that I wanted to analyse and quantify this thought/prayer energy then he told me quite firmly that I should stop. That not only was I endangering myself, but I could bring the most awful harm to others if were to finish The Project."

Starlight looks at me. She is deadly serious now. No more banter, discussions about art or sexual provocation. This matters.

"Duncan," she says, "It's not just Bryan Willan, I too am asking you to stop. To end this Project, to dismantle it and forget that you and Miranda ever thought about these things."

"But why? I can't do that. It is unheard of. I owe it to Miranda. I owe it to the University. I owe it to myself damn it. I feel sure I can take Miranda's work right up to the point where the existence of parallel worlds can be proved. With any luck we can take it further and show that we can access these worlds by the same means."

"That's what I was afraid that you would say, and what I really did not want to hear from you." She says, and then, very quietly to herself, "it will mean a bit of rescheduling."

"Val and I also spoke to Bryan about angels"

"They are very much part of Christian theology."

"Do you believe in them?"

"I'm not sure about the word 'belief' in this context."

"At one stage you suggested that I should think of you as an angel."

"Yes, but as you well know, that was an attempt to assist you in coming to terms with my presence. I didn't say that I was an angel."

"Starlight I don't think that you are a dream . . ."

"There you go again – always handing me compliments."

"No. Be serious. I was going on to say that I don't think that you are appearing to me as if in a dream. On the other hand you seem to posses powers that ordinary mortals do not. I would really like to know more."

"There are things that 'ordinary mortals' as you put it really should not know – not even friendly philosophers."

"It's all to do with this thought-energy thing isn't it?" I say.

"Possibly."

"And perhaps to do with the existence of more worlds than this one?"

"Probably."

"Bryan Willan was talking about prayer and about heaven and hell."

"Most religions foster a belief in some form of an afterlife, usually as a reward for doing good or as a punishment for doing evil in this world. It used to be a very effective way of controlling a large mass of the people, and still is in some religions."

"So do heaven and hell exist?"

"Now you are asking me an impossible question."

"How so?"

"Because the existence or otherwise of such abstract concepts is within the mind of the beholder, or believer. If you believe in heaven – then it exists, but that's your heaven, just for you."

"So if separate worlds only exist in the mind of the individual what's of such importance about my research, and why must I stop?"

"Well I admit that it is of importance", says the girl who has called herself Starlight. "But you asked me specifically about the 'other worlds' of Christianity. This is a wider thing. If you were to succeed in proving the existence of energy exchange potential between this world and another using the process of thought, and if you were able to isolate and then target that energy then we could have a state of chaos."

"I'm not sure that I quite see that, why?"

"Think back to Miranda's take on anti-matter. What happens when a particle and an antiparticle collide? There's an explosion; they give off a flash of light and 'create' lots of smaller particles, the 'particle zoo' as the physicists call it, made up of six the different varieties of Quark. Now if we have a situation where anyone can pay a few hundred pounds and have access by thought-energy to other worlds, what to them may well be heaven or hell, then we have the possibility of such access being used for very sinister purposes. And remember the particle/anti-particle collision, we could be looking at a very similar, but much larger, reaction."

"Yes, but that is only a possibility. Miranda told me about a scientist called Jacob Bekenstein. He has propounded an interesting hypothesis regarding what is called the Holographic Principle. Bekenstein states that we may have to regard the physical world as being constructed principally of information, with the physical attributes of energy and matter being mere incidentals."

"That's right, and that the whole of our universe may in fact be a two-dimensional bubble with a sort of soup of information surrounding it."

"But that is beyond the research that Miranda was carrying out."

"O.K. let's look at that research. Although the start was a bit shaky you and Miranda were thinking on exactly the right lines."

"Exactly. But I still don't see where you fit in."

"Duncan, Duncan, have you not got there yet?"

The girl is looking at me. Her blue eyes seem to pierce into my brain. She has a look of real concern on her face.

"I suppose I'm being incredibly thick, but I really do not understand why you're here, or what's going on."

"Then why do you think I'm here?"

'You know, Starlight I have simply no idea."

"Then I'll have to show you. Not now, later."

"What do you mean 'later', that's too open-ended?"

"Soon then, within the next few hours. It has to be soon because I need to stop you."

"Stop me?"

"Yes, stop you from completing this Project."

Now that really takes me aback. Miranda is trying to urge me on to finish the research, even dying in silence in order to ensure its completion. Simon is so keen that The Project should be brought within the influence of his people that he was prepared to kill in order to ensure that it was. And here is Starlight, this girl who has lulled me into trusting her, saying that she is intent upon stopping me. There is another person trying to stop me, Bryan Willan, if he can still be considered a person. He has warned me quite clearly that I must give it up.

"But you can't stop me. I've got to go on. You've no idea how important this all was to Miranda, and indeed to everyone else."

"To whom is it important."

"To me, to the University, to the whole scientific community, to the world."

"Its importance is illusory. It'll not matter if you hypothesise the existence of the two parallel worlds. It will not be a problem if you suggest that these can be quantified by means of antimatter. What we really cannot have you doing, Duncan, is finding a way to target thought-energy to communicate between those worlds."

"So you must stop me."

"You must stop yourself."

"I'm not sure that I can."

"Then that's what I am here for, do you understand now. I'm here to help you."

I understand sufficiently to know that I am in the gravest danger of agreeing to throw away the best work of my late wife.

I look towards the Sanctuary. The five sections of the reredos with the crucified Christ at the centre glow golden in the morning light. Can I fight the whole of Christendom? I imagine Josefina de Vasconellos' St Michael thrusting out through the jaws of its dragon leading out all the angels that are now lined up behind the Christ figure. Serried rank upon serried rank of golden figures are glowing in the light from the great fifteenth century east window. They are pointing at me and crying 'NO'. I hear the sounds of marshal music, of cymbals and trumpets. I am within the Book of Revelation. The angelic hoard is converging upon me and I will be crushed by it, subsumed into it. It is impossible to resist. St Michel turns from his sculpture and raises his sword. He is about to slay the dragon. The dragon is a depiction of the Devil. I am the dragon.

But there is more. In my fevered imagination there are foul crawling slimy things emerging from out of the great stone tomb opposite me. There are horns and forked tails. It is a multi-headed Beast and behind it are all manner of ghastly tortured things bearing staves and lances. 'YES' they are all saying as they place themselves in front of St Michael, restraining his sword arm. There is a great lashing of tails and slavering from jaws at the thought of such rich harvest; the harvest that is The Project. The breakdown of the barriers of morality would be complete, not just between earth and hell, but also between heaven and hell. There would be no order. There would be chaos. Satan triumphant!

Great battle is joined in this small rural outpost of the universe. Angelic hoard and Satanic masses fight to the death in a cacophony of sound. I cower down. This fight is for me; for the future of The Project; for my very soul. I hear the very Bells of Hell ringing as if in triumph.

The Bells of Hell go ting-a-ling-a-ling
For me but not for thee:
For thee the angels sing-a-ling-a-ling,
The devil tolls for me.
Oh! Satan, where's thy sting-a-ling-a-ling?
You dig my Grave for me,
Where the Bells of Hell go ting-a-ling-a-ling
As they do welcome me.

I come to with a start; it is my phone that is ringing.

"Hi Helen, "I say feeling very shaky. She tells me that they are ready for the tree planting "Yes, sorry, I'm on my way."

I look round. There is nothing to upset the contemplation in this quiet, peaceful old building. The girl who calls herself Starlight is not here.

Twenty Two

Deanstones is a large grey stone house just off the main Square. That it had stood there for many years was evidenced by the pieces of dressed stone that could be discerned in the lower parts of its walls. These had no doubt been 'acquired' by enthusiastic builders following the dissolution of the Priory and the demolition of the vast array of out-offices that it would have boasted. It must have been rich pickings for a few.

Helen, bearing her six foot of Damson, entered by the street door and with some difficulty managed to plonk her tree down in the hall. The house was sound enough but had the slightly musty air of an unlived-in building. The heating had been left on low but the place needed warmth and ventilation. Helen set about putting matters to rights. She turned the thermostat up, opened windows and lit a fire in the sitting room grate. She understood that keeping the heating on should keep the frost out of pipes within the house. Those pipes in the outhouse and serving the two garden taps were vulnerable. Fortunately there had been little frost so far this winter. Helen found an adjustable spanner and a shallow bowl and set about draining pipes. She might be a wired city sophisticate nowadays, but she had been raised as a straightforward Cumbrian lass and a very practical one at that.

Once she had dealt with the pipes she took the tree out into the walled garden then went back to Val's car and removed the urn from the passenger foot-well. Val had not locked the car and Helen was amused at the idea of a thief making off with the car and discovering Miranda's remains.

She carried the urn through to the garden and set it carefully on the ground next to the Damson. There was an old stone seat underneath the ivy-clad wall to the side of the garden. Helen sat there as she had when she was a small girl. Her thoughts turned to her companion of those years, her dead sister.

Miranda had loved this home, surely it was the right place for her to be? Helen wondered if she was worrying too much about it, after all Miranda would know precious little about where her ashes were being buried. But it was not just about Miranda, it was about a persona; a continuum, about the feelings of those that had known and loved her sister. Strange how as soon as her sister had died so had her own determination to sell Deanstones. The house would remain hers; she would not sell it. And now, with this new link to her dead sister there would be even more reason for her never to part with it.

Helen was worried also about the decision the previous evening to allow Simon to continue without accusation. It was not because she was now an accessory to murder; she accepted that. But she felt very strongly that Simon must be punished as soon as possible for what he had done to Miranda. Perhaps she should not have let Duncan take so much of the responsibility for the decision, but she knew that he was only sticking up for his dead wife's dying wish that The Project should continue.

She wondered about the effect all this was having on her brother-in-law, if that is what Duncan still was. This Starlight thing was very odd. Could she be real, or was she just a figment of Duncan's imagination? She seemed to be acting a bit like an angel, without actually being one. Perhaps a combination of Miranda's death and Simon's duplicity was affecting the balance of Duncan's mind.

She thought about Val and her love for Miranda. It was good to know that her sister had found someone in her life with whom she was able form a lasting emotional bond. It was a bit of a surprise to her that this person had been a woman, but she liked Val and was delighted that her sister had been happy in the relationship. She hoped that Val would want to rent Deanstones. It would make it easy to establish and maintain a friendship with this calm and perceptive psychiatrist who had meant so much to her sister.

Helen came out of her doze to find that Val had wandered in through the house and was standing opposite her and looking at her curiously.

"Sorry, Val, I didn't hear you come."

"You must have been well away," said Val. "I knocked on the front door and just came on through when I didn't get a reply. By the way there is a lot of smoke coming out of that fireplace in the sitting room."

"Oh blast. It's those bloody jackdaws."

Helen jumped to her feet and rushed to do battle with the sitting room fire. She crumpled up some newspaper, set it alight and let the air current take it up the flue. Nothing happened. She did it again with similar effect. The third time there was a sudden crackling and bits of smoking twig started to fall down the chimney. She retreated to the garden and looked up at the chimney. Smoke was billowing out.

"You've got a chimney fire," said Val.

"Not yet, and I hope not at all. Just burning the nests."

Val looked at Helen and smiled. "You've got smudges all over your face, your hair looks like a barn-yard and you have at least one broken finger nail that I can see."

"Not the Helen we all know and love," she replied, "this is the Country Helen. I think you had better come upstairs and see if you can help sort me out."

Val busied herself in the bathroom trying to remove soot from Helen's face with tepid water and some tissues. She asked Helen if she had been enjoying a snooze before her exertions with the fire.

"Yes, sort of," said Helen, trying to get soot off her hands, "but there was a kind of daytime dream going on inside my head. I could imagine that Miranda was speaking to me, telling me things."

"What sort of things?"

"First that she was happy to be remembered here, second that she was sorry to have imposed upon us by wanting us to keep quiet about Simon, and thirdly that she has a lot of faith in Starlight's abilities."

"So that's what you think as well?"

"Yes, it is."

"Will you accept that voice inside your head was in fact your own subconscious breaking through into your conscious thoughts?"

"Val, I really don't know. It did sound very real, she even sent us, you especially, her love."

"But that's just as well explained by your own, very sensitive, imaginings."

"There," said Helen, "Do I look a bit more presentable now?"

"You'll do," said Val.

They made their way downstairs, looked in at the sitting room fire, discovered that it was now behaving as a good fire should, and went out into the garden again. Helen grabbed a spade from the small potting shed.

"Where are you going to put her?" asked Val.

"I'm not sure. When we were young there was a lovely old apple tree just over there. I remember my father rigging up a swing from one of its branches. Miranda and I would play there for ages. It was rooted out years ago, perhaps that would be a good place."

"The apple didn't die from Honey Fungus did it?"

"No, I think it was just old and started to fall apart, why?"

"Damsons are very susceptible to it."

"Oh. Well I think it should be OK," said Helen rather vaguely.

She turned away and pulled up DUNCAN on her iPhone. She was sure that he would like to join them and help plant the Damson. The mobile seemed to ring for very a long time before he answered.

Helen turned back to Val, "Now what about this house, Val, what do you think of it?"

"It's just gorgeous. I love it."

"So how would it fit in with your working life?"

"The garden room would be so good for a Consulting Room. There's direct access off the lonnen and the outside loo is next to it, so the whole setup would be ideal for my clients. The house is probably a bit big for what I need, but it really is so welcoming."

"What about getting to Lancaster?"

"I only need to be in college two, perhaps three days each week. It's less that an hour's drive, or I can get a train from Grange."

"So you would like it?"

"Helen I would love it."

"Just one thing though that may put you off. I'd like to keep a room here for myself so that I can come up here every so often and just chill out, away from city life. Would that be too awful?"

"Helen, it would be lovely."

"So no rent, you just pay the outgoings and look after the place."

"I couldn't accept that. I must pay you."

"Well you're caretaking the house. And instead of rent you can have the most scrumptious meals ready for me whenever I come up here."

"I'd love to do that anyway. But I must sign a proper tenancy so that I can pay you some rent."

There was a ring at the front door.

Without waiting to be invited I let myself into the house.

"We're out here," shouts Helen.

I join them. There is a spade propped up against the outhouse wall. "Where do you want me to dig?' I say.

"I'll do it, "says Helen. She sets about digging a hole about a yard square,, She carefully takes the turf off first laying it to one side, and then heaping the soil onto an old builders' bag that she discovers in the shed. Val and I watch her in some admiration.

"There we are," she says panting slightly after five minutes exertion. "Now if you just take the tree out of its pot, Dunc, and sit it in here." I do as I am bidden. Helen gives the root ball a bit of a knock to loosen it up. She then pulls some of the soil back around the tree until it can just stand without falling over.

"Right. We need the ashes," she says.

Val picks the urn up and hands it to Helen. Helen unscrews the lid and peers a little uncertainly at the contents.

"There's quite a lot of her."

"Yes," I say, considering it best not to mention that there are still some bits of Miranda gracing my garage floor, "and she's quite heavy."

"I'll get some water," I say. There us a watering can conveniently standing next to the shed. I pick it up and sill it from the standpipe, Val takes it from me and soaks the area around the newly planted tree.

"Do we need to say something?" says Helen.

I feel a bit embarrassed and uncertain, 'I think we ought to."

Val comes to the rescue. "There is a piece, she says, by a local poet, I have it here." She fumbles in her coat pocket, eventually finding a rather tatty piece of paper which she unfolds. "I do hope that it is appropriate, for the occasion," she says.

"Go on," says Helen.

Val starts to read:

Remember me in the summer sun, high larks singing,
The rushing beck, the heather-scent, the open moor inviting,
The endless days, the ripening wheat, the bat-studded gloaming,
The hay-time lates, the velvet nights - As a cloud shadow passing.

Remember me in the Autumn mists, sharp game-birds rising,
The web-draped hedge, the cartridge smell, wild wind storming,
The clarty plough, the rain-cold kale, the days-end toweling,
The orchard glut, the harvest-home - As a 'gone away' a' blowing.

Remember me in the snowy lane, the laden boughs drooping,
The crackling lake, the rook-stark trees, the bird-bath-braking,
The beet-mud road, the toasting fork, the lantern-hung caroling,
The warming hearth, the cheering cup - As a Yule Log burning.

Remember me in the bud-burst spring, the leafing and flowering,
The green-tipped field, gamboling lambs, chorus at morning,
Grieve not with saddened heart, the time was mine – for passing,
My life was good, remember me - in each new life that's dawning.

Helen scatters Miranda's ashes around the roots of the Damson and I fill the hole with soil, replacing the turf.

"Val, that was lovely. Where did you find it?"

"It's by a local Cumbrian poet, a great friend of mine called de Gwyneth, I've known him for years. I wasn't sure if it was entirely appropriate in that it is in fact a 'Countryman's Lament' for his much-loved Retriever, rather than an elegy for a neuro-scientist."

"She was a country girl at heart," says Helen, "and it was just what Miranda would have wanted."

"Well done, Val," I say, and really mean it.

"It's all so perfect," says Helen, "this, my parent's home, Miranda returning here, the garden, the damson tree, the ashes, the three of us, Val wanting to live here. The whole thing has got to be an illusion. The reality is totally different. Miranda being killed quite deliberately by that awful Simon, Duncan having to mislead everyone about Miranda dying, people wanting to barge in and grab The Project, the Hospital and the University desperate to save their own skins. That's the Reality."

"Helen," says Val "don't despair. You've described the muddled world that we all live in. But if there was no downside how could we all feel what happiness is?"

"Like stopping hitting your head against a brick wall." I say.

"No, far from it. Have either of you heard of Konrad Lorenz? One of mine really, a psychologist, he was jointly awarded a Nobel Prize for work on animal behaviour. Well he identified a phenomena that he described as Entropy of Feeling."

'What's that," asks Helen.

"Lorenz asks us to imagine that we have climbed and puffed and sweated our way up a mountain. With aching limbs and parched throats we achieve the summit. There before us is the most wonderful view that we have ever seen. We are engulfed in an experience of pure joy.

Now let us say that the mountain in question is Snowdon. The next person to experience exactly the same view has arrived by the summit railway. This second person steps out of the carriage, has a quick look at the same scenery, says 'very nice', takes a photo and wanders off into the café. He has experienced at best a fleeting pleasure – certainly not Joy.

The point is that without struggling to achieve your goal, whatever that might be, there is but limited satisfaction in gaining the end."

"Wow," I say.

"Exactly." says Helen.

She cleans of the spade and puts it away. She turns the heating down again whilst Val and I shut the windows. She checks that the sitting room fire has burned out. Then she shepherds Val and I out into the street and locks the front door.

Twenty Three

We are seated at a scrub table in the cosy pub in Cartmel Square. There is a friendly log fire glowing in the open metal grate bringing a feeling of warmth and welcome to the room. Horse brasses adorn the low beams and a collection of photos of Cartmel in past times hangs from the walls. The slate flag floor is a little uneven so our table, despite its sturdiness, rocks as we lean upon it as if possessed by the spirit of the sea. Helen shoves a couple of beer mats under one table leg, partly curing the problem. Val removes an amiable Westmorland Terrier from the comfortable seat that she then sits on. The dog looks mildly put out, but takes its expulsion in good part and goes wandering off to a neighbouring table in search of food from friendlier humans.

We have ordered a selection of sandwiches and I am now telling Helen and Val about how I once again met Starlight; this time in the Priory.

"Presumably she had some reason for coming?" Helen asks.

"She told me that her main purpose was to warn me off finishing The Project. It upsets me a bit because I thought that she was encouraging me to go on with the work, if for no other reason then as a tribute to Miranda. I told Starlight that I was very keen to finish it, but she seems determined that I should not do so."

"Did she say anything else?" asks Val.

"Yes, we talked quite a lot about angels and about the existence of parallel worlds."

"I see," says Val, "so has she now affected your thinking about The Project?"

"Yes she has a bit. She seemed fairly relaxed about the principle of thought transference between two or more worlds, although she was not keen that the work should explore the science behind that. But where she really threw a wobbly was over any further exploration of the use of thought-energy, especially any attempt to isolate it so that it could be manipulated. She really tried to put me off that."

"I suppose the transference does happen, though," says Helen, "look at Starlight herself."

"I'm not sure but that may well be right. What I don't understand is how Starlight obtains her mass. I'm wondering whether what I see is the real Starlight or some sort of image of her. Much of her form could have materialised as a product of some other process, possibly an energy transfer, or perhaps just imagination."

"Your rather vivid imagination, I presume?" says Val.

"Well yes, I suppose so. Apart from Luigi, and possibly a security man, I know of no one who has seen her beside myself. I'm not sure what would happen if other people were to see her. Would they see the same body-form or would their imagination create a totally different Starlight."

"Possibly," says Val "but that could get very complicated if several people see the same imaginary form in different guises. Mind you people who see angels describe them differently even though they should be seeing the same entity."

"She did say that it was, in very rare cases, possible for thought-energy to move mass between worlds. She was determined that I should not explore that at all. It may well be why she is so set upon persuading me to drop The Project."

"This thought transfer between parallel worlds is in itself interesting," says Val. "There's been some research done in my field on the question of multiple personality disorder and schizophrenia in relation to parallel universes."

"Do you think that this might have some relevance to The Project?" I ask.

Val explains that there is a line of thinking within her profession that accepts parallel universes to be a lot more accessible than might be supposed. It might be possible that whilst our body remains firmly rooted in our own universe our mind has the capacity to jump between different planes of existence. She says that recent neuro-scientific studies into schizophrenia, lucid dreaming and other altered states of awareness indicate that there might be a very ready ability to break through from one universe to another.

"This could apply equally to parallel worlds?" I say.

"I don't see why not."

I ask Val if the studies that she is referring to show an ability for certain people to move almost at will between different planes of existence.

"I don't think that 'at will' is quite correct," says Val. "It would be an involuntary thing rather than a conscious decision."

"So in studying the psyche you'd be looking for some kind of trigger that enables the mind to make such leaps?" asks Helen.

"Again, I'm not sure about the word 'mind'. I rather thing that we would be looking at certain thought processes rather than a highly controlled part of the brain. Certainly there's likely to be some trigger event that sets the whole thing going."

"So what happens when our bodies die? They contain not just our physical presence, but also our mind, our memories, that which makes us unique individuals?" says Helen.

"We're getting in a bit deep here," says Val, "and we're very much in the realm of speculation."

"This," I say "is where most of the main world religions start to talk about our soul. We are looking at the essence of our being. The question is does it have any sustainability once the mind-vehicle has died?"

"What does your Starlight make of this?" asks Helen.

"I'm not sure that she has said anything about it directly. But then she never does seem to say anything in a clear direct manner, she's always using some form of analogy."

"Like a parable," says Val.

"That's perceptive. Yes, just like a parable."

Our soup and sandwiches arrive and we tuck in with gusto. The Westie comes back to enquire if we think we might have been given just a little too much to eat. It gets fairly short shrift.

It seems strangely appropriate; the three of us are sitting here in the twenty-first century discussing philosophical and theological matters that must have been at the very heart of this place over eight hundred years ago. It is interesting to speculate on how far we have come in that time. Although in material terms the change is immense I am beginning to see that philosophy has moved a bit, but theology hardly at all. Even the relatively recent discipline of psychology is only new in terms of the codification of its principles.

"Even in today's society," I say, "Is it not extraordinary that we are still seeking answers so similar to the ones demanded hundreds of years ago. Nowadays we talk about energy and life-force, in those days they would have called exactly the same thing our immortal souls."

"That's right," says Val, "for 'immortal soul' in my language read 'essential me'. But as you say it is the same thing."

"May I join you? That sounds rather in my line."

We look up to find John Sommerville, pint glass in hand, beaming at us.

"Yes of course, Vicar," says Helen. "How very good to see you, this is my friend Val Staples, and Duncan you've already met."

"Oh yes, Duncan and I bumped into each other, quite literally. Good to meet you, Val, I hear that you visited the Priory earlier."

'Yes indeed, it's a truly fascinating place. It's such a mixture of architectural styles and yet it all comes together to form such a beautiful building"

'Bit like the C of E," says John. "Soaks up all sorts of differing views, but comes out looking good in the end. Helen, it is so good to see you here, but did I hear that you are thinking of selling Deanstones?"

"No. I plagued poor Miranda to sell the place, but now that it's my responsibility I really do not want to part with it. The good news, and this is hot of the press, is that Val is going to live there and make it her home."

"Oh, I am pleased," says John, "We need people who are active in the community. There are so many second homes here, and it just tears the heart out of a small village. Now can I join in with this philosophical discussion that I was ear wigging as my pint was being pulled."

"Yes, of course" I say, "we are rather lacking the religious input."

"Then here I am," says John taking a long pull at his beer and then in an absent-minded way helping himself to a ham sandwich from the stack on the table.

"Oh Dear!" he says, waving the once-bitten sandwich in the air, "look what I've done!"

"Typical of the Church" says Helen with a grin, "demanding their tithe."

"Don't listen to her, "I say, "just carry on and help yourself, there's far too much for just the three of us and it will only end up inside a Westmorland Terrier if you don't get stuck in."

"Yes, "says Val harking back to John's original question." We were discussing various aspects of this Project that Duncan is grappling with."

"Where does your Project stand in all this?" asks John.

"It's entirely complimentary to Val's position. I think that we've now more or less accepted that it's possible for thoughts to transfer between our different worlds although quite what the mechanism might be for controlling this is far from clear."

"And your profession Val, considers that under certain circumstances thought can jump between these worlds?" says John.

"It is a position that has fairly recently been taken by some fairly eminent figures in psychology."

"And for my part," says John "the Church would have to stand by its teaching over the centuries that promoted the existence of angels as beings that can cross the divide between this world, heaven and hell. I ought to say however that it's not been part of that doctrine that angels necessarily have mass. They are beings without substance, certainly when they are in this world.

"What's so extraordinary about all this," says Helen, "is that everyone is coming to the same conclusion from different disciplines and totally different standpoints; Duncan as a philosopher, Val as a psychologist and now you, John, from a theological perspective. Perhaps I should put in my pennyworth from a commercial viewpoint. I can see that Virtual Ventures, or whoever they really are, would be incredibly stupid to pass up a chance to exploit these ideas, but it's difficult to see how thought-leaps, to coin a phrase, could be commercially exploited unless you could gain a very high degree of control over when they happened. You would also need control over the individuals they passed between. However the real commercial potential lies in the possibility of the transference of thought-energy into mass and using this to move substance between different worlds."

"This is incredibly dangerous ground," says John. "Duncan, you told me that Bryan Willan warned you against further experimentation in this area. I have to say that from the Church's perspective he was right. By far the best known such manifestation within the Christian religion and that is of Christ himself, who is described as 'God made Flesh'."

"From the psychological point of view I can offer no such example," says Val "but I can certainly see the danger of giving substance to our illusions. We deal with many individuals who have lost touch, at least in part, with reality. To provide a corporeal confirmation of their imaginings would cause chaos. A light-hearted example might be the number of real Napoleons that would be created – and what would happen if two of these materialised fantasies actually met."

The sandwiches, despite my prediction, have all been consumed and we have all but finished the excellent coffee, served in large cups accompanied by small squares of flapjack.

My mobile rings. It is Simon. I listen to what he says and then slip my phone back into my pocket and turn to the others. "I had agreed to meet Simon in the Lab this afternoon, he has arranged for me to meet with him and one of the Principals of the organisation that is interested in taking us over. However knowing that I had intended to travel to Cartmel he has rather conveniently he has arranged for us to meet up near here, at a place on the west side of Windermere."

"I hope you're intending to say 'No'," says Helen.

"I'll listen, and possibly learn, but the answer has to be that I can't sell out."

"Good!" say John, Val and Helen in unison.

We leave John standing in the Square, as honest a man as any parish might hope to enjoy.

Twenty Four

We solve the ensuing logistical nightmare by Val driving us back to Milnthorpe. Helen and I bid her farewell and set of back North again in the Alfa.

"Dunc," says Helen as we make our way up the Lyth Valley, I am not sure if I can keep my cool with Simon. It's one thing dealing with the man when we suspected he might have been closely involved in Miranda's death. It's quite another being civil to him with the absolute knowledge that he killed her."

"That is exactly how I feel," I say. "But we really do owe it to Miranda to treat him just as she did. We'll have to let these people have their say but whatever happens to The Project I'm damned if I'll let Simon have any part of it."

Simon has chosen a strange spot for a meeting. We cross Windermere on the ferry and then pull into the first car park we come to on the Claife shore.

"Where on earth is this?" says Helen.

"You can stay here if you want to. It's a bit of a climb to get to the Station."

"Station? Dunc, what the hell are you talking about?"

"Not a rail station, a Viewing Station. In the eighteenth century it became the vogue for specific locations to be identified as prime viewpoints. At some of these places buildings were erected, the better for the discerning to 'take the view'. Most had large windows which made for easy viewing through a Claude Glass."

"Dunc, you are talking in riddles"

This is hardly the moment to bring my sister-in-law up to speed on the eccentricities of the picturesque movement. I simply explain that a Claude Glass was a tinted mirror that was used to provide a particular effect upon the observation of landscape.

"But surely that would mean turning your back on what you wanted to look at?"

I shrug my shoulders. To do otherwise would have taken us into a philosophical discussion about perception.

"I think I'd better come and have a look at this place," says Helen.

"Oh good, I'm pleased. I may well need your support."

We make our way up a steep path that joins a much wider track. It rises steeply from the valley bottom and is easily wide enough for the two of us to walk side by side. Every so often we pass large rocks with holes bored in them.

"For torches." I explain.

Helen looks at me blankly.

"So that guests would have the way lit for them when they came up here for a party," I say.

"Hmm, more like Acid House I would say." My sister-in-law is a child of the eighties.

Claife Station has been re-roofed since I last visited it. It is a tall stone building about the size of a decent, detached house perched on a wooded crag overlooking the lake. There is an aura of faded grandeur about it. There are two floors, the lower one being rather squashed in comparison with the height of the upper one. As we approach the door is opened by a large man in a rather ill-fitting chauffer's uniform.

"You are expected," he says, "follow me."

There is a kitchen on the ground floor, and some sort of storage space. It all looks rather cold and unused. We do not pause here; instead we mount a short stone staircase to the main viewing area. The room is hexagonal in plan. There are three enormous windows on adjacent walls, the view from two of them partially obscured by tall trees. On the centre wall of the other three there is a fireplace providing welcoming warmth from a large log fire.

Simon is standing next to a hefty oak table talking to a well-built fit looking man. He seems a little surprised to see Helen. "Hi, Dunc, glad you managed to find your way up here."

"Been before, quite a bit ago."

"May I introduce James O'Connell."

The man moves forward and takes my hand in a firmly, perhaps rather over firmly, and squeezes hard. I manage not to wince.

"And my sister-in-law, Helen Marston," I say.

O'Connell approaches Helen, takes her hand and in an old-worldly gesture kisses it "Ah yes. Sister of the late Miranda Marston I presume?"

He does not wait for an answer but turns in the direction of the man in the chauffeur's uniform "Be sure that we are not disturbed, Joe."

Chauffer-man slides out the door leaving the four of us standing slightly awkwardly around the table.

O'Connell motions to us to sit, pulling a chair out from the table for Helen in a rather over-extravagant manner. "Forgive the rather crude surroundings," he says. "We are well met here and I am delighted to welcome you both. I do hope that this will be the start of a long and fruitful relationship."

"We are here to listen," say I, "not to commit ourselves to anything."

"Just so. Perhaps it will be best therefor if Simon were to start our little discussion."

Simon thanks Helen and myself for coming and says that he thought it was very helpful to have O'Connell with us as he will be in a much better position to provide the answers to several areas of questioning that I might wish to pursue.

"It really is time to come to a decision now, Dunc," says Simon, "when we last had a chat about the idea of introducing new capital and owners into The Project you said that you needed a little bit if time to think about it, so I do hope that you have come to the right conclusion. How do you stand now?"

I look around this room. The firelight casts moving images across the two adjacent window-less walls. There is little furniture besides our table and chairs. Outside, through the three great windows, the afternoon light is just starting to fade.

O'Connell has noted my lack of attention to Simon's question and seems to have been following my train of thought. "It's a truly magnificent vista is it not?"

"One of a series of such eighteenth-century viewpoints."

"I rather think that those of artistic temperament had the energy to work hard for their pleasures in those days, Professor Fielding. They were keen to foster an interest in the picturesque."

"They had the money and the time. Speaking of which I'm pleased to see this spot restored to something like its original state. It was a ruin for too long."

"Come over to the widows," says O'Connell.

We both get up from the table and move over to look out on the three different aspects of Windermere. The man has the air of a very select tourist guide as he stands just slightly behind me almost whispering into my ear.

"Consider these windows as our three worlds, Professor Fielding. This central one is of clear glass giving an unaltered view of the real world, our world, as it now is."

He subtly guides me over to the right-hand window and turns me so that I face into the room with my back to the view. He reaches out to a recess in the wall and produces a rectangular mirror which he holds up in front of us."

"A Claude Glass," I say. How quaint that there should be one here, how apposite."

"If you would care to perceive," he says.

I look into his mirror and see the vista behind me, but instead of a neutral view I see that the mirror has been cleverly designed so that it provides a red-tinted version of the aspect from the window.

O'Connell's mouth twitches, almost a smile. He guides me quietly over to the left -hand window and repeats the exercise, but this time the view is tinted blue.

"My apologies. Professor, we should not have had to resort to mirrors to create our illusion. We should have arranged for glass of different colours to be installed in the widows, just as it was when this station was built. We do not own this place and we did not know that we would be in a position to invite you here until earlier today, so we have had to make do with Mr Claude's invention."

"I appreciate the trouble you have gone to. May I ask the reason for it?"

"Oh, Professor Fielding, a thousand apologies, I thought you understood."

What is this man up to? I thought we were going to have a rather negative discussion about selling out The Project. Instead we are playing with the toys of eighteenth-century aesthetes.

O'Connell is still speaking. "The middle window represents our present world, the one we're all in at this present time. The view is clear and straightforward and entirely as expected. The window for which we created an illusion of red is a different world, a world perhaps viewed through rose-tinted spectacles we could say. Some people might refer to that world as heaven."

"And of course the illusory blue-tinted world is that which might be thought of as hell."

"Exactly. The reason for building this viewing station is so we stand in one place and gain three different perspectives of exactly the same view."

"And that of course has relevance to The Project."

"Indeed it does; in an allegorical sense. We can stand at the threshold of three worlds that have a basic similarity of form, but which we know exhibit totally different attributes."

"That is clear. But you seem almost more familiar with the concept of these worlds than I am, or Miranda was."

"That is not the case," says O'Connell, "It is you who are the expert, however it is right to look beyond the present boundaries of your Project and consider the implications of your work in the future."

He guides me back to the table and crosses towards the fireplace. He motions to Simon who places four large glasses on the table. O'Connell retrieves a jug from an alcove by the fire and pours a measure of an aromatic amber liquid into each glass. "Mulled wine," he says. "A toast to the picturesque movement and the eighteenth century."

We all raise our glasses, toast and drink.

"Now, Duncan," says Simon, "what about it. Are you happy now that you can see what good hands Miranda's project will rest in?"

"What about you, Simon, what do you think I should do?"

I already know what his answer will be, but I need to hear it directly from the man himself. As expected Simon tells me that he thinks that the offer is really interesting. Quite apart from Simon's close relationship with O'Connell I am well aware that he always has his eyes open for the main chance and probably sees that there's a once in a lifetime opportunity in it for him.

"I would be really keen to go for it, Dunc. It would be the very best opportunity to not only tie up the Paper, but also to continue with the research. I am sure that is what Miranda would have wanted. As you will have deduced the resources that James O'Connell can bring to the practical application of The Project are almost unlimited."

"I'm not so certain." I turn towards O'Connell, "I know next to nothing about you, who you are and who you may represent. You must appreciate that I could not possibly consider you as a suitable candidate or organisation without a great deal more information about you. I mean have you worked in this field before, I have never heard of you, and what other research projects are you involved with."

O'Connell says "I can understand the reason for your questions, but just for now I would prefer not to go into any detail in answering them. We will be working through a company that we have created called Virtual Ventures. It is probably best to consider this organisation as a business angel. It has no scientific expertise as is only concerned with the funding, and of course the outcome, of The Project. It is the intermediary between you and my organisation."

"And who might you be?"

"That I am not at liberty to reveal. I can assure you however that we are a very well-placed organisation, entirely UK based and with the very best interests of this, our country, at heart. Indeed it is for this reason that we wish to subscribe to this Project of yours."

I am far from satisfied with this lack of concrete information. Why should a large British organisation not contact me directly rather than work through an intermediary? Miranda would have been concerned to ensure that anyone financing The Project should be doing so in the interests of scientific research. These people are neither involved nor interested in the science, so what is their interest. O'Connell had said something about ' the very best interests of our country', hmmm I wonder if that is worth following up on.

"If you cannot, or will not, tell me who you represent perhaps you could just flesh out the reasons for your interest in this Project. You seem to be prepared to go to an awful lot of trouble to achieve ownership of our work. Why?"

"Perhaps you will excuse us for a moment?"

O'Connell takes Simon by the arm and walks him over towards the 'blue' window talking in a low voice. They have a short discussion and return to the table.

Simon speaks, "James and I both understand your curiosity. He has explained that he cannot reveal the name or nature of the people that we work for, but he thinks it might be appropriate if I explained a little about the reason why his people are keen to become involved with you."

Simon has suddenly, it seems to me, become one of 'them'. He is no longer a junior colleague of mine, but is clearly now reporting to O'Connell. He has taken the silver penny.

"Dunc, we both know that if this Project succeeds, and there is every indication that it will, then the potential that it opens up is enormous."

I look a little blank. I must be too much the academic, but I cannot see that the proving of an interesting hypothesis about thought-energy and parallel worlds is going to be anything more than an interesting scientific accomplishment.

"Don't you see?" Continues Simon, "we will be opening up a whole new era for mankind. We will not be physically restrained to one place or one time, we will be able to influence events, thoughts, actions of other people in real time?"

"You mean it might be used as some sort of mind-weapon?" I say.

"Of course. There will be foreign governments and criminal organizations that will be desperate to have access to the practical implications of our work."

I begin to see why Simon and O'Connell are so keen to become part of all this. But if it is as important as they are convincing me that it is then surely it should not be the sole property of one organisation, or one government. I know I am a hopeless academic, but to my mind it should be shared by anyone in the world who wants to use it. But Simon has opened up a train of thought about who O'Connell represents.

"O'Connell, am I to assume, from what Simon has told us, that you represent the British Government?"

"Simon has said no such thing. It would be wrong of you to assume anything. As I explained I am not at liberty to reveal my exact position in this matter."

"Let's get back to business," says Simon. "These people are offering you a great deal of money, massive support and political acceptability, what more could we wish for?"

Miranda had nurtured The Project in our scruffy little Lab back at Lancaster. She had worked there in far from ideal conditions for many arduous hours. The place is a bit shabby, it is small, it is dingy, there is very little equipment, and what there is had been acquired second-hand. In the early days Miranda scoured laboratories throughout the country begging and borrowing the bits of equipment that might be needed. Yet, despite these handicaps, perhaps even because of them, she came within a whisker of proving that the mass that comprises dark matter sustains at least two parallel worlds. She was poised on the very edge of making an even more crucial breakthrough, proving that it was possible to use thought-energy to access these worlds. If only she was still with me, instead of Simon, the thing would be just about wrapped up by now.

I would be betraying all this if I were to agree to the offer that is being put to me. I have got to do my best to keep The Project out of the hands of these people who, even if they are the Government, will use it entirely for their own ends and not for 'the good of mankind'.

However if we do not get funding, or if I lose Simon at this stage, it will leave me with an enormous amount of work to do, some of which is way outside my field of expertise. Would I be able to bring to a conclusion all that I started with Miranda? Am I capable of finding the right people to finish the experimentation phase? I think so, but it would take more time and I would need to employ at least two postgraduates. But yes, if it comes to it, I can probably afford to let Simon go and The Project will still carry on.

The other thing of course is how Simon would fare with The Project if he takes his, slightly sketchy, knowledge of it to these people of his. How would he manage, not as part of the University but with a privately funded piece of research? With the money and personnel that they would seem able to resource he might just make a go of it. After all he has access to nearly all of Miranda's notes.

"Gentlemen, I would like to thank you both for the immensely generous offer that you have made me, but I really think I should not sell out."

Simon looks across at Helen. It is clearly worrying him that she has come with me, there does not seem to be much reason for it. I tell him that Helen and I were visiting Cartmel together. Simon looks as if he might be satisfied with that.

"Helen, you could help us a bit," says Simon, "we seem to have reached a bit of a sticking point. You are a woman of the world. Perhaps you can persuade Duncan to our way of thinking?"

Simon tells her that he is keen that I should accept the offer. It would mean much better facilities, almost unlimited funding and a great opportunity for us to really make our names with it. Indeed there might even be the possibility of a Nobel Prize.

I tell Helen that I am uneasy about the whole idea and would much prefer to stay with the University and finish the work that Miranda had started.

Helen is a shrewd and experienced businesswoman. She understands people who are motivated by money but also recognises risk. Her role now though is to give as much support as she can to the wishes of the dying Miranda. Miranda wanted The Project to continue, and wanted it to be part of the University. "I can see why you want Dunc to do this Simon, in that it would give The Project a chance that it just won't get at the University, either now or in the future. On the whole though I have to say that I agree with Duncan. If your real motivation is the successful conclusion of this research, and if it can be done at Lancaster, albeit a little more laboriously, then I would suggest that you stay there. And, Simon, surely it is the quality of the work that makes for a Nobel nomination."

"Look here, Helen," says Simon, "I really can't go along with that. You simply haven't given enough credence to the technological side of developing this project further. That can't be done with the present resources of the University, the initial investment required would be immense, and frankly we should be very thankful to James and his people in that they that can provide all that we need."

I know full well that Simon has been hooked by the people who are making this proposal, indeed this was obvious from the moment Helen had shown Val and me that tape. I am very concerned about dealing with O'Connell, even if he is part of HMG. I remember Starlight warning me to keep clear. Helen came to the same conclusion from a very different set of criteria. I am also all too aware as to how utterly ruthless they can be. In any case it is all I can do to be civil to Simon. It is Simon who was responsible for killing Miranda, and I am certainly not going to work with him any more than I have to. If Simon leaves The Project now it would be set back by many months and mean a lot more work for me, but really that might be the best possible outcome.

"Simon, I can quite see why you find this offer very tempting; however my loyalty lies to the faculty and to the work that Miranda and I started some two years ago. Whilst it would be wonderful to have the facilities that are being offered I have decided that this Project will remain at Lancaster and with the University."

"Dunc, I think you might be making a decision that you will very much regret."

Is there just the slightest hint of a threat in the way Simon says those words? I begin to feel distinctly uneasy. "We'll continue as we are," I say.

I sense that Helen is becoming frustrated. She has done her best to persuade Simon that we should stay with the University but clearly to no avail. Simon is looking sulky, but conversely it seems that O'Connell has not seen my decision as that much of a setback.

"Professor Fielding," says O'Connell, "I wonder if you have had sufficient time to consider our very generous offer. Perhaps you owe it to The Project, and of course to your late wife, to give this offer a bit more time, a little more consideration."

This was the man who plotted Miranda's death. "No." I say, "I'm quite clear about the situation. The project stays with Lancaster."

"We can can be very persuasive," says Simon.

Helen has been suspiciously quiet for some time. "Simon," she says, "Where were you on Monday?"

The change of tack takes everyone by surprise.

Simon recovers quickly, and after a moment says "At Lancaster, on campus. Had a lot of stuff to catch up on so I was incarcerated in my room most of the day, if I remember correctly."

"I don't think that you do. Perhaps you would like to try again."

Simon glances away from Helen. He is not telling the truth and looks decidedly furtive. "What is it to you anyway?"

"I know exactly where you were. And it most certainly was not in Lancaster."

This is alarming. Why the hell is Helen doing this? Perhaps she is trying to put some pressure on Simon so that she can play him off against O'Connell. It is a risky game and I am far from happy about it. Presumably she is intending to show Simon, and possibly O'Connell, that she has damning evidence against them.

"So are you going to admit it?" she says.

"Admit what exactly."

"That you were in London on Monday"

"Really, Helen, you forget yourself," says Simon. "Whether I was in London or Timbuktu on Monday, or any other day, is really of no concern of yours whatsoever."

"But if it involves this offer that you have been pressing upon my brother-in-law then it certainly does."

"Again Helen, this is none of your business."

I look sadly at this man that had once been my friend. "Bit of a parting of the ways, Simon" I say, "I am sorry that it had to come to this. I am grateful for your trouble, and to you Mr. O'Connell, for the offer. I would wish you well in the future, but fear we must leave it at that."

"I do not think that the time is entirely propitious for you to be thinking of leaving us," says O'Connell. He jingles a small skivvy bell.

"I do not mean to be rude," I say, "but I think that we are done here."

Joe enters the room. O'Connell signals to him to stay by the door.

"Now," says O'Connell to Helen, "what is all this about Simon not being in Lancaster on Monday?"

"Oh, I might have been mistaken, I just thought I saw him. Sorry, my stupid fault."

"Where were you that day, Miss Marston?"

"At my office, in London."

I doubt whether this information will help her much, by admitting that she was in London she is saying that she must have seen Simon there.

"So where is this office?"

"In the West End"

"Don't play games with me, Miss Marston. Whereabouts in the West End?"

"Near Harley Street." Do I sense that O'Connell relaxes slightly?

"And you work for yourself?"

"Yes, my partner Reinout Schmidt and I run a small business."

"May I ask as to what you do?"

"Oh, it's a sort of service business, doing photocopying and internet hosting for other companies," she says.

O'Connell does not seem at all convinced. He is calling up a number on his phone. "Julia? Yes, it is I. You know that office suite that you booked for us the other day; can you tell me from whom we leased it?"

There is a pause, then some words that I do not catch.

"You're sure of that," says O'Connell, "Who did you deal with?" More words.

"It wasn't a Helen Marston?"

O'Connell's phone crackles with the noise of someone speaking.

"I see, I thought so. Thank you, Julia, that is all I need."

O'Connell kills the call with great deliberation. He says nothing for a while.

"You own a company called 'Rooms for Business'. It is a statement. "You have offices that you let out in Queen Anne's Gate." Another statement. "So how did you know that Simon was there?"

"I really don't know what you are talking about," says Helen.

"Nonsense. Now you must have some sort of surveillance. Are all your rooms bugged?"

"I run a respectable and respected company. Yes, I do run Rooms For Business, and we do indeed lease office space near St James' Park tube station. Of course the place is not bugged, that is a ridiculous idea, we just have a security camera to ensure the safety of our clients, and that is how I knew that Simon was there."

"Why should I believe that?"

"Because it is the truth."

"Who else did you see?"

Clearly Helen did not want to say anything, she is damned if she says she saw O'Connell, equally she will be seen to be lying if she says that she did not.

I decide to intervene. "Look, I don't know what your problem is but clearly this is a case of mistaken identity. If Simon was in Lancaster then it cannot possibly be him that Helen saw on the video."

O'Connell rises to his feet. He seems to have grown bigger. "Quiet, Professor."

Helen picks up the cue from me, "I have no idea what this meeting was all about. If Simon says that he was not in London that day then obviously it could not have been him that I saw."

"So where is the camera?" asks Simon

"Oh. In the lobby area," says Helen.

"So you thought you recognised me, even with my hat on did you?"

"Well I thought so, yes, but probably just because of your red hair. Obviously I was mistaken."

"Liar. I was not wearing a hat. Your camera must be in the boardroom, and no doubt there is sound recording as well."

"We do not have voice monitoring."

"I don't believe you"

"I have no idea what this is all about. Whatever it is let's just forget about all this nonsense and behave like reasonable adults. Duncan and I are due back in Lancaster this evening."

She had played it as well as she could, but had been caught out in a very amateurish way by that business with the hat. I am not sure if either Simon or O'Connell believe her about the sound monitor. I can sense that Simon is uncertain, but O'Connell is not so gullible. The trouble is that it is going to be impossible for Helen to prove that she had not heard everything that the three men had been talking about. The audio surveillance has put her in a very vulnerable position, especially as both men realise that she is bound to have accessed it.

"Helen," says Simon, "will you give me your word that you have no idea of what we were discussing in your boardroom?"

"Yes, of course. I really don't want to know what goes on in relation to the running of my clients' businesses. I have enough hassle in looking after my own."

"You know that I was there." Says O'Connell.

Helen decides it is best to play it straight. "Yes."

"Who was the third person besides Dr Pennick and myself?"

"Someone called Strickland."

"How do you know his name?"

Helen realises her mistake as soon as the words leave her lips.

"I recognised him of course," she says in a desperate attempt to pretend that she had not heard mention of Strickland's name on the recording.

O'Connell catches Joe's eye and nods. 'Most unfortunate," he says, "such a pity." He turns to his back on us, and stares into the fire.

Simon gets up as if to approach Helen.

Joe grunts, "Mine now, Boss."

"Really, Joe," says Simon, "I am not sure . . ."

"Leave it Boss. It's mine."

Joe, moving quietly for so large a man, is beside Helen. He walks her to the far wall. She cannot see the gun in his right hand.

"No." I cry as the weapon is raised to her temple. I make to rush forward. There is a blinding flash followed by complete blackness.

Twenty Five

Slowly the world is coming back to me. I have no idea how long I have been lying here. I am partially numb with the cold that has taken up residence in every limb. My head hurts like hell. Jeez what a mess! I stagger to my feet and run my left hand uncertainly up to the side of my head. It feels wet and sticky. I look at the hand and can just make out that it is covered with something dark. Blood!

Oh hell! This is not what happens to me. I start to shake.

It is all coming back to me now. I have a snapshot memory of Joe quietly holding Helen by the arm; the raised gun; the explosion. Helen is dead. She was as good as dead before I tried to intervene, and I was too late.

Christ my head hurts. Where am I? Why did they leave me? Did they think that I was dead as well? Surely I can only be a danger to them alive. I really cannot figure out what is going on, and my head is throbbing with pain. There is no way that I can cope with all this by myself.

There is just the faintest trace of light, a minuscule red glow. It is the remains of the log fire. I am still at Claife Station. I must get out of here and find my way back to the car. I fumble my way to the stairs. In the kitchen I find a box of matches. There is no one here. Striking a series of matches I climb back up the stairs. The room is deserted. Whatever they have done with Helen's body they have not left it here.

I am downstairs again, and out into the darkness of the night. I bash and crash down the path through trees. The soggy snow rubs off the branches as I push through them depositing itself down my neck and up from my wrists. My feet are just cold wet lumps. More than once I fall to my knees and the cold melt-water runs down my shins.

I miss the small track down to the car park and end up by the lake. I am getting colder, exhausted, numbed. My head has stopped bleeding but it goes on throbbing. I make it to the main road and stagger up along it for a couple of hundred metres. The Alfa is where I left it.

I collapse into the car.

I start the engine and twist the heater control up to full red. I keep my foot gently depressing the throttle so that the engine warms up more quickly. It takes an age for hot water to get through to the heater, but at last warmth begins to flood into the cockpit and envelop my chilled body. I close my eyes and let the heat seep into my bones. Slowly the numbness leaves me but with its departure come stabs of pain from hands and legs. I try to inspect the wound to my head, but fail. I just cannot see enough in the driving mirror. It will have to wait.

As warmth returns to my body my brain starts to re-engage with those last moments up at the Station. I cannot see what they could have done with her body and I certainly cannot understand why they left me there, alive.

My mobile is ringing.

Helen was sitting comfortably on an intercity train heading south. She was pleased, but not surprised, to find that she was travelling First Class. She was warm and comfortable. She did not have the foggiest idea of how she came to be there. She could not recollect boarding the train at Oxenholme and yet her ticket said Oxenholme to Euston. Oh well she supposed she must have been under a bit of strain recently, anyway she would be back home in less than four hours.

Opposite her sat the only other occupant of that end of the carriage, a pleasant looking young lady with rather spiky blonde hair who smiled at her in a friendly way. "Feeling better?" She said.

"To tell you the truth I'm feeling a bit odd," said Helen.

Her memory was becoming slightly less fuzzy. She recalled climbing with Duncan up to that strange building in the woods. They had met some people there. That was right, Simon and a man called O'Connell. What then swept over her was a sudden and overwhelming anger with Simon. This man had killed her sister.

"Something happened to me. There were these men, one of them was called Simon; they wouldn't let us leave." She was getting the facts in order now "There was someone called Joe. He had been told to kill me. He was about to do so. Then something happened. I have no idea what it was."

She looked really startled by what she had said, "He was going to shoot me, honestly."

Why was she saying all this to a total stranger? She looked more closely at the girl. Perhaps she was not so young as she appeared to be. She seemed very calm, very self-assured.

"I know," said the girl, "Probably best not to think about it too much."

"I need to find Duncan, he's my brother-in-law. He's still up there with those men and may be in terrible danger. I think he's been hurt."

"Duncan's OK," said the girl.

"You know him."

"He knows me."

Helen's thoughts were starting to become clearer. "I know you," she said, "or rather I know of you. You must be the girl that he calls Starlight."

"Just so."

"He's told me about you. I think he rather fancies you."

Starlight smiled and Helen immediately realized how attractive she was when her vivacity showed through. "I dare say he does, but that's not the point."

"Did you save me?"

"It was best that you did not stay there."

Helen was sure about that. Mind you she would have liked to have put an end to Simon. She was very worried about Duncan, despite the assurances of this girl called Starlight.

"Yes, you are of course right. They decided to kill me you know."

"You put yourself into the very greatest danger."

Helen thought about that for a bit. "I suppose I did. That was probably very stupid of me. You know the awful thing is that I could now cheerfully kill them."

"Taking lives is not good," said the girl, "Believe me, I know."

Helen wondered what she meant by that. Was she just emphasizing a point of moral philosophy, or could she mean that she had personal experience of not taking, or taking, lives?

"I think I need to thank you," said Helen. "It sounds a bit odd, but I think you must have saved my life."

"You're welcome."

"You did save me?"

"The important thing is that you are here now, and that you have done the very best for your dead sister."

"I suppose you're right," said Helen, "but I hate the idea of those scumbags getting away with murder. If I come across any of them again I may well end up in a prison cell."

'No," said Starlight. "It really is an awful thing to take a life, and in practical terms you're unlikely to get away with it."

"I suppose you are right. But they have got away with killing Miranda. Is there nothing that I can do about punishing them for that?"

'Just leave it all with me. They will not trouble you again. Now I must be getting off at Lancaster. Oh, and I rescued the bag that you left it in the Alfa. I would suggest that you phone Duncan as soon as you can and tell him that you are fine, he will be worried about you."

"Where are you going?"

"Job to do. Nice meeting you, bye."

'Thanks" said Helen to the back of the departing girl.

As the train started to draw out of Lancaster Helen reached for her iPhone.

The Alfa is still in the car park. My phone is ringing. I pick it up and look at the screen. Helen!

"Helen, is it you? Oh, thank God! Where are you?"

"Duncan, I'm just fine. It's O.K. I'm on the train."

"What train? Where? What happened to you, I thought you must be dead."

"Duncan, it really is O.K. Something strange happened and I found myself on this train to London with your girl, Starlight. I think she saved my life. I asked her what had happened but she never quite gives a straight answer to a question. The important thing is that you are OK as well."

"Starlight? You've met her? So she cannot be an idea in my head. How did she rescue you?"

"I think she changes time or place and moves things around a bit. She couldn't have physically carried me here, she is only a slip of a thing, but there is something a bit 'out of this world' about her.

I think that she can do things that seem impossible to us. Duncan where are you, are you all right? What happened to you?"

"They must have just left me at the Viewing Station. I have had a bit of a knock on my head, but otherwise I'm fine. Just a bit wet and cold."

Where are you?"

"I'm still in the car park."

"You had better get back home. I'll give you a ring there once I make it back to Islington"

"Helen, do look after yourself. Bye."

With a good deal more restraint than was usual for me I quietly drive the car out of the car park and head south towards home. To my surprise I find myself to be shaking slightly as I join the M6 and take to the slow lane with about as much élan as a wayward dustcart.

So Starlight saved Helen from that Joe and the other two. She seems to have the ability to turn up at rather disjointed moments, but just when she can say the right thing or, as in this case, physically intervene at a point when she is most needed.

Thinking about Starlight leads me to wonder again about her attending my lecture. She clearly was not a student, so how did she know that it was happening. Also she seemed pretty clued up about the subject. Then, when we met again later in the day, this girl went on to have a serious discussion with me about Dada – not just the movement, but the change in artistic thinking that it inspired. She used Magritte's 'La Magie Noir' as an exemplar. Could this surrealistic image relate in any way to the metaphysical status of Starlight?

Helen had this brief encounter with Starlight. Helen is the only person other than me who has spent time talking to the girl. That confirms Starlight's physical presence, but Helen's undoubted rescue points towards Starlight being more than just flesh and blood. But then all humans are that, we can deal with abstract thoughts. It is just that Starlight seems to be able to take it further than an ordinary human. Clearly there are close connections between what this girl is capable of and the work on thought-energy that Miranda and I were exploring.

So deep is my train of thought that the Alfa positively crawls into the depths of its garage. It has never before been treated thus. If a car could have felt anything that Alfa Spider would have felt indignant. Why bother to own a decent car, admittedly a bit temperamental and Italian, but none the worse for that, and then drive it as if it were no more exotic than a dilapidated wheelbarrow?

I make my way into the house, hang my jacket in the back lobby, and walk rather slowly to the living room. I am still feeling cold despite the warmth in the car and I continue to shiver slightly. There is a fire laid in the grate and I put a match to the firelighter. Perhaps it will warm me up a bit, I still seem to be having a bit of a reaction to the events of the early evening. For the first time for many weeks I do not turn the on the television as I collapse into my comforting armchair.

Three men sit quietly inside the large black car. The one in front wears a chauffeur's uniform. The other two sit in the back. The car's engine is running, perhaps to keep the heater working on this cold December night. They seem, at least initially, to be in something of a doze and it takes some time for them to emerge from that state, and to realize that they are on water. To be more precise they are on the car ferry that pulls itself across Windermere on cables. The car is the centre of the three marked lanes, just a bit back from the lifting barrier. There are no other cars and the only noise apart from the muted sound of the large engine is the whirring of the diesel that is pulling The Mallard across the calm night waters.

The snow stopped an hour or more ago and has been replaced by a wonderful clear night. There is a full moon and very little cloud. If any of these men were interested in looking to the north they would see, in the bright moonlight, the snow-clad fells at the head of the lake. It is a scene of beauty, serenity and enchantment that would be wasted on those individuals. Above the shore to which they are heading, the eastern side of the lake, there are a myriad of pinpricks, the lights of many houses. Behind, on the far less populated western shore, there are only one or two such lights, denoting an isolated farm or cottage on the steeply wooded Claife shore.

If they are puzzled to find themselves thus transported they do not give any outward sign of so being. The last that any of them will have remembered is that they were in Claife Station, high up on the Western slope. They will have realized that they left both Helen and Duncan behind, and they will be puzzled as to what had occurred at the moment when Joe made to kill Helen and Simon hit Duncan over the head. They should be worried, either they have left behind two dead bodies which might easily be traced, forensically, to them; or worse they might have left two seriously injured people who could definitely implicate the three of them.

It would be difficult for an outside observer to make out if these men are thinking about anything at all, there certainly does not seem to be much in the way of conversation going on between them. Perhaps they are reflecting individually upon the worthlessness of their lives, the suffering that they have heaped upon others, the foul deeds, great and small that they have perpetrated. It is doubtful if that is the case. Remorse does not come easily to hardened hearts, and the hearts of these men are as iron.

About half way across the lake the sound of the ferry's engine alters as the motor slows down. The cables that hitherto were pulling tautly out of the water ahead of the craft start to sag as the strain on them reduces. The gentle lap of water under the access ramp settles to quiet murmur and then subsides into silence.

The twin barriers in front of the Mercedes start to rise silently, impelled by their small hydraulic rams. There is now nothing ahead of the car except the black, icy water. Imperceptibly at first, then slowly gathering its own momentum the Mercedes starts to roll very gently forwards. The man in the driving seat, wearing an ill-fitting chauffeur's uniform, appears to spring into action, presumably becoming aware of the danger that he is in. He could be seen grabbing at the handbrake and stamping his feet down hard as if attempting to push pedals through metal. He appears to fumble at the ignition, tearing his fingernails as he grapples to extract the keys. The Merc's engine continues to run and the car maintains its very slow but steady forward progress.

One of the two men in the rear, the slightly rotund, red headed, one, makes an effort to help by forcing himself over the top of the front passenger seat and yanking at the handbrake; wrenching it upwards, to no avail. The other man, better built and fit looking, adds his efforts. The handbrake is wrenched from its bracket. This car is not going to be stopped. The men, almost as one, abandon their attempts to halt the car and scrabble for their respective door handles, wrenching at them with desperate energy

No doors open.

The engine continues to purr gently.

The car maintains its remorseless forward roll, perhaps picking up speed very slightly.

The men can now be seen to be smashing at the windows with their shoes in a futile effort to release themselves from their prison. Their fate is written in the fearful expressions on their faces.

The car starts to tip as the front wheels rotate in clear air, the underbody of the car scraping along the edge of the ferry ramp as the rear wheels continue to push it ever onwards out into the lake.

If any of these three men were in a state to do so they might have looked back over their shoulders at the control cabin above and to the right of the car deck. They would perhaps see, silhouetted against the full round moon, a youngish looking female figure with spiky hair. She has a fixed expression and her sad deep blue eyes never waver.

After a while the ripples on the surface of the lake subside, the barriers return to their horizontal position, the drive motor of the boat accelerates to its optimum speed and the ferry continues on its journey to the eastern shore.

Helen was surprised to find no lights on in the house at Bewdley Street. It was after eleven thirty when she paid off the taxi outside her front door. Surely George had not gone to bed this early?

She hung up her coat, dropped her bag at the foot of the stairs and walked into the sitting room. There was a small envelope addressed to her lying on the coffee table. Helen picked it up.

My dear Helen,

Our Continental cousins have sprung back to life. They have confirmed, in a manner that does not quite conform to the Queen's English, that the job in Paris is now mine. I am inclined to agree with them that I am by far the best person for it and so have little choice but to follow this particular star. You can rest assured that I will be doing everything in my power to return this wayward land to its rightful place – under the auspices of the true descendant of Eleanor of Aquitaine.

My vision for our future relies heavily upon the Chunnel and your eagerness to imbibe the occasional glass of the vine water with me in The Marais. Marriage seems a trifle superfluous to this vision.

You have a very nasty habit of becoming enraged with me at the smallest trifle, such as the breaking of an engagement, so I thought it best to remove my wonderful body and various accoutrements from your presence. I will of course be at your service just as soon as your return to equanimity permits. Further immediate discourse between us would no doubt lead to things physically hurtful. On reflection I think you will agree that we really wouldn't have done marriage very well.

Yours as ever,

George.

"The dirty stinking testosterone-infected scumbag of a rat," said Helen by way of mild reproof.

Twenty Six

There is something going on in the room. I am dimly aware that I can hear semi-familiar sounds. I open one of my eyes with considerable reluctance. I am tired, my head aches and see no reason as to why I should be disturbed.

Things are not as they should be. A person is silhouetted against a glow of firelight. Someone is making up the fire, turning the logs, adding some more, bringing it back to life. There is no light in the room other than from this source.

Starlight turns to me, "That's better," she says.

It is not that I realistically expected her to return to my house, but her presence is not a surprise. She said back at the Priory that she wanted to explain more about herself. I open both eyes. I am almost wide-awake. What does surprise me is how pleased I am to see her.

"I suppose you just let yourself in?"

"Yes."

"And you are staying for a bit?"

"That depends."

"Depends upon what?"

"How long it's necessary for me to stay with you."

Just for a moment I am tempted to suggest that she should stay forever, but I know that pleased as I am to have her with me at the moment there can be no question of such a long-term arrangement.

The room is becoming brighter now as the logs start to flare up. I can make out the familiar furniture, an amalgam of Miranda's good taste and some pieces that we inherited from distant relatives or could not quite bring ourselves to junk from long-forgotten student lodgings. It is a large room by modern standards, almost square and with a high ceiling. There are some pleasing reproductions on the walls and just a couple of originals by local artists. The far side of the room is shelved out in the manner of a library so that almost the whole wall presents a solid phalanx of books.

I move rather gingerly expecting, following my exertions of the early evening, that my limbs will be stiff and sore. To my surprise I do not feel too bad. Even my head is no longer throbbing, although I can feel a bit of a bump where Simon struck me.

I need to talk to Starlight. There are so many unanswered questions. I need to know more about her interest in The Project. But more pressingly I really need to find out what happened at Claife Station.

"I'm not asking for detailed explanations, but I'm really confused about the last few hours and what you've been up to."

"I've been looking after your interests'"

"And would they be similar to your own?"

"Possibly."

"What are those interests?"

"That you must discover for yourself, as my involvement becomes clearer to you. You will find that we are working towards the same ends."

"But what you did at Claife Station was outside the boundaries of common experience, beyond the laws of Newtonian physics."

"Even a philosopher must be aware that we have moved on from Newton, for over a century we have been singing to a different tune."

"Yes, that's true. Quantum physics has changed the way that we understand our surroundings, from the smallest particle to the whole universe. But we still live our normal lives within the confines of what we call 'common sense'."

"Everything that I have just done has a logical explanation. It may not be entirely Newtonian, but there is no 'magic' in it."

"What happened at Claife Station?"

"I simply intervened. I don't often do that. It tends to get messy. There's also the problem of free will, which is a really vital part of the human condition, so we're very cautious about intervening. It tends to end up with an awful lot of things going awry."

I note that she said 'we'. I must return to that later. "You carried out some sort of teleportation of Helen to the train? Is that what happened to the others."

"Duncan, dear," says Starlight, "you really have been reading too much science fiction. What's worse you haven't been listening to me. Teleporting indeed. What do you think I am, a signed-up member of the crew of the Starship Enterprise?"

I feel a bit embarrassed. "Sorry, I say. I'm only trying to make sense of things. I don't find it easy to grasp."

"Well you don't need to invoke Scotty. I told you that there was no magic involved in anything that I do."

"What happened, what did you do?"

"It seemed best to take Helen to Windermere station, it's only a mile or two from where we were. We changed at Oxenholme and boarded the Euston train. We had a little chat and then I got off at Lancaster leaving her to continue her journey. She was entirely happy by the time I left her. She's a very nice person, even if she is a bit too fixated on monetary reward as being the driving force of her life."

"I suppose it was just after you left her that she rang me?"

"We did talk about her phoning you. She knew you would be concerned about her well-being and she was very keen to let you know that she'd survived the incident at Claife."

"What has happened to that awful man, O'Connell? And where is Simon and that side-kick of his, you know, the bouncer type?"

"I saw them shortly after I took Helen to the rail station."

"What do you mean you 'saw them'? Where are they, and more importantly how much of a danger are they to us now?"

"You won't be troubled by them again," says Starlight.

"Where are they? Have they gone away?'

"Yes, in a manner of speaking, they have. It might not be a good idea to pursue their fate any further. There's some work to do elsewhere. A job that is required elsewhere just to finalize things for them in all eternity."

"What do you mean by 'elsewhere? Are we talking about a different world?"

"Possibly."

"Are you going to tell me anything more?"

"About those three? No."

It's apparent to me that there will be no further discussion on the fate of the three men. I know that Starlight is telling me the truth when she says that they will not be bothering us again, and under those circumstances I suppose that what has happened, or will happen, to them does not really matter. It is a relief to know that they are not going to bother any of us again.

Starlight, still standing, looks over at me. "You've been doing a lot of thinking."

Indeed I have. It is the relationship between my research work and the activities of this girl whom I now know to be in command of extraordinary powers, that interests me. Miranda and I constructed an elegant hypothesis concerning the possible manner of communication between our world and other worlds. It is now entirely probable that Starlight is herself proof of that hypothesis. It is just a matter now of translating that into a provable theory.

"I have been wondering how you view the research project."

"Yes, I thought that might be it."

"It's just that Miranda and I were convinced that we were onto something important. There really did seem to be a very strong probability of targeted access to these parallel worlds using thought-energy. If it wasn't for Simon messing everything up she would've been able to identify what makes things work."

"Make what work exactly?"

"The biological basis of thought transference. I am sure that Miranda succeeded in this just a few milliseconds before that bastard blasted her brain."

I am increasingly aware that Starlight is looking at me with a strange mixture of affection and sorrow.

"Duncan," she says, "you have been totally truthful with me. I know that to be so. I also fear that within your research notes and indeed inside your head there is a grasp of this subject that's going to have serious consequences. But I've not been entirely open with you."

"Too bloody right!" I say with feeling. The memory of that walk in Langdale is all too vivid and I can recall almost exactly the conversation that we had in the coffee house. "Your interpretation of the word enigma would shame a sphinx."

Starlight smiles. This is one of a very few times that I have seen her express a fully human emotion. I grin back at this delightful girl.

"I did promise that I would reveal more to you, but you must realize that in doing so I will be putting you in a position of serious danger."

"I think I have to accept that." I reply.

"Duncan, your role is just to watch. Whatever I do you must stay sitting down. In particular you must not, under any circumstances, try to touch me. Is that understood?"

I nod.

"Say that you agree. This is important."

"Starlight, I will stay here in this chair whatever happens,"

What is coming now? What have I let myself in for? It crosses my mind that I am still asleep, dreaming once again of a visitation from an enigmatic and desirable girl. It is probably my advancing years that cause me to dream thus.

Starlight kicks off her trainers, pulls off her blouse and slides out of her jeans. She is wearing nothing else.

"No." she says as I half make to leave my chair. "You made a promise to me that you would stay there, to do otherwise would be very dangerous for both of us."

For a second time I nod my acceptance. "I'm sorry, I'll stay where I am. I promise."

Like most men I can always be summoned to enjoy a bit of sex, but as much as she titillates me sexually I find, to my surprise, that I am more interested in where her thoughts are leading me rather than having quick shag with her.

She has removed her clothes without seduction. As if she is about to hop into a bath. She now stands before me stark naked with a rather distant smile on her lips. There is, inside my head, the faint sound of music. The firelight flickers on her supple body. The light from the flames seems to wrap itself lovingly around her. She has a good figure, not thin, in fact quite curvaceous, what might be termed 'juicey'; one that might have been sought after as a renaissance painter's model. She expresses absolutely no embarrassment at exposing herself fully to me.

Starlight holds her fingers momentarily to her lips. She turns her head and body half away from me and rests her right hand on the side of the sofa. She lifts her left arm above her head stretching her left breast upwards as she does so, and then, very slowly, she brings that hand down over her head and down her body until it rests by her side just out of my sight. As the hand comes down so her head turns a luminescent grey that spreads to her neck. The life seems to drain out of the grey area as it moves on downwards taking in her breasts, her upper arms and her torso to waist level. Behind her I seem to catch a glimpse of a blue sky and white clouds. She is Magritte's 'La Magie Noir'.

She holds the tableaux for perhaps half a minute before, with a swift upward sweep of her hand, she restores the marble to flesh. She grins a very human grin and it seems that her voice comes straight from her mind to mine without the intermediary of lips and ears. "I would have preferred 'Le Faux Miroir I think." And her laughter fills my head.

Now something different is happening to her. As I watch the flicker of the firelight grows stronger and faster. The music plays louder. She starts, very slowly to turn to her right so that I firstly catch a left profile of her, then a back view, and now her right profile. Her body seems to be just slightly translucent, almost glowing. She stands full frontal again and as I look into those deep blue eyes I begin to see in my peripheral vision the whole of her body bathed in a white glow that grows more and more intense.

She is turning again now, faster and yet faster and the white plasma that has enveloped her body is trailing behind her, like a muslin wrap, unable to keep up with this gyrating human form. The music is reaching a crescendo. Her rotating body catches up with the trailing end of the luminescence and as it does so it starts to disappear into the light, becoming one with it. The column of white becomes more and more intense until I can scarcely bear to watch it. Her body has gone. She has gone

The music dies gradually to silence and as it does so the column of light thins until all that it comprises is a pencil-thin column of white light that stretches from floor to ceiling. It is pure. It is serene. It is untouchable.

And now her voice is in my head again. "This is the way, Duncan, this is the way that it has always been. This is the way it must stay. To change the way would bring untold destruction to us all. That is why Simon and his kind must be stopped." Her voice grows sadder "What Miranda and you were researching was not of concern whilst it was just an idea. But Miranda embarked, just fleetingly on a journey that she was not prepared for, and one that you crave, and that cannot be allowed. The knowledge that might make that journey possible must once again become unknown. It must all end here. You have to destroy every last vestige of your work, and then, and only then, you must come to me."

The pencil thin beam flickers slightly and loses some of its intensity. It starts to widen and shorten changing from white to cream to the colour of flesh, and as it thickens it becomes a human form again, rotating fast, then slower and slower, until within the space of less than a minute Starlight is standing naked before me once more.

With a quiet deliberation she stoops, picks up her clothes, and moves silently to the sofa. She curls up on it with her back to the world, shuts her eyes, and goes to sleep.

Shortly I move quietly from my chair. I go upstairs and rummage around for a bit, returning with a white duvet. I gently place it over the sleeping girl. I tuck the ends in around her naked limbs. I give the dying embers of the fire a push with my foot so that no log will roll out in the night.

I sit down again in my chair and, companionably, go to sleep.

My sleep is not peaceful. Thoughts come hurtling at me from all directions I can hear Miranda calling to me, urging me to carry on, to complete The Project. I can hear Bryan warning me that by doing so I will imperil the World and myself. I listen to the quiet wisdom of Val, the no-nonsense clarity of Helen, the bumbling but sincere concerns of John Somerville. Above all I see Starlight. She has clarity of purpose and steadfastness of will. I can only do as she demands; it is my destiny.

I feel fear. I experience deep and very real dread of what lies ahead. How did it come to this? Why has fate picked on me to bear this burden? I do not have what is called Faith. I am, let us be honest here, a fairly pretentious little prick. I am a capable but not outstanding philosopher. I have been a poor husband. I am a bit of a pillock when it comes to Alfas. But surely all these relatively innocuous misdemeanours do not warrant such a sentence as has been passed on me. That of removal from the human race.

I sleep, fitfully.

Twenty Seven

Even before I open my eyes at eight o'clock on the shortest day of the year I know that Starlight has left. I ease myself from the chair that I have slept in and start in a slightly crumpled manner to potter around the house. She has folded up the duvet and must have had a shower before she left as there is a wet towel hanging on the rail in the bathroom.

I do not want to dwell on the events of yesterday evening other than to consider in practical terms what it is that I must do. I realize that this is hardly an emotional reaction to what was an extraordinarily moving experience. I am a careful person, I measure, I analyze, I deduce and I theorize. I may be affected as a man, but I cannot afford, as a philosopher, to be anything other than objective, analytical.

I walk through to the kitchen, fill the kettle with sufficient water for a mug of coffee and switch it on. I turn and see that there is a note on the kitchen table. I pick it up and with a certain grim anticipation I unfold it:

Long Meg. Today. 3pm.

Now that is concise, clear and to the point, just way that I like people to be thinking. I know Long Meg as an ancient circle of stones near Penrith. I have many things to do beforehand, and a pretty good idea of what lies in wait for me there.

I find a rather stale couple of croissant that must have been bought by Helen. I shove them into the microwave. They will lose their crispness, but at least they will be warm. I pour a large cup of coffee; spread some damson jam on the now very floppy French breakfast and wolf down food and drink. I discover I am very hungry I have not eaten since lunchtime yesterday.

I pick up the phone and dial Val's number. It rings for a while and then a rather drowsy voice answers "Hello, 352"

"Val, it's Duncan."

"Hi, Duncan. You OK?"

"Well in a manner of speaking I suppose I am. Val I need a big favour from you."

"Try me."

"Could I collect you just after lunch and then drive up to Penrith with you. I need to stay up there, and I just wondered if you could bring the car back for me."

"No problem. Stop here and have a bite to eat on the way. See you about twelve thirty?"

"Thanks, Val. See you soon."

I retreat upstairs, enjoy a long shower, dress myself in some fresh clothes and brush my hair. I then sit down at my iMac in the corner of the Living Room and pull the keyboard towards me.

I write several letters to banks and building societies. I download a couple of forms from the 'net sign them and place each in an envelope. I then compose an e-mail to Helen. Before sending this I print off a copy, add a few handwritten words, sign it and fold it into an envelope addressed to her at Bewdley Street.

I have done all I can. I look around the house, lock the door and set out for the Campus.

Just inside the main entrance to the Physics block is a small cubicle used by the security people. I say 'used' but it strikes me that there is very little security here at all. I suppose a large wagon and half a dozen men dressed in balaclavas loading it up with bits of shiny equipment might just raise an eyebrow or two. Otherwise we seem to be able to go about various nefarious tasks unmolested.

I am however currently in need of a suitably uniformed enforcer, and as luck would have it there is one in said cubby-hole clutching a Micky Mouse mug of tea. I have a word with him. He nods and calls a colleague on his radio.

"That will be fine, Professor Fielding. If you just shove the stuff into black bags we can incinerate it for you."

"I need to see it go. Is it O.K. if I come over to the incinerator?"

"Yes, of course Professor Fielding. Just give me a shout when you are ready and we'll give you a hand."

I collect several black bin-liners from the janitor's room and carry them up to my study. The room looks even more chaotic than usual, perhaps due to my having dumped various papers all over the floor to free up chairs for their secondary purpose – that of providing seating.

I search meticulously for every scrap of information that I have that relates to The Project and start stuffing it into bags. I have never done anything like this before. Each and every project that I have completed has been properly archived so that, in future years, a fellow researcher could pick up the threads of what I have achieved and run with it. Not this time. Everything is consigned to the bags. It is a tedious business but I am determined not to leave anything relating to The Project. When I have all the paperwork safely imprisoned within black plastic I turn to my computer. I spend 10 minutes wiping everything of mine off the network server. I wipe it properly, overwriting twice with zeros. I then find a small screwdriver in the middle drawer of my desk, remove the hard drive from the iMac and chuck it into one of the bags. I put the screwdriver in my pocket. I will need it again.

I rummage around in the left-hand drawer of my desk and find the key that I am looking for then stride down the corridor and unlock the door to Simon's room. Although the room is so much tidier than mine it is a bit harder than before as I have to search very diligently to make sure that I have got everything. Surprisingly there is not very much paperwork, although that is balanced by the enormous amount on his computer. Again I wipe the server and remove the hard drive from his PC.

I now have three further bags of material to add to the five from my room. Using a trolley and the service lift I take all eight bags down to the Lab.

Down here my task is even harder as I have to search out all the experiment notes that Miranda, Simon and the team have ever made. I have to make absolutely certain that there is nothing left that could possibly be associated with The Project. It takes me over an hour, but I am very thorough.

I buzz Security and within five minutes a janitor and a uniformed guard appear with another trolley. We load the bags from the lab onto their trolley and wheel both trolleys out of the building and over to the central boiler room.

"Still got one we use for rubbish," says the janitor with a degree of mischievous pride.

"Thought we had to recycle everything now?" I say.

The janitor winks at me, "we have our little ways," he says.

Between the three of us we stuff every one of the bags into the furnace. I watch, fascinated, as all the work that Miranda and I had poured our souls into over the past two years ignites. There is a slightly greenish tinge to the flames, perhaps caused by the hard drives. I feel slightly sick. It is the end of so much. There's no going back. It is over.

I give the janitor ten quid for his pains. I pass the keys for the Lab, for my room and for Simon's room to the security guard. "Thanks," I say, "we won't be wanting these any more."

I leave the building. I take one last lingering look at the campus, tweak the Alfa into a gentle rumble, and point it firmly in the direction of Milnthorpe.

Helen did not get up quite as early as usual on the Saturday, but she had finished breakfast by eight thirty. That George was not in res did not seem a major omission. Being honest with herself she did not relish the idea of marrying the man, it was more the wallet that came with the package. Their relationship was one that lacked any possible kind of commitment. Paris was an ideal distance apart for them to enjoy each other's company! She had decided that she would allow a Georgian toothbrush to reside in her bathroom, but she would make its owner grovel like hell before this dentine scrubber would be admitted once more to Bewdley Street.

She poured herself a second cup of coffee and wandered into her sitting room.

The last couple of days had shaken her up a bit. As recently as Wednesday morning, when she had left London for Lancaster, her life seemed satisfying and organized. She enjoyed running Ro-Bus and got a great kick out of doing so amidst the cut and thrust of what was still a male dominated world. Her profits were up, new clients were contacting her every working day and many of her previous customers were returning on a regular basis. She wondered if it might be the right time for expansion to another city. She would need to appoint a manager to take charge of the existing offices leaving her free to establish a branch in, say, Manchester. She rather liked the idea of Manchester, still an expanding city despite the recession. She would need to look into this.

She considered again her relationship with George.

"I never loved George," she said to herself, "but I do find him witty, entertaining and convenient."

She allowed herself a wry grin at this; it hardly seemed the best basis to found a marriage upon. She wondered if George's recent flight, the second in as many weeks, had more to do with her wedding ultimatum than the offer of a job in Paris. He had tried marriage, and had a couple of fairly spectacular, and very expensive, failures. He could hardly be blamed for making every effort to avoid a third. Total rejection of The Scoundrel would however leave her with a small mortgage problem. She had better make sure that George and his bank account could discover a path back to her heart. She would let him off the marriage thing. But he would pay for it.

If Manchester was on she could find a small pied-a-terre there and spend the occasional weekend at Deanstones. She wondered if Val would mind. It dawned on her that she was asking rather a lot of Val, but then it seemed as if Val really wanted Deanstones and had certainly not blanched at her keeping a room there for her own use.

She thought again about that strange little note that she now knew to have been written by Val. It had almost certainly saved her from marrying George and might yet have started her along the road to expanding her business.

She had also met, in her vulnerable and befuddled state after the incident at Claife Station, a charming and impressive girl who called herself Starlight. How real she was and what she was doing was far from clear, but her involvement in the lives of Duncan and herself had been no accident. It would seem that Starlight was intent upon stopping Duncan from completing The Project, and there appeared to be a very good reason. Helen had been amazed at the research that

Miranda had been involved in, aided by Duncan – and fascinated by the way that both psychology and theology could be related to it.

She fired up her laptop. Not much had come in since she checked her e-mails on the train yesterday. There was the inevitable spam. She looked again; a message from Duncan:

> *Dear Helen,*
>
> *I am going away for a long time. This is my clear and logical decision. It is most probable that I shall not return. Do not ask after me or try to find me. It would prove a hopeless quest for you.*
>
> *I need to make arrangements regarding my possessions and I think the simplest thing is for me to give everything to you, absolutely, and without reservation. You must appreciate that this is not a Will, but a gift during my lifetime of all that I own, including house, car, money, etc. They are yours to do with exactly as you want.*
>
> *In the very unlikely event that I should return one day then I shall be quite happy to start from scratch and fend for myself, however I think that this would be a very remote possibility. I have made a hard copy of this note, signed it and posted it to you, as you will need proof that this is my intention. I have signed the transfer for the car, written to my bank and also informed the building society.*
>
> *Please look after yourself. Sometimes I wonder about the stressful life that you lead in Town.*
>
> *With much love,*
>
> *Duncan*

Helen had a fairly clear idea about what was going on, what Duncan meant. She knew that Starlight was involved. She thought of

Duncan's involvement with Starlight. It was not that they might be going off together to start a new life. Their relationship was not like that. There was however something very final in what was happening, or going to happen. Helen was sure that it would affect The Project.

"Duncan is a grown up," she thought, "and I am not one to question the motives of slightly distant brothers in law, let alone try to influence them. If he really wants to leave all his goods and chattels for me to sort out then I will get on and deal with the situation as I find it."

She composed a reply:

Hi Dunc,

Surprised to hear your news. It would be a shame to lose touch. Do please try to send me the occasional message by whatever means you can.

I will deal with all your belongings, etc. so do not worry about that. I will put all proceeds into a long-term fund. It will be in my name, but if you do decide to return we can easily sort that out and you will have something to get you going again.

George has buggered off to Paris. Reluctant as I am to agree with the rat I have to admit that wedding bells are not going to chime – but we can manage a Paris-London relationship (providing he still pays half my mortgage!).

I just might come up North for a few days to decide if I should expand the business into Manchester. I will keep in touch with Val.

Whatever you are up to please do take care.

Love

Helen

Well, that had moved things along a bit. It was amazing how everything was falling into place. She had better start drawing up a business plan for the changes that would be needed to Ro-Bus. Helen wondered if she might need another phantom business partner for her northern office. Dr Reinout Schmidt was all very well for London but did not seem quite the man for the North. She started toying with ideas, perhaps Sir Clive Higgenbothom "pronounced Highem, you understand", third Baronet, money made in cloth or cotton, a family of muck and brass, . . .

Helen's thoughts wandered off.

Twenty Eight

Perhaps we are being a little foolhardy in opting to wear coats and sit out on the terrace so as to make the most of this sunny midwinter's day. Val produces some excellent, but very filling, homemade chicken soup which is accompanied by crisp French bread and unpasteurised Brie.

I tell her about the extraordinary goings on of yesterday evening and how I feared that Helen was killed, but that we had both survived the experience.

"Oh, that's such an awful thing to happen to you both, thank goodness you are all right," says Val "but what exactly happened when you were knocked unconscious?"

"That I don't know. Starlight said that she 'intervened'. For my part I knew nothing until I came to myself in a very groggy state – and everyone had disappeared. Helen of course found herself on a train with Starlight and from what I subsequently learned we owe our salvation to this strange girl."

"Do you know what she did?"

"Well I know now that she has exceptional powers, but she told me that she never does anything that is outside the bounds of natural possibility. She does not work miracles. She led me to believe that she took Helen to Windermere station and they caught a train to Lancaster."

"I suppose that might just be possible," says Val.

"What she did with Simon and Joe she just would not tell me. She merely said that they would not trouble us any more. I may be wrong but I got the distinct impression that they're now dead."

"She killed them?"

"She certainly didn't admit that, but it does look awfully like it to me," I say," and I am quite sure that she's capable of doing such a thing. She also said something odd about their lives being sorted out somewhere else."

"You've spoken to her recently?"

"Yes, I have. But look here, Val, I always seem to be burdening you with my near-dream experiences."

"Don't worry, Dunc, I'll just put it down as a professional hazard. Medics spend whole dinner parties discussing other guest's in-growing toenails and no doubt solicitors find themselves holding forth to people about suing their neighbours."

"Oh, I'm so sorry. I really will just shut up."

"No, Dunc, I didn't mean to stop you - go on you silly old dear."

I have every reason to be grateful to Val. I very much want to tell her about my latest experience with Starlight. Just for a moment, I thought that she meant for me to keep quiet and I would have no chance of telling anyone about the extraordinary happenings of the previous night. I need to tell someone, someone who will remember, who will have both discretion and the skill to communicate my experience only to those who will need to know.

I describe my encounter with Starlight at the house. Val listens carefully to what I'm saying.

"Whatever she does, "says Val, "she does for good reason. She's portraying herself in this way to make a really important point, but lightheartedly from what you say?"

"Oh, yes, she did the Magritte transformation with a smile, and burst out laughing when it was over."

"But it became more serious after that?"

"Yes, the Magritte thing was almost a sideshow; a sort of demonstration to get me in the right frame of mind. It was the column of light transformation that was really important, I'm sure of that."

"What can we make of it?" says Val. "You tell me that you don't think it was power that she was displaying?"

I consider that carefully, "No, that was definitely not power. I reckon that what I saw was energy in its purest form. I think she may have been showing me, demonstrating, something about the raw energy of life."

"And why would she be doing that"

"Hmm, that's difficult, but she knew she had to convince me to stop working on The Project. I'm fairly sure from what she said in the Priory that she was reluctant to do it this way. She probably knew that it was the only way she was going to get through to me."

"And she did."

"Yes, it's done now, there is no going back."

"I presume that you are sure in your own mind that Starlight does really exist, and that she's not an energy force that you have conjured up within your own psyche to provide you with a social conscience?"

"Val, I don't know." A feeling of uncertainty that I find hard to describe to her gnaws at me. "All I can say is that Starlight and all that has happened seems to me to be totally real. That does not mean, objectively speaking that it is real."

"Well something is influencing your Super-Ego. It's either reality in the form of this Starlight girl of yours or it's the stirring of your sub-conscious self deep within your own mind. I am not sure that it makes that much difference in the sense that it is your Super-Ego taking control of the situation. "

"I see what you are getting at," I say, "but I thought the Super-Ego was all about control and guilt?"

"You are partly right, but there's more to it than that. Starlight – let's assume that she's real - is tapping into that part of you that aims for perfection, which looks for your spiritual ideals, your personal goals and, as you rightly say, your conscience. It's the organized part of your personality that nullifies the drives, fantasies, feelings, and actions that are engendered by other parts of your personality."

"That sounds about right. And when added to her very weird powers it makes her one hell of a force to be reckoned with. A force for Good I think. And if she does not exist then all that force would be coming from within me would it not?"

"Yes. And you need to be very careful about that. The mind is both powerful and fragile, and I worry for you. Dunc."

"Well I prefer to think of her as being real, or at least a 'real phantom'."

"It's as good a way as any to cope with the situation. I also wonder whether if Starlight is influencing your Super-Ego she is also perhaps working on those other parts of your mind that make up your full personality."

"What are they?"

"The Ego and the Id. The Ego is the place where your conscious awareness resides, it is about reason and intellect."

"And the Id?"

"That's where your basic drives are located. It's the unconscious you that seeks pleasure without any form of negation."

"Hell, Val, is everyone this complicated"

"Oh yes! That's why I am in work. But you only have to look at a child carrying around its 'comfort blanket' to understand why, at certain times in our lives, we need to invent external means of emotional support."

"And you think that I am doing that with Starlight?"

"I can't say. But I know that you're deeply troubled and it's one explanation of what you have been putting yourself through."

"I look at my watch. It's time to go.

We dump the bowls and plates in the sink and move out towards the car.

"This really is so good of you, Val."

"It's a pleasure – and I get to see the Eastern Fells on a glorious day."

It is with a light heart that I swing the Alfa northwards towards Penrith.

Val asks where we were going and it is with a guilty start that I realize I have not explained that our destination is Maughanby stone circle near Little Salkeld. I tell Val that the circle is better known as 'Long Meg', but that is really only the name of the largest stone.

I am unsure about how much I can tell her about what I am going to do, and decide that the minimum will suffice. I explain that I am meeting Starlight at Maughanby. Val looks at me curiously but asks no question. She says that she is quite happy to drive the car back home. "I'll leave it in your garage tomorrow morning. What do you want me to do about the keys?"

"Well this is a bit of a cheek really but I wonder if you would mind hanging on to them for the time being. The house keys are on the same ring and I will not be needing them for a good long time. In fact I sent an e-mail to Helen this morning asking her to look after the place, so she may well be in touch."

"That's fine," says Val, "but I do wish you'd tell me what is really going on."

I tell her that I am really not quite sure myself, but that I am certain that Starlight has plans for me and that these will not include my returning to Lancaster for a very long time, if ever.

We turn off the M6 at Penrith. I drive through Langwathby and then Little Salkeld arriving at Maughanby Stone Circle just before three o'clock. There is not much area for parking, but as no other cars are here that is no problem. I turn the car around so it is pointing in the right direction for Val to drive it straight back towards Little Salkeld.

I start to gather up my things and to stow them in the limited storage provide by Alfa Romeo Cars plc. I flick open the laptop and connect via dongle to the Internet. There is a faint chime and Helen's reply to my earlier message appears on the screen. I read it carefully and hand the laptop to Val. "Yours to deal with now", I say.

Val reads Helen's note then hits the reply button:

> *Dear Helen,*
> *I look forward to seeing you. You are very welcome to stay with me.*
> *Love Val*

She clicks on 'Send' and closes the Mac. I am watching her. She gives me a smile. "It'll be just fine", she says.

With deft fingers I open the case of the Mac Book, take out the screwdriver for the last time and remove the hard drive. I find a mall chunk of rock and smash at the disc completely destroying it. Val looks at me.

"Last vestige of The Project," I say. "It's all destroyed now, no trace whatsoever."

"You've junked all your notes, all your apparatus, the Paper?"

"Yes, all gone."

"I see," says Val, "that final, hey?"

"That final."

We both get out of the car. Val comes around to the driver's side. She gives me a searching look.

"I'm worried about what is going on with you Dunc. I am frightened about what you are getting up to and really uneasy about what Starlight has in mind. Would you like me to stay here with you?"

"No. Please do not be alarmed. I am happy with this. It is what I want, what I have to do. You go back home. I will be just fine. Val, I want to thank you so much for coming with me today. You must not be concerned about me."

Val moves closer to me. She takes me in her arms and gives me a great warm hug. She kisses me on both cheeks. Then she slips into the car.

"All my love to you and Helen." I say, but my words are all but drowned out by the song of 3.2 litres of V6.

As the Spider makes its way down the lane away from the circle I turn and walk slowly towards the stones. With just a few words of Wordsworth's sonnet inspired by the very same stone circle ringing in my ears:

'A weight of awe, not easy to be borne…'

I can see that the bright winter sunlight is casting long shadows from the stones. The whole scene is one of a peaceful winter afternoon in an English rural landscape. Despite the opening lines of Wordsworth's sonnet there is nothing awesome or sinister about it. The stones are just stones with a farm road passing between them and a couple of mature trees standing solidly within the ring.

Perhaps I should be a bit more receptive to things spiritual. These stones were positioned here, presumably with considerable effort, some five thousand years ago. Quite what the purpose of the circle was remains uncertain, but it must have been a meeting place, most probably with religious significance. But try as I might I can only see it as just a charming ring of stones set in a field.

Twenty Nine

I walk into the centre of the ring and look to the west. One large stone stands outside the circle, Long Meg herself, and sitting underneath this sandstone finger is Starlight. I walk slowly across to her.

"I came." I say.

"Yes. You were bound to do so." She smiles, pats the ground next to her and says, "Come and sit with me for a bit."

I sit next to her looking out over the circle of stones.

Her words have rather disturbed me, "Do you believe in pre-determinism then?"

"You took what I said the wrong way. I meant that given the circumstances, how you feel about me, and the status of the research Project you had little choice but to come."

"I understand. But I've come for a reason other than to satisfy my curiosity have I not?"

"Yes."

"I've destroyed all the paperwork"

"Yes."

"And everything else to do with The Project."

"I know."

"I 've made preparations for leaving."

"Yes."

"And told everyone that I need to tell."

"Good, well done."

"I hope I've done all that I need to do?"

"Just so."

The shadows slowly lengthen and although the midwinter sun shines as brightly as before it has dipped just a little nearer to the horizon so that a slight chill pervades the air.

"You came to this world to stop me?"

"Nearly right. I certainly came prepared to stop you if the situation demanded it."

"Simon wanted me to go on."

"Yes. He wanted fame and he wanted money."

"And it was our own Government that was backing him."

"And would have backed you. They saw tremendous power, and possibly millions of pounds, coming their way, so they paid Simon to keep them informed about your progress, and arranged for Miranda's death so that Simon would have a clear field in persuading you to sell up."

"And they tried to kill Helen."

"In their eyes Helen just had to be silenced."

"Then you intervened?"

"Yes, in a manner of speaking I did."

"Miranda wanted me to continue."

"Yes, but she did not know as much as you do about the consequences of success."

"Are you now able to tell me where you come from, and who you really are?"

We sit there together, looking away from the distant fells and the low sun in the west. We sit with our backs against the ages old Long Meg stone, facing the ancient circle. Starlight very gently takes my hand in hers.

"I'll try to be as truthful as I can," she says." And I 'll not tell you anything but the truth. But there are still some things that it's best that you do not know.

I realize that this all seems complicated to you. You want to know about me. But I am little more than a figment of your imagination. That does not mean that I do not have substance or that for you I cannot be flesh and blood. But it is your power of thought that's creating the mass that you see as me. Furthermore as you rightly concluded you create within your own mind the form that mass takes, so you see me as you want to want to see me."

"So why does Helen see the same 'you' as I do?"

"That's because once you have imagined me then that particular form sticks with me, it combines with my intellect, my soul if you like, and shows itself to others just as you've imagined it."

"That's why I was getting mad at you every time you were so evasive," I say. "And that's what all that stuff was about on Sergeant Man. My trying to conjure you up without using my senses."

"Exactly. But we're only talking about my physical presence, not the things that I say to you, not my thoughts, not my self. That's a real identity. That's me. You're not creating that."

I can feel the reality of the situation slipping away from me. I can no longer tell if my senses are sending true information to my brain. I am not sure if my senses, anyone's senses, can do that at all times and in all places. It's all a matter of interpretation, and to a certain extent imagination. I am beyond being able to tell what is illusion and what, at least in Newtonian terms, is real. Starlight is not real in a corporeal sense. Perhaps she is all illusion? Perhaps the meeting with Bryan was also nothing but illusion?

"Amazing how close this is to the Christian religious tenets." I say, "We were talking at Cartmel Priory of two other 'places' that we cannot normally access from this world – the Church would have them as heaven and hell. We are now also talking of insubstantial beings that have their own will and that can indeed pass between these worlds. At one stage you said that I might find it easiest to think of you as an angel. You said that you were not an angel, but by your own admission you have the very same attributes that the Church assigns to angels."

"Christianity, like most of the great religions, has evolved its own notion of spiritual reality. It's a good, fairly clear, concept and there is not much wrong with it. In Christian theology they would have me be the angel Paschar."

"I'm not sure I have heard of that. I assume that this Paschar is an angel?"

"The angel of Vision. The one that dissolves illusion so that the Truth can be seen."

"I see, yes. They had it about right, didn't they? That's really what you are."

"It's important to realize that it is but one interpretation of a reality. It's your choice as to which religion you follow. It is also your choice to follow no religion. It must be your choice to accept or deny the existence of these other worlds or states of existence. You ask of me what I'm here for. That's a hard one to respond to truthfully. Everything that has a meaning has a presence in all these 'states of existence', let's call them worlds."

"Can I just recap a bit," I say. "We've agreed that there are other worlds within one universe. Are you suggesting to me that each of us has a counterpart 'me' in those universes?"

"In some ways," says Starlight, "but don't fall into the trap of thinking of the other worlds as heaven and hell, that's just Christian theology."

"Normally there's no interchange between these universes, but there are certain life forces, equivalent to the Christian notion of angels, who can make the transition."

"I want you to be careful there, "said Starlight, "We're not talking about transfer of mass except in truly exceptional circumstances. All that's required is what we might call the 'Spirit of Me' to make the transfer. You can then conjure up my substance and dress out that spirit in whatever way you wish. Of course when I met Helen she did the same, but you had already described me to her, so she had in her mind the same picture of me as you had."

"So why did you come? What did you want of me? What do you truly want of me now?"

"I came because we knew that Miranda was about to make this breakthrough. We needed to find out whether it was purely conceptual or if there was the possibility of real practical substance to it. I found it was the latter, and that meant closing down The Project. Unfortunately you were, and still are, very much in the way, in that you have a sound understanding of all that Miranda was doing. This is one of the hardest things that I have to do, destroying the work and the aspirations of decent people like you, who are genuinely seeking after knowledge and truth."

"But it has to be done?"

"Yes, it has to be done. I had no compunction in dealing with O'Connell, or with Simon and that Joe. They murdered Miranda, would have murdered Helen, and then used you and the knowledge that they gained for commercial and evil purposes."

"But won't they exist in at least one of the other parallel worlds?" I ask.

"You are too good a philosopher," says Starlight with a grin. "You're not letting me off lightly. O'Connell, Simon and Joe do have spirits in one of the parallel worlds, evil spirits as here, but they will be dealt with."

"By whom?"

"There's more than just what you see of me, you know. I'm with you here as thought only, but I too have a real body, not just an imagined one. I'll show you something, something that is happening, elsewhere, right now.

Duncan, look steadily into my eyes. Don't look away, just look at me. Stare into my pupils."

I do as I am bid. Her dark blue eyes seem to acquire an infinite depth. I can feel myself sinking into them. I am moving into a scene that's being played out somewhere far away.

Ego slips his feet out of the stirrups, flicks the reins deftly over the ears of The Horse and dismounts, rather stiffly, from his steed. The dusty road behind tells of the hot, thirsty journey that has brought them thus far, to this jumble of pinnacles, these rocks known as the Tablelands, the ambush point he has been hoping to reach.

He has made sure that the Others have been able to track his route all day.

He saw the Targets back at that dilapidated fuel store and smiled grimly as they set off from there in the wrong direction. They would soon return, but it bought him the small amount time that he needed.

The outback shimmers slightly in the intense heat as he tries to focus his eyes on a spot near the red-tinted horizon. It is moving, and at considerable pace, towards him. "Hmmm," he thinks, "that took them no longer than I expected."

In his normal unhurried way he unclips the M16 from his saddle-pack. It is time for action.

"Company approaching!" he says in a casual manner to Id. The Dog looks at him with a weary gaze that says quite clearly that he has seen all this before. If his master is getting serious with this rifle then lying out in the open is no place for a dog. Id lopes off behind the outcrop and lies down, panting, near The Horse. A moment later he hears Ego's whistle, he is needed, probably as range finder. He slinks over the top of the crag and crouches down just above his master and in line with the approaching dust cloud. He knows that Superhorse has the better temperament for carrying out this sort of job; but what Ego needs now is some solid backup, something he feels instinctively comfortable with.

The spot, just as the two of them expect, resolves itself into a large black Mercedes. It is coming at them fast now raising a great rooster tail of dust. Ego deems it appropriate to metamorphose the assault rifle into an M72A2 LAW. He can quite easily make his kill with the rifle, but it's probably best to obliterate the machinery as well. He cocks the bazooka and raises it to his shoulder.

Ego has the car in his 'scope. "Three occupants," he says, just to keep Id in the picture. "All IC 1 male, one with red hair in the passenger seat, big feller doing the driving, last one is sitting by himself in the back."

Good that is all three of them. He has been worried that they might have split up at the fuel dump leaving the big guy sweltering in the heat as an insurance.

"Wait until you can see the whites of their eyes," says Id.

"Hell, that's too close. We are in the twenty first century now," says Ego gritting his teeth and squinting along the sights. "Minimum range is 35 feet for this thing."

"O.K., boss." Id quivers slightly with the concentration and in anticipation of the outcome. "Steady," he says, "150 yards, Steady, 120, . . . Now!"

Ego fires.

Gases burn within the LAW tube at 760º Centigrade. Stabilization fins spring out of the rocket sides as it clears the launcher and hurtles at 475 feet per second towards the onrushing target. The missile ploughs with total destructive force straight into the car and explodes in a great burst of flame. The occupants are annihilated. A black plume rises into the blue of the sky.

"Bit over the top that" says Id, "your fantasies are getting the better of you."

Ego nods in agreement. The Dog is right. Perhaps it would have been better to do the job with the M16, "mind you," he thinks, "at least I don't have to destroy the car. Job done!"

The Horse appears from the other side of the bluff. "What a mess," it says, "I hope you don't want me to start clearing it all up."

Ego surveys the twisted wreck of Germanic engineering, tosses the empty rocket launcher into the smouldering heap and turns to The Horse. "Not this time, Super" he says, "There is nothing left to do except put a good few miles between ourselves and this fandango."

"Just as well you got in some chow time then," says Id to Horse, "looks like we'll be travelling nights."

Superhorse Horse looks slightly ashamed. It has failed to engage with Ego and Id in this small action "Takes my mind off what's going on" it says. And might have added "And stops me butting in with a bit of conscience which is just going to get in your way."

Ego walks around the remains of the car and picks up a few scraps of paper that have survived the inferno. "O.K., guys," he says, "Time to move out."

"The airstrip?" says The Horse. "Three days travel I reckon, half that if we do overnighters."

"I do hope she will be there for us," says Ego.

"She always is," says Id.

The sun beats down. Time passes. Man, Horse and Dog continue westward across the vast outback.

Reality, such as it is, returns. I look away from Starlight. My head is swirling. I feel giddy, and very elated.

"So, it really is out there? Parallel worlds do exist."

"You said it."

"And it's possible for some types of being to move between these worlds."

"Again, they are your words."

"Normally only thoughts can make that jump, and that's no problem to you, is it?"

"I would say not."

"And some people call those thoughts 'Prayers' and some people call those that make the breakthrough 'Angels'.

"Exactly"

"And when we die there's another place where a different us is still living?"

"That I will not tell you."

I have reached the end of my questions, the end of my quest. I have knowledge within my mind that cannot be shared with others of this world.

"I'm all that there is left for you to deal with," I say.

"Yes," says Starlight rising to her feet and pulling me up beside her. We turn and walk hand in hand away from the Long Meg stone towards the stone circle. I have anticipated this since first thing this morning and feel strangely at peace. I am not long for this world. How strange that phrase sounds. 'Not long for this world' has a clearer and more positive meaning for me now. It has not been like this since I was a small boy at Sunday school.

Val was far from happy about the way she had left Duncan. He was clearly in a troubled state. This would, she thought, at least in part be brought on by the physical destruction of the work that Miranda and he had put so much into over the past two years. There was more than that though. In her professional opinion he was acting in a manner bordering upon the schizoid. He was exhibiting signs of delusion, and appeared to be adding substance to his own imaginings.

She was no more than a quarter of a mile away from the circle. She parked the car at the junction with the minor road. She was already regretting leaving Duncan on his own. Goodness knows what he planned to do and what sort of state he was in. She slipped out of the Alfa and started to walk back along the road that she had just travelled.

She knew that Duncan was sure that wherever he was going to he was not going to return. So much was clear from his e-mail to Helen, but did that mean that he intended to kill himself? Or was it just that he wanted to construct a totally new, and different life. She had a deep and worrying conviction that it was the former. She was concerned about this obsession of his, his conviction that a girl calling herself Starlight had entered his life to influence his conscience.

She hastened on a bit. Ahead of her she could now see the circle, but the sun was just setting and a shadow had passed over the stones. She could see some shape or shapes at the very centre of the circle, but she was too far away to make out much more than that. Could it be a figure, or possibly two figures? She was not sure. She started to run.

We walk towards the centre of the circle. There is no one about, no wind, no movement.

Starlight is speaking quietly. "This ancient stone circle is one of just a few places on Earth that at certain times posses the power of a portal. It provides a gateway through which it is possible to transpose not just thoughts, but also thought-energy, and by definition, mass. There is no going back from here. You'll pass through into another world where your energy and mass will be absorbed by the spirit of you that resides in that world."

"I must go now?"

"It is the shortest day. This circle was built by The Ancients so that at sunset on the shortest day the shadow falling from the Long Meg stone strikes the exact centre of the circle."

"We are at the centre now."

"Shush, my darling," says the girl whom I had once known as Starlight.

She draws me to her and opens her mouth against mine. The shadow from the Long Meg stone is upon us. I feel only the power of this kiss. It fills my head, my body, my very being. I am travelling down this kiss into another being. I feel nothing else. The final second of sunlight has expired.

The shadow falls.

Epilogue

Whilst the operation had been of very limited success things were not too bleak as far as Hugh was concerned. By involving SIS with their recommendation of Simon's involvement he had managed, at least to some extent, to distance the action from his own department. He would have to be careful, but with delicate handling he could nullify any long-term disadvantage to his career and thereby not compromise his end of term gong.

He was again being interrogated my Michael Pederson who was showing signs of grave concern, if not imminent panic. "But from what you tell me we have lost three operatives. What will I tell the PM?"

"Perhaps we are looking at this from the wrong direction," said Strickland.

"Nonsense, man. I knew it was going to be a cock-up. Didn't I tell you that the whole thing was a disaster? Now we are up to our necks in it."

Hugh was studying with the intense interest of an art historian a very fine Landseer that was hanging on the far wall. "I think," he said at last, dragging his attention away from the painting with noticeable reluctance and speaking in a thin dry voice, "that we should concentrate on the facts and not be side-lined by anything of less consequence."

"There is nothing inconsequential about this whole thing. It is murder, and that Fielding fellow has got away with it."

"The point is, Minister, that we have achieved our ends."

Pederson looked over at Strickland. Perhaps he could sense a very small gleam of hope.

Strickland continued, "We have ensured that the threat posed by this research has been totally nullified. Did I tell you that Fielding just this morning scrapped every trace of The Project. There is no chance whatsoever of it falling into unfavourable hands."

"You are sure?"

"Oh yes, we have a minor operative on the Security rota at Lancaster. Fielding destroyed everything."

"What about Professor Fielding himself. He probably knows too much about HMG involvement, he certainly knows too much about The Project."

"I think that particular loose end will be tied up within a couple of days. Apparently the man drives a fast car. I have issued the necessary instructions. You probably do not want to know the details, but I will make sure it is discrete."

"No I bloody well don't. Operational matters are entirely within your province. Now tell me, is there anything we should learn from this sorry affair."

"It is all taken care of, Minister, but I wonder if perhaps we were just a shade too trusting on an inter-departmental basis."

"You mean that we never vetted this Simon person?"

"We know better now." Said Strickland. "I am sure that our Friends Across the Water did their best."

"That is such a stupid name for the Secret Intelligence Service."

Hugh moved over to his desk and surreptitiously pressed one of an array of small buttons concealed underneath it. Almost immediately there was a discrete knock at the door.

"Come in," said Strickland.

A functionary came up to him and whispered something in his ear. Hugh looked over to Michael, "Minister, I hate to bring our conversation to an end so abruptly but it appears that you are required in the briefing room regarding the Atlas Alpha project. I think we can consider this matter closed. If anything occurs beyond purely operational considerations I will of course ensure that you are fully informed."

"Sorry to have to leave you, but duty calls." The florid little man puffed his chest out in anticipation of his next meeting, gave a perfunctory wave of his hand towards Strickland and followed the functionary from the room.

Hugh sat at his desk. He allowed himself just the faintest of smiles. There would be no repercussions as far as his involvement was concerned. He reached out for a thin blue file and started to fill out a requisition form for a new Mercedes.

About the Author

I have had an interesting and fortunate life, first as a Land Agent, then as owner of a passenger boat company in the English Lakes, and now as an author living a large part of my life in northern Greece where I don't much like the climate but enjoy the lifestyle!

I have written poetry and novels, some under a nom de plume. I had the enviable experience of being employed by The National Trust first in North Wales, then as their Regional Agent in Northwest England, which included much of the Lake District.

However it was time to move on when the N.T. , quite rightly, grew up into a corporate institution, and I failed to grow up with it, preferring the more personal and idiosyncratic approach. With the blessing of my previous employer I set up and ran a passenger boat company on Coniston Water, with two boats each carrying 60 passengers. It was a small business employing a maximum of seven people, but it was great fun. We were ahead of our time in converting our two 1920's launches to hybrid solar power (yes in the English Lakes!).

When I found that the physical effort of the winter work was getting a bit much for me I moved on, both physically and mentally and found myself, slightly to my surprise, writing books in Greece.

Gordon G Hall
Halkidiki May '25